Lisa Hall

The psychological thriller everyone is talking about

'A well plotted psychological thriller with the mother of all
twists. It's certainly one of the best debuts I have read in a
while, it's compelling and shocking, and very cleverly crafted.'
– The Book Review Cafe

'Hall packs a punch with this one and the ending left me gasping.'
– For the Love of Books

'A gripping psychological thriller with a level of tension
that will leave you breathless.'
– Tracy Book Lover

'It is disturbing and chilling. It feels very real. And a quick
mention for that twist! I did not see that coming AT ALL. I
usually spot these things and I didn't! Clever! Very clever!'
–Northern Crime Reviews

'*Between You And Me* is that kind of book. The one that
makes you feel like you're there, you're experiencing
the emotions, the hurt, the pain.'
– Bibliophile Book Club

'Lisa Hall has written a harrowing, disturbing and chilling novel
which I couldn't help but devour in a matter of days. She's one
of those authors you don't see coming and BANG best seller,
up there with the greatest crime writers like Stuart McBride and
Lee Child. She's one to watch.'
– Brunette Lifestyle

D0264168

between you and me

LISA HALL

CARINA™

Carina
An imprint of HarperCollins*Publishers*
1 London Bridge Street
London SE1 9GF

www.carinauk.com

This paperback edition 2016
8

First published in Great Britain by
Carina an imprint of HarperCollins*Publishers* 2016

A catalogue record for this book is
available from the British Library

ISBN: 978-0-00-819450-5

Set, printed and bound by
CPI Group (UK) Ltd, Croydon, CR0 4YY

LISA HALL

loves words, reading and everything there is to love about books. She has dreamed of being a writer since she was a little girl – either that or a librarian – and after years of talking about it, was finally brave enough to put pen to paper (and let people actually read it). Lisa lives in a small village in Kent, surrounded by her towering TBR pile, a rather large brood of children, dogs, chickens and ponies and her long-suffering husband. She is also rather partial to eating cheese and drinking wine.

Readers can follow Lisa on Twitter @LisaHallAuthor

To Team Hall – for making me who I am.

PROLOGUE

It happened so quickly, and now there is so much blood. More than I ever thought possible. One minute, he was shoving me backwards, into the kitchen counter, the air thick with anger and words spoken in temper that could never be taken back. The next, he was on the floor, the handle of the knife protruding from his ribs. I don't even remember picking it up, only that I had to stop him. I back away, pushing myself up against the cold, granite surface, across the room from where he lies. I feel light-headed and sick, sweat prickling along my spine. He reaches up to me with a shaky hand, slick with his own blood, and I draw back even further. He is slumped on the floor, back resting against the kitchen counter, a lock of hair falling over his brow. He is pale, a sheen of sweat shining on his forehead. A coppery, iron tang fills the air and I want to retch. Turning, I lean over the kitchen sink, where I heave and heave but nothing comes up. I wipe my mouth on a tea towel and push my shaking hands through my hair. I need to try to think calmly, rationally. I need to phone for an ambulance, and I need to get my story straight. I'll tell them that he slipped and fell on the knife, a brutal, heavy knife usually used for carving the Christmas turkey, not carving into other people. That we weren't arguing, just talking. It was an accident; one minute he was fine, the next he was on the floor. I'll tell them that I didn't see what happened – I have to protect myself. I can't tell them that I snapped. That a red mist descended and for just a few seconds I felt like I couldn't take it any more, the shouting, the aggression and the lies. That in just a split second all rationality left me and I grabbed the knife and thrust it firmly into my husband's stomach.

CHAPTER ONE

SAL

The first time you hit me it was a shock, but not a surprise. Surely, this is the natural progression of things? Starting with the little things, like wanting to know where I've been, who I've spoken to, escalating to a little push here and a shove there, until now, when a slap almost feels like a reward – and I'm thankful that it wasn't something worse, that there are no bones broken this time.

I remember the first time I saw you. Nothing on earth had prepared me for it and the sight of you hit me like a punch in the guts. Is that ironic? You stood there, in the Student Union bar, talking to a guy on your course I had seen around campus previously, a pint of Fosters in one hand. The sun was streaming in through a window behind you and you looked majestic, standing tall in a faded pair of Levi's and battered Converse, your fair hair standing out around you like an aura. I was with a group of people from my own course, planning on spending the evening with them, hashing over that day's lectures over a few drinks and then maybe heading out for a bite to eat. Once I saw you, I knew my plans had changed and that I had to pluck up the courage to approach you. How would things have turned out if I hadn't asked you if you wanted another pint? If you hadn't accepted, and we hadn't spent the entire evening holed up in one corner of the SU bar? If I hadn't answered your call the next day and accepted your invitation to lunch? If we hadn't spent the whole of that following weekend together, in your flat, ignoring your roommate, the phone, the world outside?

Maybe I would be married to someone who doesn't think it's OK to hit me. To throw things at me if I have a different opinion to the one I 'should' have. Someone who doesn't think that being happily married means the other half of the partnership towing the line at all times, no questions asked. Maybe you would be settled with someone else, someone who knows the right thing to say and the best way to handle you. Maybe you would be with someone you don't think defies you at every opportunity, although I don't, I really don't. You just think I do, regardless of what I do or what I say. Maybe both of us would be happier.

CHAPTER TWO

CHARLIE

A file the size of a house brick lands on my desk and Geoff appears, throwing himself down in the chair opposite mine.

'Another bunch of stuff for you to work through – looks like you're not going home early tonight!' he wheezes, his face bright red as he struggles to catch his breath. Geoff is the size of a house himself, his enormous belly straining at the buttons of his grubby white shirt. Geoff is a colleague, my equal, but as he's fifteen years older than me, he treats me like a five-year-old. The man has a serious lack of ambition, and a serious case of body odour.

'Honestly, Geoff? It's 8pm – surely you don't think I'm even considering going home yet?' I give a little laugh as I pull the file towards me and start leafing through it; despite the fact I still have a ton of paperwork next to me that needs going through before I can even consider leaving the office. I feel the beginnings of a migraine tapping at my temples, no doubt brought on by tiredness from a 5am start and the stress of the never-ending paperwork that comes with the case I'm working on. The pressures of being a corporate lawyer are well known – the long hours, the stressful cases that take over our lives and eat into our personal time with our families – but it is all worth it in the end. The salary and benefits make sure of that.

'Well, don't stay up too late. You don't want to leave that pretty little family of yours too much; someone else might snap them up!' Geoff heaves his massive bulk from the leather chair across the desk from me, leaning over to ruffle my hair as he leaves.

'No chance of that, Geoff.' I grin at him through gritted teeth, the thud of my headache growing louder and making me wish I could slap his meaty fingers from the top of my head. He breezes out of the room, as much as a twenty-stone, fifty-year-old corporate lawyer can, and I reach for the phone. I dial our home number, leafing through the new documents while I wait for Sal to pick up. Engaged. I hang up and redial, using the mobile number. It rings and rings, and I picture it sitting on the kitchen side where Sal always leaves it, the hideous Johnny Cash ringtone that Sal insists on blaring out. It rings out and goes to voicemail.

'Sal, it's me. Who the fuck are you talking to? Call me back.' I slam the receiver down, and lean back in my chair, grinding the heels of my hands into my eyes to relieve the pressure that beats away there. I don't need this shit – I have enough on my plate to deal with in the office, without wondering who the hell Sal is talking to at eight o'clock at night.

An hour later, when my call still hasn't been returned, and I've tried the house phone numerous times, but to no avail, I bundle up the files and stuff them into my briefcase. I can't concentrate on work all the time I am wondering why Sal isn't answering the telephone. All sorts of scenarios cross my mind, ranging from Sal knocking the phone off the hook so as not to be disturbed with some illicit lover, through to Sal on the phone to some other person (Sal's sister? Sal's mum? Someone I don't even know?), planning to leave me. I don't know what the hell Sal is playing at, but I'm not happy. I thought I had made the rules perfectly clear – if I call, Sal should answer. I spend every waking hour working my butt off to make sure I can provide for my family – I think the least Sal can do is answer the phone when I call. I smooth down my fair hair, sticking up at all angles where I've been pushing my hands through it in an attempt to calm myself while I concentrate on those bloody files Geoff dumped on me, grab my black jacket and head out the door. When I get home, Sal had better be there – and if Sal is there, I'll want to know why the bloody hell my calls this evening have gone unanswered. I'm not being ignored by anyone, least of all the person I chose to spend the rest of my life with.

CHAPTER THREE

SAL

I hang up the phone and breathe a sigh of relief. My sister can talk the hind legs off a donkey, and although I love to speak to her, I dread her calls, knowing as I do how you don't really like for me to speak to my family. You think that we don't need anyone else, in particular anyone else from my family. The difficulty with that is that I come from a large, chaotic, noisy family, who have a lot to say and only seem to want to say it to each other. I try my hardest to put them off when I can, just so I can avoid the inevitable row that follows when we do see them, but it's difficult, and I'm not always sure that I want to put them off. My parents came to England from Italy in the 1980s, but haven't lost any of their Italian ways – they love to have the whole family together in one room as often as possible, and the highlight of their day is if I take Maggie over to visit. As their only grandchild so far she is doted on, but you disapprove, saying that they interfere in our lives and that they shouldn't have a say in how we bring Maggie up. I don't always agree, but you have made it abundantly clear in various ways that in our house we do things your way, and, to be honest, the repercussions just aren't worth it. So I don't see as much of them as I would like any more, but my sister, Julia, has relocated back to Italy to be with her husband's family, and she doesn't see how it is here now. I don't want to tell her how things are either, that the long, rambling phone calls put me on edge every time, with me completely unable to tell her that I need to get off the phone.

I run lightly up the stairs to check on our daughter. She's curled up tight into a ball, only the top of her head visible above the duvet, the nightlight casting a warm glow across the bedroom. Nearly five, she has the most beautiful glossy, dark curls, a legacy from the Italian side of the family. She gives a little snore, and rolls over onto her other side and my heart squeezes as I gaze at her sleeping form. No matter what happens between us, no matter how difficult things get, I will always put her first. I will stay and tolerate your demands and rules, if only it means she has a stable family life, with two parents who love her.

Checking the *Frozen* clock that hangs on Maggie's wall, I realise that it won't be long before you are home, so I head downstairs to check on the lasagne that has been keeping warm in the oven, and to open the bottle of Malbec I bought earlier. Creeping down the stairs, avoiding the telltale creaky floorboard in order not to disturb Maggie, I hear the key in the door before I'm even halfway down and it's obvious by the way the front door slams shut that tonight is not going to be a peaceful night.

'What the fuck, Sal?' you hiss into my face as I reach the bottom of the stairs. I wince, worried that the slamming of the front door will wake our sleeping daughter. Holding up one finger, I listen, but no sound comes from the bedroom above.

'Charlie, please – Maggie's asleep. What do you mean, *what the fuck*?' Whispering, I skirt round you into the hallway so I can get you into the kitchen and away from the staircase before you start to shout and risk waking Maggie up. You throw your briefcase down and are following me into the kitchen when I see it. My mobile, sitting on the side where I left it, turned to silent after Maggie insisted on playing some ridiculous game on it and I had to turn the volume off to stop it from driving me insane. My mobile, sitting on the side, showing several missed calls from Charlie, alongside a text announcing that CHARLIE had left a voicemail. Oh, shit.

'Charlie, I'm sorry. The volume was switched to silent. I didn't realise, I promise. Maggie was playing a game; it was driving me bonkers. I had to turn it to silent before I went mad. I'm sorry, Charlie, really sorry. It was a mistake, that's all.' I know I am babbling, but your silence is making me nervous, even though I know it is ridiculous to feel this way over a missed call. I look over to where you're standing in the doorway and, seeing you take off your black jacket, use the opportunity to open the oven door and pull out the steaming hot tray of lasagne.

'Look, I've made your favourite: lasagne. Come and sit down. I've bought some wine; we can eat together.'

'Who were you talking to, Sal? Huh? Who were you on the phone to that was SO FUCKING IMPORTANT that you couldn't answer my call?' Throwing your jacket onto the dining chair, you're across the room before I even realise, standing so close to me that I can feel your hot breath in my face. Carefully, I lower the hot tray of food to the counter and turn towards you. I think about lying, but past experience has taught me that you always find out, which just makes things worse in the end. I decide to brave it out.

'It was Julia. She was calling from Rome. She and Luca are staying at a hotel for a few days while Luca has business with a guy there. She was just calling to catch up, that's all.' I grab a dishcloth and wave it half-heartedly across the draining board in an attempt to avoid eye contact. To avoid the way you'll be looking at me like I'm a bit of shit, anger and disgust crossing your perfectly aligned features, something that happens only too frequently these days.

'To catch up, and to slag me off, no doubt. Jesus, Sal, do you think I'm some sort of idiot? I know what your family think of me, I know what you say about me behind my back!'

'God, Charlie, NO. We didn't speak about you – Julia asked how you were, that's all. I told her you were fine, busy at work, you know. Nothing else, I swear to you, please. Please, Charlie.' I try to take your hand, to reassure you that what I'm saying to you is true, that I'm not lying to you. Your icy-blue eyes bore into mine, as you try to decide whether to believe me or not.

'My phone was on silent, Charlie. Maggie was playing a game on it and it drove me crazy, so I turned the ringer off. That's all, I promise. I wasn't ignoring you.' Decision made, you turn on me, slapping my hands away from yours.

'You're a fucking liar, Sal. You always have been. You've lied to me from the word go and, to be honest, I don't think you know how to tell the truth. I know what you and your family think about me; I'm not an idiot. I know you all think that poor old Sal could have done so much better. So what were you and Julia plotting? How to get rid of me? How you'll leave and build a new life in the sun with your fucking sister? Is that it?'

You're screaming into my face now, spittle landing on my cheek as I turn my face away from you. Raising my hands to ward you off, unsure as to whether a blow will be forthcoming or not, I shake my head, trying to get the words out before you hit me, trying to tell you, *No. None of those things. Just talking.* I don't get the chance before you start yelling into my face again.

'What, you think you're going to raise your hands to me? I don't think so, Sal. You need to remember who's the boss here – who's the one that goes out to work all hours so that you can live the life of fucking Riley? ME, that's who. I have to deal with all the stress and demands, getting up at the crack of dawn every single day so you can live the life you want to lead. So you can sit on your arse at home, playing games with Maggie and slagging me off to your sister, you fucking ungrateful *shit.*'

You turn and, twisting your sleeve down over your hand so you don't get burnt, grab the hot tray of lasagne, hurling it to the ground, smashing the porcelain dish into millions of pieces, before stalking out of the kitchen. You don't notice the shards of china cutting into the tops of my bare feet, and the steaming hot mince making burning arced splashes up my legs.

It takes me the best part of two hours to clean up, after I sit with a cold wet cloth pressed against my legs where the hot meat splashed up and scalded me. Tiny blisters have risen on my shins and calves and I know that tomorrow, despite the warm weather forecast, I will have to cover them up. Fighting the beginnings of a headache brought on by fear and exhaustion, I wipe up tomato sauce that has splattered all up the kitchen cupboards and sweep up the shards of porcelain. I mop the entire floor with bleach to get rid of the garlicky smell and make sure that not a single piece of china is left on the floor to pierce Maggie's bare feet in the morning. I put antiseptic cream on the scalds on my legs, and wearily climb the stairs, praying that, as it's after midnight, you'll be asleep.

As I slide into bed, the sheets feeling blissfully cool on my hot, sore legs, you roll over towards me and I hold my breath, not sure if this is the start of another onslaught. I stiffen, waiting for you to speak.

'I'm warning you, Sal.' Your breath is hot and sour in my face, as I lie dead still. 'I'm not having it. It's your fault the dinner was ruined – if you hadn't slagged me off to your sister, and then lied to me about it, it wouldn't have happened. You bring all this on yourself.'

You roll away from me and assume the position you always do when you're ready for sleep. I lay still, head pounding, and blink back hot tears until sleep takes over.

CHAPTER FOUR

CHARLIE

Sal and Maggie are already in the kitchen when I come downstairs at 6am the next morning. Despite the row last night, I slept well and I'm feeling good, ready to face another day dealing with Geoff and his brick-sized files at the office. It looks as though Sal, on the other hand, didn't get a wink of sleep, with dark eyes bloodshot and surrounded by deep, purple circles. I don't feel any sympathy; if rules were followed there wouldn't be any arguments. Sal doesn't seem to understand that I don't do things to be horrible, or to make life difficult for anybody – I just want a bit of respect. After all, that's what marriage is about, isn't it? If there are rules, then order naturally follows, and that makes life easier for everybody. If only Sal would respect me, respect my idea that *rules are there to be followed*, there would never be any rows.

Sunlight streams in through the kitchen window and I grab a cup of coffee from the pot that's brewing, pull on my trusty black work jacket and lean over for my briefcase. Drinking deeply from my coffee cup, I feel a pang of guilt on noticing that, despite the heatwave that's been forecast for this week, Sal is wearing jeans. I'm guessing that means not all the piping-hot lasagne hit the floor last night. Still, that's not my fault and I reiterate in my mind my mantra that rules are made for following. You'd think Sal would have learnt by now. I kiss Maggie on top of her head, where she sits at the breakfast table, drawing something that looks like it should be in a sci-fi movie.

'See you later, munchkin.'

I tip the rest of my coffee into the sink and head to the front door, noticing as I do that the sunlight pouring in through the window only serves to highlight the cobwebs hanging in one corner of the kitchen ceiling. I hear Sal murmuring something to Maggie before following me out.

'See you later.' Sal offers up a watery smile, eyes surrounded by dark circles showing the lack of sleep following last night's argument. I don't feel guilty. The phone call shouldn't have happened. If Sal hadn't taken the phone call, there wouldn't have been a row; it's as simple as that. I take Sal's face in both my hands and kiss both cheeks.

'I'll see you tonight. And remember, Sal, I meant what I said. I don't want you speaking to Julia – not about me, not about us, not about anything to do with our family. Do you hear me? If you had just done that in the first place, last night wouldn't have happened. You need to respect me, and our marriage, OK? I love you, and I'm the only one you need. Remember that. Oh, and Sal?' I turn back to where Sal stands on the front doorstep. 'Sort that kitchen out; there are cobwebs everywhere. It's fucking disgusting.'

Sal nods, and I turn and stride off towards the train station, a spring in my step now I know Sal is back under control. I don't watch to see the front door close.

When I reach the office, Geoff is already lurking outside my office door waiting for me to arrive. Giving off an air of desperation and the usual fug of body odour he bounces around in the doorway as I try to get settled at my desk.

'So, Charlie, get a chance to look at that info I gave you last night? Otex are keen to seal the deal with this little communications outfit and Vygen are sniffing round. I've had Vygen's lawyer on the phone – Alex Hoskins? I heard you knew Alex from uni or somewhere?' I frown and pull my laptop out of its case. Geoff is clearly excited about this deal, bouncing around like a little kid. If it all goes smoothly he will look good, seeing as he is head of our department.

'Um, no, Geoff. Not yet. Last night was a bit hectic, you know? I'll make it my priority this morning. I want to get the deal sealed before Vygen get any more of an idea about it; we could stand to make a ton of money from this deal. And, yes, I do know Alex from uni. Let me deal with it next time Vygen call.'

I switch on my laptop and pull the files from my briefcase, hoping Geoff will get the hint and leave me in peace. Instead, he perches his huge arse on the edge of my desk and peers at me knowingly.

'Oh, yeah? Heavy night last night? Stop off in the pub on the way home, did you? Ahh, your secret's safe with me, don't you worry!'

He pats my hand with his grubby little paw and hefts his bulk off my desk and lurches out of the room. Ugh. Reaching into my bag I pull out a travel-sized bottle of hand sanitiser and disinfect my hands before sitting back in my chair and pushing my hands through my hair. Alex Hoskins. What a blast from the past. Tall, fair, with amazing legs and a ferocious attitude to go with it. Alex had been at uni with Sal and I, back in the late '90s, and while we had occasionally clashed, there had been an underlying spark of attraction. We had had a bit of a thing going on, nothing serious, but then I met Sal in the Student Union bar and that was it for me. I never looked at anyone else again, and I've made damn sure since then that Sal has only had eyes for me. If Alex Hoskins is working for the rival company that wants to buy the communications company that my client is after, though, things could get interesting. I decide that I will wait for Alex to call me – I don't want to look like

I'm chasing. I open the files and make a start on reading them through, highlighting parts of interest and making notes on my computer. It's vital for me that this deal goes through smoothly – its success means a promotion for me, more money, which means the financial burden that I shoulder for our entire family should ease a little. It's not easy being the solo breadwinner, but if it means Sal stays at home, where I can keep an eye on what goes on, then so be it. I call through to Anita, my secretary, and tell her to hold all my calls, unless I get a call from the Vygen lawyer, Alex Hoskins. That call I will take.

CHAPTER FIVE

SAL

'God, Sal, you look like shit.' Laura pops her head round the back door, the sun glinting off her red hair as she pushes the door open with one hand and shoves her sunglasses onto the top of her head with the other.

'Thanks, Laura, you really know how to make someone feel special.' I don't mean to snap but I'm tired and ninety-nine per cent certain I do actually look like shit. I feel like it, that's for sure.

'Oh, touchy. Rough night last night? Did Charlie get in late?' Laura pushes her way in and slings her bag onto the kitchen table.

'You know how it is when Charlie's got a big case on. And apparently, this is a huge one – the firm stands to make a bajillion quid or something, if Charlie can pull it off. It means major pressure, even a possibility to make partner if it all goes to plan. And you know how badly Charlie wants to make partner before the big 4-0. So, yeah, Charlie did get in late, and it was a bit of a rough night. I just need some sleep, that's all.'

'Ha. I know that feeling: Fred had me up four times in the night, didn't you, dude?' Laura smiles down at the chubby little boy as he toddles into the kitchen behind her. Looking me over, she frowns. 'Jesus, Sal, aren't you hot in that outfit? It must be nearly thirty degrees outside; speaking of which, has Maggie got sun cream on? She's outside playing dolls under the apple tree, I've left Lucy out there with her.'

'What? Yeah, she's got sun cream on; they'll be fine out there, and it's shady under the tree. And no, I'm not hot, I'm fine.' I turn to the sink and start to fill the kettle, feeling the weight of Laura's gaze on me. I am too hot in my jeans. It's June and the heatwave that was forecast last week is in full force today, but the only other option is shorts, and that would mean revealing the red, angry scald marks left by the splashes of food from last night, and that would mean questions. Questions that I really, really don't want to have to answer. Questions that I'm not even sure I have the answers to – I have no idea how events like last night's ended up being almost the norm in our relationship.

Laura settles herself at the kitchen table, spreading out across it with Fred's juice bottle, a pot of grapes, Fred's dummy and Lucy's security blanket. She brings over a hell of a lot of stuff for someone who only lives next door.

'Are you sure you're OK, Sal? I thought I heard shouting last night, that's all. You know how thin these walls are; I just … well, I just wanted to check, that's all.' She doesn't look at me, pretending she is busy with Fred's juice bottle.

'Laura, I'm fine, I promise. Charlie must have just had the telly up too loud; you've just said these walls are hideously thin! Nothing to worry about, honestly. And I appreciate your concern, but believe me, I'm big enough and ugly enough to look after myself.' I squeeze her shoulder as I lean over and place a cup of tea on the table in front of her and swing Fred up for a cuddle. Nearly two, Fred still has that chubby baby feel about him that I miss so much in Maggie now she's four and almost ready for 'Big School'. I would have loved another baby, a boy, to balance out our family and keep Maggie company. I would have loved lots more, coming from a big family, but you weren't keen on even having one more, let alone three or four, saying, 'We can provide a better lifestyle if we only have one child, Sal. Don't be an idiot.' I can't help feeling that Maggie is missing out somehow. I give Fred a big nuzzle and blow raspberries on his neck until he shrieks with laughter and squirms to be put down. Lowering him gently to the floor, Laura lets Fred run over to the toy box in the corner of the living room, ready to search out toy cars and bits of Lego that I'll be scooping out from under the sofa later on.

Laura sips at her tea and eyes me closely. 'So, if you're not too tired, or too hot …' – she winks at me – 'what do you want to do today? Shall we take the kids to the park? Get an ice cream and slag off all the yummy mummies with their bugaboo pushchairs and glamorous white-jeans-and-heels summer park outfits? It's roasting out there, and before you know it, it'll be September, Lucy and Maggie will be starting school and you'll spend all your days cleaning and tidying like a proper housewife.'

'Fuck off.' Smiling, I throw a tea towel at her and she bursts into laughter, her mouth open so wide I can see her back teeth, filling-free thanks to a dad who practises as a dentist.

'To be honest, I think I'm going to give it a miss today, Laur. I am really shattered from last night, and I've got a ton of stuff to do today. I might just fill the paddling pool and let Mags go crazy in there this afternoon.' I look at her apologetically, not sure of her reaction, but I really can't risk going out today, not after last night.

'Loads to do? Like what? What could be more fun than spending the afternoon in the park with your fantastically gorgeous, pale-skinned, red-headed mate, in a thirty-degree heatwave, while she bitches and moans about the perils of being so fair-skinned in said bloody heatwave?' Laura laughs again, and I am relieved. I need to learn that not everyone reacts in the same manner you do to things. I remember why she is one of the best people in my life, despite what you say about her behind her back. I laugh, too, and then decide to tell her my plans.

'I'm going to look for a job. I've decided that once Maggie starts school, I want to go back to work. I only stopped working for Maggie. Charlie could earn twice what I earned, and we agreed that I would stay home and look after the baby, but I think it's time. Charlie doesn't want another baby and I don't want to sit around here, twiddling my thumbs all day while Maggie is at school. And I want Maggie to know that it's OK for both parents to go to work, that it's not a case of one parent going to work while the other stays home.' I look down at my feet, suddenly feeling a bit shy that I've actually told someone.

'Shit, Sal, that's brilliant.' Laura stands, and comes over to give me a hug. 'But what is Charlie going to think? I mean, I thought the whole "stay home and bring up baby" thing was most important? God, I envy you, Sal. Since Jed left me bringing up these two on my own, I can't see myself ever getting back out there in the real world.'

'I think Charlie is probably going to go mad, in all honesty,' I say. I am not looking forward to talking to you about it, which is the reason why I think, if I look for a job now, and tell you when, *if*, I land one, hopefully the fallout will be less. Don't get me wrong: I know there'll be fallout – it's almost something to be expected now any time I do something that you don't approve of – but I'll be able to use the salary and the fact that I'll be around in the school holidays as a bargaining chip. 'But I can't sit around all day here, Laura, not without Mags to take care of. I'll go mad.'

'I know, Sal. You still need to be your own person.' Laura kisses my cheek, and scoops all her debris from the kitchen table into her bag. 'Listen, good luck. I'm going to take Fred and Lucy to the park, sneer at some yummy mummies and bitch to myself about lobster skin and red hair. You let me know if you need anything, OK? And Sal? You can do it. I know you can.' She squeezes my hand and scoops Fred up from the Lego that's exploded all over the living room carpet.

Once I've waved Laura and her brood off, I fill the paddling pool and clear up all the Lego, including the rogues that have hidden under the sofa, just waiting until someone sneaks down for a midnight glass of water before they pop out to savage bare feet. I *am* going to look for a job, starting today, but I didn't want to tell Laura the real reason I didn't want to take a trip to the park. I didn't want to tell her that I need to be at home, just in case. Just in case Charlie rings and I'm not here. I need to be home in case the house phone rings, and if I'm at the park and Charlie calls my mobile, I might not hear it. I just want one peaceful night tonight, and if it means staying indoors and waiting for the phone to ring, then that's what I'll do. I check the ringer on my mobile for the hundredth time, making sure the ringer is turned up to full volume and not on silent. Just in case.

CHAPTER SIX

CHARLIE

I manage to get through a ton of paperwork in the office today and, with Anita's help to keep any distracting calls at bay, feel like I'm actually getting somewhere with the Otex merger. The only slight dampener on my day is that I don't hear from Alex Hoskins, but no big deal. It's Friday and it can all wait until after the weekend. I make a note in my online diary to call Alex on Monday.

'Charlie? Do you need anything else?' Anita pops her head round the door of my office, her summer scarf already tied jauntily at an angle and her huge handbag on her shoulder. 'Only, it's just that it's Friday … and my daughter is bringing the baby over tonight – we're going to have dinner and then...' She hesitates.

'It's fine Anita – go. Like you say, it's Friday and family has to come first.' I turn on my most prize-winning smile for her, all gleaming white teeth.

'Thanks, Charlie – you are the best, and I mean *best*, boss. Have a brilliant weekend!' With that, she flicks her scarf over her shoulder and heads off towards the lifts.

I stretch out, and peer through the blinds that separate my office from Geoff's. His computer terminal is switched off, and his jacket and briefcase are gone. Taking this as a sign that he has also had a productive day on his side of the Otex merger, I decide to pack up early and head home to Sal and Maggie.

I've called Sal repeatedly today and the phone has been answered every time, each time within a few rings. Hopefully, yesterday's tiff has hammered home the idea that I really don't see the need for Sal to have so much contact with that side of the family. We don't have any contact with my family. I moved down to London from Lincolnshire to go to university and haven't looked back since. My mother is still living in the house I grew up in, that shabby little terraced house with its worn-out carpets, stained kitchen lino and tiny rooms full of dusty, old-fashioned furniture. I couldn't wait to escape from there and, after living under my drunken father's violent regime for so many years, university felt like my life had begun again. There's nothing for me there and I haven't been back since, not even for my father's funeral, when that last glass of whisky proved to be just a little too much for his poisonous old soul to take. I'm not the same person that walked out of there eighteen years ago. I won't go back there again, ever.

'Honey, I'm home!' Sal comes out of the kitchen, smiling nervously as I shout my arrival through the front door, holding out my gift of Haribos. Sal is the only grown-up I know that actually likes Haribos, even after that awful Channel 4 programme showed the actual ingredients used.

'Did you have a good day?' Sal accepts my kiss on the cheek, and the bag of sweets, and leads me into the kitchen where I can smell something delicious simmering on the stove. I am glad to be home and the bitter taste of last night's argument has dissolved, meaning I am feeling more affectionate towards Sal.

'We had a perfect day,' Sal says. 'We stayed home and played in the garden all day, the weather was so lovely. We had a picnic under the apple tree, and Mags ran through the sprinkler for about two hours. Oh, and look, we checked on the veg patch and picked our own little harvest!' Sal opens the fridge to show me a large ceramic baking bowl filled to the brim with fresh strawberries, and another, smaller, bowl filled with tiny new potatoes. 'Dinner will be ready soon. Why don't you run up and get changed and I'll open the wine.'

I head upstairs to our bedroom to change into something cooler, the windows wide open in an attempt to get some air moving through the house. Even though it's close to 7pm, it's still ridiculously hot and muggy. I lie on the bed in my underwear, hoping for a cool breeze to wash over me, but the air is thick and still. I hear Sal singing in the kitchen while preparing dinner, something low and sweet in Italian, and I smile to myself before pulling myself upright and grabbing a pair of shorts. Sal is obviously making an effort after ruining our evening yesterday. Maybe – just maybe – some lessons have actually been learnt and I feel optimistic that tonight will be a better night.

After a meal of poached salmon and new potatoes from Sal's vegetable garden, Sal puts Maggie to bed and we settle down for a night in front of the television. Sal brings through another bottle of wine, and the bag of sweets, and I finally feel relaxed. My family are all under one roof, together, with nobody snooping around, poking their nose in, interfering in how we do things, and Sal seems to have realised that all we need is each other. Sal is showing me respect today, by doing what I asked, and the effect of that is that everyone is calm, relaxed and happy, which just goes to prove my point. Anyone looking in from the outside would see us for the perfect family. Which is, of course, what we are.

CHAPTER SEVEN

SAL

Our Friday evening is just about perfect, as far removed from Thursday evening as it possibly could be, and I can't help wishing every evening could be like this. We almost seem like a normal family. My plan to keep Maggie at home all day so I could be near the phone seems to have worked, as I manage to answer every time you call (I think, at the last count, by 4pm, you had called me six times), and when you stride through the front door just before seven o'clock, waving a bag of sweets at me, your mood is buoyant. I heave a sigh of relief and come through from the kitchen to greet you. Your good mood is infectious and I find myself humming under my breath as I cook – an old Italian love song that my mum used to sing to me at night when I couldn't sleep. It's moments like these, little fragments of our lives together, when everything is peaceful and you're happy … these moments are part of the reason I stay when things are bad. There is nothing that compares to an evening indoors with you and Maggie, a nice family meal eaten together, time spent as a family, with no arguments, recriminations or fear. These few and far between moments are what I wanted when I married you, when we had Maggie. These moments are what I hang in there for, when you're screaming at me, or throwing something at me because I've let you down again.

After a meal complemented by vegetables that Maggie and I have grown in our vegetable patch, we settle in for the night. Maggie and I are very pleased with ourselves today, after plucking a bumper crop from our little mini-allotment. We created our patch at the back of the garden last year, as soon as Maggie was old enough to start helping out. I dug the patch over myself, weeded it and set up a little fence to try to keep the rabbits out. We visited the local farmer and requested his help with fertiliser (it turns out that horse poo comes free of charge) and then, once it was all ready, Maggie helped to plant various fruits and vegetables. It's become a little parcel of pride for me, down at the bottom of the garden, a small achievement that doesn't mean a lot to anyone else, but when I stand back and look at it, I think, 'I did that.' You, on the other hand, don't think it's anything terribly special and can't see the attraction in growing things from scratch, telling me that it probably works out cheaper just to buy the vegetables ourselves. You don't understand that it's the sense of pride that comes with it all that makes it all so worthwhile.

We finish the second bottle of wine, and before long you're snoring softly on the couch. Every day is a long day for you, and by Friday the hours seem to catch up with you. I think back to our uni days, to when we first met, and we would stay up until all hours, just talking about nothing and enjoying being together.

After that first meeting in the Student Union bar, we are inseparable. You call me the next day, to see if I want to meet for lunch, and of course I say yes, despite feeling terribly nervous. I hadn't had a lot of luck in relationships, and although I come from a large, vibrant family, it is easy to hide the fact that you are the shy one when everyone around you is so noisy. I can't quite believe my luck that I have managed to pluck up the courage to speak to you in the first place, and that now, after spending an evening in my company, you want to see me again. We meet outside the local coffee shop, on a day not unlike today. It is hot, the air thick and muggy, making every action an effort, but it doesn't stop me from looking forward to our date. There are butterflies in the pit of my stomach as I walk towards the coffee shop, worrying that you will have changed your mind, but as I round the corner you are already there, sunlight bouncing off your fair hair, a huge picnic basket slung over one arm.

'It's too hot for lunch inside.' You greet me with a kiss, with no sign of the nerves that I am suffering. 'I've brought us a picnic. We can go to the park, eat outside, get to know each other a bit better.' You wink at me, and take my hand with your free one. As we walk towards the park, the butterflies in my stomach calm to a mere flutter and I know, just know, this is going to be the start of something big.

We spend an incredible, long, hot summer together and by the time September rolls around and it is time to head back to university life you have persuaded me it makes more sense for me to move in with you than to go back to my shared house with three other flatmates, despite us only knowing each other for a matter of months. You share a house with only two others; your room is a huge, light, airy double room as opposed to the tiny box room that I inhabit in our grungy student house, and your place is nearer to the university than mine. Your final convincing argument is the car. I have a car, and you don't, although you have your licence. I am one of those lucky ones whose parents have splashed out on a car prior to my starting university in the hope that I will use it to come home every holiday. I say 'splashed out', but it is a 1988 Ford Escort, never one hundred per cent reliable, and the exhaust fell off within three weeks of them buying it.

'Just think, Sal, if you live with me you won't have to use the car half as much – we'll be together in the evenings anyway, and you'll be able to walk to lectures from here. You know it makes sense.'

You have it all planned out and, after a few weeks of you presenting your arguments like a typical lawyer, it just seems easier to go along with it. So I do just go along with it, despite the fact that I'm going to miss the friends I've house-shared with since my second year at uni. That summer I don't get back to see my parents even once. I am flattered that I have become such an important part of your life so quickly. But nothing stays the same for ever; things change and, while I am pretty sure I am still the most important person in your life, I'm not sure how it went from being a good thing to being something that, to be honest, I sometimes find quite frightening.

CHAPTER EIGHT

CHARLIE

I wake up with a start on the couch, after snoozing for an hour. The wine we drank after our meal was enough, coupled with the early starts and late nights that go alongside working on a case as huge as the Otex acquisition, to send me over into oblivion for a little while. Sal is smiling down at me when I wake, dark curls falling over one eye.

'God, sorry, Sal, did I snore? Jesus, I'm shattered.' I yawn, a huge jaw-stretching yawn.

'Ha, no. You're OK. I know you're tired – the case must be taking its toll on you. No, I was just thinking about when we met. Remember that summer?'

'How could I forget?' I pull Sal in for a hug and squeeze tight, last night's row completely erased from my mind. 'Picnics in the park, your crappy old car that could barely get us from A to B without something dropping off it, drinking cider in the sun – those were the days!' I laugh. Those *were* the days, once I persuaded Sal that moving into my place was the right idea. Those flatmates Sal shared with were a nightmare – all they wanted to do was take Sal away from me, with their promises of gigs to see obscure bands that no one except them (and Sal) had ever heard of, and wild house parties, full of dodgy punch and people being sick on the stairs. An actual nightmare. One of them actually had the nerve to tell me that he thought I was 'too controlling' of Sal – he soon shut up once I told him I knew he had slept with his lecturer and did he want me to let the head of department at the uni know? It's amazing what information you can pick up when everyone else around you has had too much to drink, while you stay sober – that and the fact that the lock on his bedroom door was incredibly easy to pick. Once I had Sal moved into my place, I could decide who Sal saw, where Sal went, everything. I could keep Sal with me, all night, every night. There's nothing controlling about it – it's just keeping an eye on your other half.

'It seems like a long time ago now.' I smile at Sal, 'And here we are still, together, despite it all. Together through thick and thin, that's us, Sal. We don't need anyone else, you know that. I love you more than anyone. More than anyone ever has or ever will. Remember that, Sal. I'd die if you left me.' A tiny frown drifts across Sal's brow before Sal stands and, disentangling our arms and legs from each other, holds a hand out to me.

'Enough of that. Come on, sleepy head. Let's go up to bed.'

CHAPTER NINE

SAL

The weekend passes without any incidents, and the calm and tranquillity carry on into the following week. Things always seem to follow the same pattern – I do something you are not happy with, you go crazy, and punish me in various ways, depending on how you feel – sometimes you'll get physical, other times I will just be cold-shouldered for days at a time – then, when you decide that I've been punished enough, that's it. It's over. You remind me of how I am nothing without you and how you will die without me – you love me that much; and then I am expected to behave as if nothing has happened. Sometimes I wish I were strong enough to stand up to you, to tell you that things aren't over when you decide – that maybe I'm not ready to forgive you just yet. Maybe I want to cold-shoulder you and sulk until I feel I am ready to resolve things. The one time I did try to walk away, the one time I told you that enough was enough, you locked yourself away in the bathroom, hysterical and ranting, with a packet of razor blades and a bottle of whisky. Needless to say, after that, I've never been brave enough to try again – I let you get away with it time and again, in the hope that this will be the last time. Hoping against all hope that the next part of the cycle, the perfect part where everything is OK and you're happy and it really feels as though we're a proper family, will continue and become normal for us, instead of this never-ending roller coaster.

This time, the exhausting cycle continues as it usually does; you go to work in a good mood every day, and come home in much the same vein. You spend time with Maggie in the evenings, and during the day Maggie and I work in our little vegetable garden, weeding and hoeing and picking treats to add to our dinner every night. I start to feel like I can breathe again, like I can relax and start to enjoy spending time with you, until the next time. Hoping with all my heart that there isn't going to be a next time. On Friday evening you make an announcement.

'I've got a big client day tomorrow. I have to take the Otex guys on a corporate golf day; things are not moving along on that case as quickly as they would like and Pavlenco isn't happy. I need to keep them sweet, so I'll be leaving early tomorrow morning.'

'OK,' I say. 'Maggie and I will miss you. Do you know what time you'll be back? Maybe if you're back early enough, we could all do something together?' I am secretly a little bit relieved that you won't be around – things are so much easier when I don't have to worry about tiptoeing around you, although Maggie will be upset that you're not there. With a bit of luck you'll have a good day and this relaxed, contented part of the cycle can continue unbroken.

'Late. It's breakfast, eighteen holes and drinks afterwards. I'm not sure what time we'll finish, but I'll call you when I'm leaving. You'll be home all day anyway, won't you? You don't have anything planned.' It's a statement, not a question, and I don't want to risk riling you, so I agree.

'No. No, nothing planned. I'll just do some tidying up, potter round after Maggie. The vegetable patch will need weeding, so we can sort that out. Hopefully, this weather will keep up and Mags can play out in the paddling pool.' The heatwave still hasn't broken and, although I am happy to wear shorts around the house, my legs still haven't quite healed enough for me to brave wearing shorts outside yet.

'Well, good. You two can have a lovely day in the garden again, can't you? And I'll need my work shirts ironing before Monday.'

'Of course, don't worry, it'll all be done. You go and have a good time.'

'It's not about a good time, Sal. It's work. You'd understand that if you actually still went to work. It's about keeping the client sweet, making sure this merger goes through, so that I still have a job and can keep supporting you. I don't think you quite understand the pressure I'm actually under, trying to make sure this deal goes through smoothly.'

I swallow and nod, your prickly mood meaning I am on edge again. I should have known it wouldn't last, that the cycle would continue.

'I do, Charlie, I do understand. And we really appreciate everything you do, Maggie and I; we do appreciate it, I promise, all the long hours and hard work, and we love you for it.' Placated, you nod and I breathe a sigh of relief. For a moment there I wasn't too sure which way things would go, and I realise that I am constantly living on a knife-edge, where even one sentence taken in slightly the wrong manner can mean the difference between war and peace.

Saturday morning dawns bright and sunny, the heatwave persisting for another day, it seems. You are back to being in a good mood, thankfully, after last night's tense exchange between us, and when the Otex guys turn up to pick you up in a huge black car with tinted windows, I help you out with your golf clubs. Before you get in the car you turn to me, a frown wrinkling your brow as you clasp my forearm.

'See you later. Don't call, because I'll be on the golf course most of the day. I'll call you when I'm done.

And don't worry about dinner. I'm taking these guys to Gaucho for a meal after.'

'OK.' I kiss your cheek and smile into the car. 'Have a good time. I'll see you later.'

As I wave you off, Laura appears in her front garden. 'Morning,' she calls, waving me over despite obviously having only just woken up. She's standing in her pyjamas with flip-flops on her feet, red hair tangled around her shoulders.

'Where's Charlie off to today?'

'Golf. Some corporate thing with the Otex lot – you know, the big merger case? They're playing all day, and Charlie said not to do dinner, so I'm alone all day.'

'*Free* all day, you mean.' Laura gives me a wicked smile. She doesn't particularly like you, saying that you are too controlling and need to learn to lighten up a little. You, on the other hand, think Laura is 'rough', and don't particularly like her either. The thing with you, though, is that it's never made obvious if you don't like somebody – you are charm personified to his or her face. Your ability to put on a completely different persona for other people is quite unsettling at times; it's like you're completely changed, not at all the Charlie I know. You can easily hide the fact that we've just had a row if someone turns up unexpectedly, while I have every emotion written all over my face. While I do agree with Laura's opinion to a certain extent, as the other half in our relationship

I have to defend you when Laura starts picking at things. Another reason, among others, why I can never tell Laura quite how bad things can get between us.

'So? You're not just going to stay in, are you? It's another beautiful day and I've hardly seen you all week! You can't just hide away in doors waiting for big, bad Charlie to get home. Let's go to the beach – the kids can play and have a splash, we can get some chips, ice cream, maybe take them for a walk along the pier? What do you say?' Laura looks at me expectantly, her hands tying her pyjama cord into knots. I pause and think for a moment. You said not to call, because you would be on the golf course all day, so surely that means you won't be able to call me until after you've all finished? If I take my mobile with me, I can always say I've taken Maggie to the park for a play on the swings, but chances are, if you're going for dinner with the Otex guys, I'll have until at least early evening before I hear from you at all. The sun is beating down on me already, despite the early hour, and I realise I just can't face the thought of another day at home, trying to keep Maggie occupied. At the thought of Maggie, stuck indoors for yet another day because you don't trust me when we go out, my decision is made.

'OK, sod it. Let's do it. Beach, here we come!' I grin as Laura squeals and bursts out laughing, making me laugh in the process.

'Excellent! Give me an hour. I have to go and shower and make myself beautiful. I'll knock when I'm ready.'

Sure enough, an hour later, Laura is tapping at the front door, a huge bag slung over her shoulder, Fred crooked in one arm and Lucy bouncing around by her feet. Maggie runs out the front door and squeezes Lucy in a bear hug.

'We're going to the *beach*, Lucy! And there's going to be chips and ice cream and we can make a sandcastle and go paddling and …' Fizzing with excitement, Maggie pauses to take a breath to carry on her epic speech.

'OK, Mags, we get it. Let's go. The sooner we leave, the sooner we arrive!' I scoop her up and carry her to the car, where I buckle her in before helping Laura pack her huge bag into the boot. Seeing Maggie this excited about a trip to the beach makes me feel hideously guilty for keeping her at home all week, even though I don't feel as though I had any other option. I am angry with myself for being so weak and pliable when it comes to you and your demands, ashamed of myself for bending to your will in exchange for a quiet life. A sweep of anger washes over me towards you, for making me feel I can't do things like this with Maggie all the time, for making me fear the outcome of a trip somewhere nice, all because of your uncontrollable jealousy and fear that I will leave given half the chance.

The day passes in a heat-filled haze, the children spending the morning splashing through the waves and building elaborate sandcastles, only to knock them flat two minutes later. Laura and I take it in turns to keep an eye on them, especially near the water, and when it's my turn to watch them, Laura drags her Kindle out of her bag and turns onto her stomach to tan her back. I walk down to the water's edge where the kids are overturning stones to see if they can find any life underneath.

'Kids, if you want to find living things I'll take you over to the rock pools. Come on. Grab your buckets and spades and we'll go exploring.' Maggie and Lucy clap their hands and make a grab for their buckets, while poor old Fred just looks bemused.

'Come on, Freddie.' I take Fred by the hand and follow the girls, who are racing ahead to the rock pools. We find a good-sized pool, water slightly warmed by the heat of the day, and start flipping over slimy, seaweed-covered rocks in search of any form of sea creature we can find – the girls shrieking in delight at a tiny jellyfish, while Fred finds a dead crab fascinating. We fill plastic buckets with seawater and the girls add their treasures to them, pieces of coral, shells and crab legs all making their way into our haul. An hour later, we return to where Laura has obviously given up on her book and fallen asleep. I ever so gently tip one of the buckets over her back, splashing her with cold sea water, and she jumps up shrieking.

'Bloody hell, Sal, you git! I'm soaked! And I was having a very enjoyable dream in which Johnny Depp was telling me how much he loves a red-head.' She shakes herself off and sits back down on the beach towel next to Lucy and Maggie. 'What have you got there?'

Maggie grins up at her. 'We've got a hermit crab, and a little tiny fish, see?'

'Sal helped us find them,' Lucy pipes up, sloshing seawater from the bucket in her haste to show her mother.

'Well, aren't you lucky?' Laura smiles down at them both. 'You're both incredibly lucky to have Sal.' Her eyes flick to my bare legs, exposed to the sun after even I couldn't justify wearing jeans to the beach, to the marks that are still visible from the hot lasagne a week ago and, grateful that she doesn't question me, I say nothing.

We spend the afternoon at the pier, watching the fishermen casting their lines, and when Fred is so exhausted he can't walk any more but refuses to be pushed in the buggy we head back to the car. By the time we pull up on our driveway, all three children are fast asleep in the back. I turn to Laura, who has been uncharacteristically quiet on the drive home.

'Thanks for today, Laur. I didn't realise quite how badly I needed it.' I turn the car off and unclip my seatbelt.

'Sal? Is there anything you want to talk to me about?' Laura gazes at me steadily, forcing me to look away and fiddle with my shirt buttons.

'What? No. Of course not. What do you mean?' I swallow nervously. There really is nothing at this moment in time that I want to talk to Laura, or anyone, about. I've tried that before and it's safe to say that it wasn't a success.

'Your legs, Sal. What happened to your legs? It looks like they're burnt. And you were wearing jeans last week, even though it was really hot, like you wanted to cover them up, or something. Then you just stayed home *all week*. Like you weren't allowed to leave the house. Please, Sal, if there's something wrong, please tell me. I'm your friend; I want to help you.' She reaches out a hand towards me, but seems to change her mind at the last minute, dropping it back into her lap.

'My legs are fine, Laura. Fine. I dropped a hot dish, that's all, and it splashed up. I wore jeans because that's what I wanted to wear and I stayed home because I didn't want to go out. There's nothing sinister going on, and I don't need you making out like there is, OK? I went out with you today, didn't I?' I feel myself getting angry and defensive, even though I know Laura is only trying to help, but I can't, *I can't* talk to her about it. It would only make things worse.

'OK.' Laura opens the car door and swings her legs out, before turning back to me, her gaze unwavering. 'But remember, Sal, I'm only next door, I'm always only next door, whenever you need me.' She pulls a sleeping Fred out from his car seat and I sit for a moment, unsure of what to say, before deciding to say nothing. Reaching in to unclip Lucy from her car seat, I breathe in the scent of Laura's perfume, a stain on the air left by her presence in the car, and wish, beyond everything, that I could tell her.

CHAPTER TEN

CHARLIE

The golf day goes well, and Mr Pavlenco and his team are happy when we all head back towards the clubhouse at the end of the day. I feel like the weight on my shoulders has lifted briefly, now that I know Pavlenco is happier. Mr Pavlenco and his team head through to the bar and I take the opportunity to call Sal. The phone is answered immediately, so I relax and find myself able to enjoy a meal and a few drinks with the Otex team before catching a cab home. The day has been a small respite in the relentless torrent of paperwork and phone calls this demanding case has generated, and although I am feeling a little better about the potential outcome of the deal, I am still aware that there is a lot of work ahead of me if I'm going to pull this off successfully.

As I walk in the door, I catch sight of Sal snoozing on the sofa – there is no sign of Maggie, and as it's past 8pm, I guess Sal has already put her to bed.

'Sal, wake up.' I lean over and hiss quietly, shaking Sal by the shoulder.

'Huh? Oh, Charlie, you're home.' Sal smiles up at me groggily and struggles into a sitting position, dark curls skewed at crazy angles. 'How did it go?'

'Excellent. The team at Otex are happy that we're doing what we can to make sure the merger goes ahead as smoothly as possible, so fingers crossed all good. What did you do today? You seem exhausted.' A tiny niggle of irritation burrows away at me, at the idea of Sal snoozing away on the sofa while I'm out slogging my guts out, schmoozing clients and bowing to their every whim.

'Oh, nothing much. It must be the heat, takes it out of me.' Sal yawns, stretching long fingers out in an arch. It is still ridiculously hot and muggy outside. 'We just stayed at home, had a spot of lunch, nothing exciting.'

'Sounds like you had a good day. And Maggie? She's in bed?'

'Yep, she was exhausted. I think the heat is a little too much for her, too, poor thing. I just hope the weather breaks before she starts school. It'll be awful for the little ones to have to go to school in this heat.'

'I'm sure it will – this is England not Africa! We need to enjoy it while it lasts. Come on. Let's sit out on the patio and open a cold bottle of wine, pretend we're enjoying this heatwave.' I pull Sal up from the couch and we go through to the kitchen to hunt out wine glasses. I grab the cold bottle of wine from the fridge and a tub of green olives and we head out onto the patio, the early evening air still warm and fragrant with the jasmine that curls upwards from the pots next to the back door.

Maggie's toys still litter the garden, where she was obviously playing with them today. Dollies with all their clothes piled up in a heap next to them lie alongside a bucket and spade, a football and a skipping rope. A pair of Maggie's pink sandals lie next to the sandpit, while a stuffed toy lies face down in the sand, and Maggie's cardigan hangs over the swing frame. I feel what was left of my good mood start to slip – how difficult is it for Sal to make sure the garden is tidy at the end of the day? I've spent all week working my arse off at the office, early starts and working all the hours God sends, while Sal does, literally, *nothing*. It's not like there's a huge amount to do, just put the toys back in the toy box, and make sure that shoes and cardigans are put away. Sal catches sight of the look on my face and scurries over to the sandpit and starts to pick up the mess that lies scattered over the garden. This infuriates me even more – the scurrying about, like I'm some irrational clean freak who flips out over mess; like I'm someone to be feared. I just want a clean and tidy house – surely that's not unreasonable?

Sal scrabbles to pick up the toys from the sandpit, watching me warily. 'I'm sorry, Charlie, I meant to get this all sorted before you got home, but I was just so tired and I thought I'd sit down for just a few minutes and … well, I fell asleep.'

Anger explodes out of me before I can stop it, like a tornado ripping along, tearing trees up by their roots. 'For God's sake, Sal, it's not like it's a difficult job, is it? To keep the bloody garden tidy? Despite what you might think, I wasn't just off having a lovely time today; it was *work*, and the last thing I want to come home to is a total shit-hole. Do you understand?' I glare at Sal, my good mood evaporated completely by the crap I have come home to. When will Sal ever learn? Marriage is about equality – both sides taking equal amounts of responsibility – not about one person doing all the work and making all the effort while the other feeds off them.

'Yes, Charlie, I understand.'

'Good.' I stride across the garden and grip Sal's jaw in my hands. 'I'm going to bed now. You can stay out here and tidy all this crap up. I want it sorted before you come up. I don't work hard all day long, even on the bloody weekend, just so you can leave shit everywhere. Right?' I release Sal, and as I sweep past the patio table on my way up to bed my hand knocks the wine bottle off-centre, causing it to crash onto the stones below, taking the wine glasses with it. I don't glance back as I hear the glass shatter across the paving slabs. It serves Sal right for ruining yet another evening.

CHAPTER ELEVEN

SAL

So, your good mood didn't last for very long. It's terrifying to see the way you can switch from calm and loving to enraged and furious within a split second. I know as soon as I open my eyes to see you standing over me that I'm going to regret sitting down for five minutes' peace, remembering that I haven't tidied the garden before stopping for a moment. When we returned from the beach Maggie was lively after her nap in the car and headed straight outside to play while I prepared us some dinner. She spent the rest of the afternoon in the garden, sitting in the sandpit playing dolls. Exhaustion had kicked in again by the time we had eaten and I ended up putting her to bed early, thinking I still had a good while to tidy up before you returned home. The next thing I knew I was opening my eyes to you looming over me, and my first thoughts were not of the garden, but a fierce hope that you hadn't realised Maggie and I had been to the beach with

Laura for the day. Luckily, it seems the state of garden has pushed any further thoughts of what my day has entailed from your mind, and you shout and carry on at me, while I quietly start to tidy up. I know the best thing I can do when you're in this kind of mood is to just keep quiet and let you get on with it – any form of argument or retaliation will just make things worse, and I really don't want you to wake Maggie up. When you announce you're going up to bed, I feel relieved that I won't have to risk a further inquisition. I glance towards Laura's house, checking for any signs that she might have overheard something. With no sign of life from next door, I carry on picking up the toys from where they lie, and watch nervously as you stalk past the patio table, your hand brushing across it, causing both glasses and wine bottle to cascade onto the patio. The shattering of the glass makes me jump but I carry on picking up toys, studiously avoiding your gaze. I breathe a sigh of relief when you head towards the house, without any further comment.

The next morning, there is a thick air of tension surrounding you and I make sure I keep out of your way as much as possible. The last thing I want is for Maggie to be around if you flip out – generally you are fairly good about making sure she doesn't witness too much; however, after last night, I am worried it won't take a lot to push you over the edge.

'I'll take Mags up to the supermarket, shall I?' I lean over your shoulder as you sit at the patio table. 'I was going to get a roasted chicken for lunch to have with some salad. We can walk up there together and get out of your hair for a bit. I'll stop off on the way and take her for a push on the swings; you can relax and read the papers.' I've made sure the patio is swept clean and the garden is tidy, so it seems you're happy to sit outside and read the Sunday papers this morning. You grunt in reply, and as you make no move to speak to me properly, or move from your chair, I assume you're OK with it.

Shopping takes longer than expected, as Maggie and I bump into our neighbour who lives at the top of the street. Mrs Wilson is pleased to see us, as always. An elderly lady, she has lived alone since her husband died, her children all disbanding to various corners of the globe and not returning home to see her as often as she would like. As a result, she dotes on Maggie and always has a little something for her when she sees her. 'Sal! And darling little Maggie. What are you up to?' Mrs Wilson places her shopping bags on the ground and lets Maggie give her a huge squeeze.

'Hi, Mrs Wilson – just a bit of shopping. Charlie's at home, so we're cooking up a storm, aren't we, Mags? Are you going our way?' I glance towards our street and Mrs Wilson nods.

'Here, let me take these.' I rearrange my own shopping bags, enabling me to pick up Mrs Wilson's shopping as well.

'Thank you, Sal – you're too kind. I'm not as strong as I used to be. And Charlie's at home, you say? Well, that's just lovely – that one works too hard for you all, you know. You're lucky to have someone that looks out for you so well.' Mrs Wilson gives a little laugh, and we start to head back towards home. We make small talk as we walk, Mrs Wilson telling me all about how her eldest son has relocated to Australia, taking the grandchildren with him. There is an air of sadness about her as she tells me about their farewell party, and I feel slightly sorry for her. You don't have the time of day for her, but I worry that she gets lonely, sitting indoors by herself, waiting for the phone to ring. I try my hardest to pop in on her when I can, just to check she's all right. Reaching her doorstep, I carry her shopping through for her and gratefully accept a quick cup of tea.

'Thank you, Sal.' Mrs Wilson hands me a steaming cup of strong, brown tea. 'You're a gem – and Maggie is a little dote. You're lucky; you have the perfect family. Make the most of it – they grow up too quickly.' I give her a small smile and look down at my cup. Perfect? I'm not too sure about that.

An hour later, as Maggie and I come strolling down our street, swinging our hands together and occasionally jumping over the cracks in the pavement, I realise you are outside in our front garden, talking to Laura. Usually, I wouldn't worry too much, but following on from yesterday's illicit trip to the beach, which I was too ashamed to tell Laura should be kept secret, my heart starts to beat a little faster, and I feel hot and clammy.

'Everything OK?' I try a wobbly smile in your direction.

'Of course, you silly thing, why wouldn't it be?' You squeeze my shoulder affectionately. 'Laura was just telling me about your little trip yesterday. I'm not surprised you didn't mention it, after being so tired yesterday evening.'

'Oh, yes. We didn't go out for too long, just to get the kids some fresh air, that's all. I meant to tell you but ... well, I was asleep when you came in.'

'You're lucky, Laura. Sal's been extremely busy this week, haven't you, Sal? Indoors all week, making the most of being home with Maggie, I should think, before school starts. I'm surprised Sal could find the time to spend a whole day out!' You put your arm around me proprietarily, clutching me ever so slightly too tightly.

Laura flicks her eyes towards me, almost an apology, as she obviously didn't realise I hadn't told you we'd been out.

'Well, Charlie, I realise that. I haven't seen Sal or Maggie all week – unusual since you live next door, eh?

I almost thought you guys were avoiding me!' Laura gives a little laugh, and Charlie joins in. Despite the supposed hilarity, you could cut the air with a knife.

'Of course not, Laura. You're our neighbour, aren't you? You must come over for dinner soon. I know this lovely chap at work – he'd be perfect for you.'

'In all honesty, Charlie, I'm not really looking, but I appreciate the offer. Dinner would be nice. Sal, I'll catch up with you in the week, OK? We can make an arrangement for dinner then.' Laura turns to go back into the house and, feeling awkward, I face you, unsure of exactly what I'm going to find. Maggie runs into the house, intent on carrying out whatever game she's cooked up on the way home. You stare at me, eyes cold like chips of blue ice.

'Get indoors, Sal. That chicken will be getting cold.'

CHAPTER TWELVE

CHARLIE

To say that I'm furious is an understatement. Sal's deceitfulness and constant lies are ruining our relationship. I find myself feeling more and more wound up all the time and it's all Sal's fault. How difficult can it be to just be honest? I don't feel like I can trust anything Sal says and it's just adding to the pressure I'm already under at the office.

When Sal and Maggie leave to go to the park, I decide I've had enough of sitting around and head out to the driveway – my pride and joy sits on the drive, gleaming, looking more beautiful than anything else I've ever owned. A 2014 BMW X5, black and sleek. Practical in that it has five seats (to keep Sal happy, though God knows we are definitely not going to have any more children, no matter how much Sal bitches about it) and expensive enough to keep me happy.

Growing up we had very little in our family. My stepdad was a hard worker who kept my mum at home so she could look after me, but for all his hard work we still went without, as my dad thought nothing of spending all his wages in the pub on a Friday night, leaving us with nothing for the week ahead. He was partial to a whisky and woe betide anyone who tried to stop him. He was a hard bastard, who ruled our house with an iron fist. I swore blind from when I was a child that I would *never* go without, once I was an adult. This car is my testimony to that – Sal has to drive it through the week and I keep an eye on the mileage, but at weekends she is my baby, for me to enjoy.

I unlock the driver's door and peer in to see if Sal is keeping it as tidy as I have requested. Sal grew up in a family that had whatever they wanted and doesn't seem to understand that things demand respect. Sal never had to wear clothes from a car-boot sale, or watch as all the other kids got to go on school trips. As I peep through into the back seats, something catches my eye on the floor. A baby's bottle has rolled under the passenger seat and lies there; the tiny amount of milk left in it already turned curdled and sour. In the footwell, in front of the bottle, lies a sprinkling of sand. I feel my pulse start to race and the first feelings of anger spread through my body, leaving my face red and my fists clenched. *Sal lied to me AGAIN.* This is the only explanation – after promising to stay at home with Maggie yesterday, after not mentioning a single word about the fact that they may or may not have gone on a trip to the beach yesterday, the proof is lying in the footwell of my pride and joy. To add insult to injury, the fact that Sal couldn't even be bothered to keep the bloody car clean just hammers home exactly how much respect Sal has for my possessions and for me.

Shaking with fury I march back into the house, powerless to stop the anger that courses through my body. There's only one way to teach Sal the meaning of respect. There's only one way to show Sal exactly how it feels when someone disrespects you and disrespects your things, the things that you've worked hard for and that you hold dear. I'll make sure that the lesson about respect doesn't get forgotten again, that's for sure.

CHAPTER THIRTEEN

SAL

You usher me back towards the house, a rigid smile on your face all the while. Feeling a little off balance, I pause for a moment before I open the front door and hold it open while trying to juggle the shopping bags. You sweep in ahead of me, leaving me to close the door one-handed. Following you through to the kitchen, I start to put the shopping away, all the time a sense of unease growing inside me.

'You never mentioned that you and Maggie went to the beach yesterday.' Your voice is like ice water dripping down my neck.

'No, well, like I said outside, Charlie, I fell asleep before you even came home and then there wasn't really a lot of time for talking before you went up to bed, was there?' I feel my spine straighten, as I stand a little taller. *Do I really have to explain myself? Do I really have to tell Charlie every time I leave the house? Surely this is not the norm for most other couples?* I'm

starting to feel as though I'm not sure how much more
of this I can take – the constant accusations of lying, the
permanent state of mistrust.

'I just thought you might have mentioned it, that's
all. Seeing as you said you didn't have any plans. You
said you were going to stay home with Maggie all day,
sorting the house and doing some gardening.'

'Laura suggested it and I agreed; it would have been
a waste of a day to stay indoors.' I am determined not
to back down on this one – I did nothing wrong, unless
taking your daughter out to enjoy the sunshine is doing
the wrong thing. 'And Maggie enjoyed herself. She
can't stay home every day, just on the off-chance…' I
trail off. My little spark of courage has burnt out and I
am worried about antagonising you further.

'*Just on the off-chance?* Just on the off-chance of
what exactly? That I might call and try to speak to my
own child? That I might call to check and see if you're
OK? Going out with that tramp from next door is more
important than building a home for your family, is it?'
Your eye twitches with that telltale tic, the one that
prewarns me you're about to lose your temper.

'No, that's not what I said! Charlie, you're twisting my
words, I never meant that; all I meant was that Maggie
needs some stimulation – I can't keep her home all the
time; she'll be going to school soon.' I place the roasted
chicken on a chopping board and turn to face you,
desperate to calm the situation before things boil over.

'Please, Charlie, let's not make this into a big deal. I took Maggie to the beach with her friends, that's all it was. It wasn't an attempt to escape from here, not a chance to neglect my duties at home or to try and get away from you. You weren't home and I wanted to do something nice for Maggie. Please don't ruin what's left of our weekend.' I take your hands and kiss you gently. You take a deep breath and just as I brace myself for the start of another onslaught, you smile.

'OK. It's not a problem.'

Confused by your quick change of mood, I give a small nod and drop your hands. I should have known that wouldn't be end of it.

The afternoon passes in a pleasant haze of scorching hot sunshine and we agree to take Maggie up to the park for a picnic for lunch. We paddle in the stream that runs through the common, watching Maggie trying to catch the tiny sticklebacks that flit through the clear water. Holding hands, all three of us run through the fountains that spurt up from holes in the ground in random patterns, trying to make it through to the other side without getting soaked, before collapsing in a giggling heap on the grass. Lying on my back, with you laid next to me, I watch the clouds scudding past overhead, a gentle breeze lifting my curls and tickling my forehead. We used to do this all the time, before Maggie came along. Just wander down to the common, dragging a picnic basket between us, lying on the grass talking and swigging Prosecco that had gone warm in the sun because we always forgot to pack the ice blocks. We would spend hours planning our future and laughing at your hideous jokes – you have such a wicked sense of humour that you never fail to make me laugh; it's just a shame we don't see as much of it as we used to. This morning's argument has faded into the distance, made almost a memory by the perfect events of this afternoon. I just wish that these moments, when we are relaxed and happy, with no tears or accusations of lies, were more frequent. When we are in these moments we are what we strive to be – the perfect family, a team with a bond that is unbreakable.

Zero stickleback, one ice cream and three hours later we head for home. Maggie, with the energy that only a four-year-old can have, runs ahead, while we stroll slowly along together, holding hands. Mrs Wilson spies us from her kitchen window and we both raise a hand to her. I feel content, and immensely relieved that this morning's storm has passed. I managed to defuse the situation before you lost your temper – does this mean you'll relax a bit more now? Maybe this means you'll change and not get so angry so easily any more. I think how nice it would be if this afternoon were to mean a turning point in our relationship – maybe things will return to how they used to be between us, before we had Maggie and everything got a bit crazy. It would be worth hanging in there, through all the crazy stuff, if it just meant we could maybe get back to that.

'Happy?' you ask and I turn to you and smile. 'You know what? I am. Today has been really, really lovely, hasn't it? We should make an effort to do things like this more often.' You smile and nod your agreement, and I am just so relieved that everything is OK.

'Sal, I'm putting Maggie to bed – do you want to get us some dinner on?' you shout down the stairs to me, a little while later. I smile and put the newspaper I'm reading to one side. You must really be making an effort to rein it all in, to make a change. Maybe this is the start of a new you, not just a new stage in the never-ending cycle that we usually live in. You very rarely put Maggie to bed, even on the evenings when you are home, preferring to let me deal with it all, saying you don't have the patience for finding numerous stuffed toys, drinks of water, chapters of whatever book Maggie and I are reading together. I go into the kitchen and dig the chicken out from the fridge. Picking up the small wicker basket that we keep by the back door for collecting our spoils, I head out the back door for the vegetable patch, ready to pick some salad to go alongside the chicken for our evening meal.

When I reach the vegetable patch I stop, my heart racing. My mouth hangs open in shock. *What the hell happened?* The gate that secures the patch is hanging off its hinges and the entire patch is destroyed. Every single thing I've grown from scratch with Maggie has been pulled from the earth and thrown into piles in every corner of the plot, so there is no chance of saving anything. This is not the work of rabbits, or of foxes; this can only have been done by a human being. And there is only one person who would know how badly something like this would hurt me. I should have known that an illicit day out at the beach wouldn't go unpunished. I put the basket gently down and sink to my knees in the hard earth, stones and small rocks digging into my skin. Nothing has been spared, not a single tiny cherry tomato, all of which have been pulled from their plants and squashed underfoot. My heart breaks a little at the thought of all the hard work Maggie and I have put into our little patch. *Maggie.* She's going to be devastated, especially as it's now too late in the year for us to even try and fix things and grow something else.

A shadow falls in front of me and I look up to see you sneering down at me.

'You didn't actually think you could get away with it all, did you?'

'What? Get away with *what*? Taking Maggie to the beach? Giving her a little bit of freedom from here? From you?' I am so angry I am past caring about the consequences of losing my temper with you.

'That's it, Sal. Lying, going behind my back, leaving my car in a *fucking state*. Leaving crap all over *my* car, which *I* pay for – not you. I pay for it, it's mine and when I do let you use it you treat like it's just another piece of shit that belongs to you.'

You loom over me as I look up in confusion. 'Charlie, what are you talking about? There's nothing in the car. I drove it to the beach and back. Nobody had anything to eat in it; it was clean. And nothing justifies what you've done here. This wasn't just mine, it was Maggie's.' I thought this was about the beach, not the car.

'Clean? If you call a stinking baby bottle full of curdled milk clean! And sand, *fucking sand*, everywhere. We haven't even got a fucking baby, Sal, so why the hell is there a filthy, stinking, kid's bottle rolling around in the back of my car?' Shit. I realise that when Laura pulled Fred out of the car yesterday when we returned from the beach, she must have left Fred's bottle in there. I was so exhausted when we got back that I didn't even think to check the car.

'So what's this then, Charlie? Revenge? I can't believe you would do this to me. To *us*. This was just as much Maggie's as it was mine. This will break Maggie's heart.' This time you have gone too far. Hurting me I can deal with for Maggie's sake, but when you bring her into it? No, no way.

'It's about *respect*, Sal. It's about thinking about other people, having respect for their things, respecting the stuff they care about. It's about not lying to your partner, covering things up so you can sneak about with other people behind my back. That's what it's all about. It's about supporting your other half in the relationship instead of just taking, taking, taking all the time, and putting me under so much pressure. Maybe if you actually gave a shit about our relationship you would understand.'

'If *I* gave a shit about us?' I feel my temper fraying, and although I know there will be consequences I can't help myself. 'Why do you think I put up with all of this, Charlie? Why do you think I let you treat me the way you do? Because I don't care? I stay because, believe it or not, I do love you, and I love Maggie and I want us to be a family! I put up with everything you throw at me so we can be a happy family – so Maggie grows up with two parents!' You look down at me, still sitting on my hands and knees in the dirt, your lip curling in disgust.

'Really, Sal? I treat you so badly? Don't you think that maybe you get treated the way you deserve to be treated?' With that, you turn on your heel, the sole of your shoe landing on my fingers as you storm off. I feel the bones crunch under your heel and a shocking, sharp twist of pain makes me feel sick to my stomach.

CHAPTER FOURTEEN

CHARLIE

I turn on my heel, catching Sal's fingers under my shoe as I storm out of the little vegetable patch and head back towards the house. I am still shaking with rage. Why doesn't Sal understand that people get treated the way they deserve to be treated? Sal needs to realise that I don't do the things I do out of hatred; I do them out of love. This is all Sal's fault – you can't lie to your partner and think you can get away with it.

I pour myself a whisky and sit at the kitchen table, waiting for Sal to come back in from the garden. Maybe I did go too far with the allotment; perhaps I did lose control a little bit. But the rage was all-consuming and I'm not too sure I could have stopped myself even if I had tried. Thinking back to that first summer we were together, I remember how once Sal had moved into the shared house with me and the two other housemates, our relationship began to feel more stable. I loved nothing more than coming home and knowing that Sal would be waiting for me. There was the odd hiccup, where I arrived home and no one was there, with no note or anything to say where Sal was, or who Sal was with, but once I got the message home that I needed to know if Sal wasn't going to be there, and ideally that Sal would be home each evening when I got back from work, things were much better. It was one Sunday, a few weeks after Sal had moved in, that it was decided I must meet Sal's family, so we travelled to Kent on a sunny but chilly October afternoon.

'They're going to love you – and you're going to love them, I promise.' Sal tucks cold fingers into the crook of my arm as we walk up the path to Sal's childhood home.

'Let's hope so.' Sal knocks and the door is flung wide open immediately. Sal's mother appears, her wide frame filling the doorway, a shock of dark curls, so very similar to Sal's, standing out around her head.

'Sally! Oh, my baby, it's so good to see you! And this must be Charlie!' She squeezes Sal hard and makes a move towards me. I hold out my hand stiffly before she reaches me, and she pauses for a moment before shaking it, smiling at me all the while.

'Nice to meet you.'

'And you, Charlie. I've heard so much about you. It's nice to put a face to the name and see exactly who's been keeping our Sal from us!' She turns towards Sal. 'And YOU! You look … well. It's been so long. We didn't see you all summer, so don't be cross but your sisters are here, too. They've missed you!' She ushers us into the house and through into a poorly lit living room, which is probably quite spacious but it's hard to tell given the number of people that have been squeezed into it. Cries of 'Sal! You're home!' and 'It's been so long!' fill the air as Sal is immediately surrounded by tall, tanned girls, all with the same shock of crazy dark curls that Sal has. I stand to one side, watching as Sal greets each and every person in the room while I just stand and wait for someone to remember I'm still there.

'And this is Charlie!' Sal turns to me, arm outstretched to point at me in the corner. I muster up a smile, raising my eyebrows at Sal, who doesn't seem to notice quite how uncomfortable I'm feeling. The sisters all turn towards me and I feel as if I'm something under a microscope.

'Nice to meet you, Charlie. I'm Julia. I'm the oldest, believe it or not.' Laughing a ridiculously tinkly laugh is the smallest of all the girls, a petite little thing with dark hair tumbling down her back. 'And as I'm the oldest, I'm the one in charge, so watch it!' She laughs again as Sal and the other girls join in. *What's that supposed to mean?* I make a mental note to let Sal know when we get home that I don't appreciate being spoken to like that by anyone, regardless of whether they are part of Sal's family or not. Sal introduces me to the rest of the sisters, who are all as loud and boisterous as each other, and we all descend on the dining room for Sal's mum's amazing Italian feast. Maria passes me the huge tray of pasta and a serving spoon.

'Charlie, is that all you're having? You'll waste away! Here, have some more.' Sal's mum heaps another two spoonfuls of creamy pasta onto my plate.

'Thank you, Maria, but please. That's enough.' I hold my hand up to stop her from loading any more on to my already full to bursting plate.

'Well. If you're sure. There's plenty more if you change your mind.' She moves away from me and attacks some other poor soul with her serving spoon. *Jesus, they like to eat.* Every plate is piled high with pasta, homemade garlic bread, gnocchi and salad. Sal, having returned home like some sort of prodigal son, is seated at the other end of the table from me, next to the head of the family, Giovanni. He, like his wife, is large-framed, which comes as no surprise seeing how much the entire family like their food, but instead of the tumbling, glossy dark curls shared by the rest of his family he has only a smattering of grey hair around the sides of his head. He is considerably quieter than the rest of his family, seemingly more content to observe and chime in every now and again, his hand reaching for his wife to pat or squeeze each time she passes by him and I realise that Sal must take after him. Sitting where I am, between Maria and Paola, one of the middle sisters, a barrage of questions is hurled at me.

'Charlie, what do you do for a living?'

'Where are you from, Charlie? Do you come from round here?'

'Where do your parents live? Do you have any brothers or sisters?'

'Are you the oldest or are you the spoilt baby like Sal?' This last question is greeted with howls of laughter, as if it's the funniest thing ever. Sal pulls a face, making them all laugh even harder.

'I'll be a corporate lawyer eventually, I'm from Lincolnshire, and no I don't have any brothers or sisters.' I keep my answers short and sweet; the less said about my family the better. If I don't give out any information, hopefully they'll all get the message. Sure enough, the sisters soon lose interest in me once they realise they're not going to get my entire life story in one meal, and go back to regaling me with tales of Sal's childhood and reminiscing about how they had such fun doing this, and has Sal told me about when that happened, etcetera, etcetera … They all talk over each other and it's difficult to get a word in edgeways. Sal sits there, next to Giovanni at the head of the table, grinning like an idiot, completely failing to realise that I am not enjoying myself.

'Come on, Sal, you can help me do the dishes while the others finish quizzing Charlie. You've got out of it all summer so far.' Julia jumps to her feet, and pulls Sal up by the hand. Sal grins at me and mouths, 'OK?'

as Julia tugs Sal away into the kitchen, Maria trotting behind carrying an armful of dirty plates from the table. I shrug and turn my gaze coldly away from Sal. What else can I do?

Finally, after what might possibly be the longest evening of my life, in which I have had to suffer hours of inane jabbering from Sal's entire family and have batted away countless attempts to discover all manner of details about my life, the meal is over and we are free to go. I endure kisses from Maria and all of the sisters, while Sal is hugged and squeezed to death and they all behave as if they aren't going to see each other for years and years. This is all completely foreign to me, and I thank my lucky stars that Sal hasn't asked to meet my mother yet.

'Well? What did you think of them? Aren't they amazing?' Sal waves frantically at the gathering on the doorstep, before turning to me once we are safely seated in the car and heading back towards our house.

'Honestly, Sal? It's all a bit much, isn't it? I mean, your mum treats you like you're five years old. And you're not a fucking god, you know, despite what your sisters might think.' Sal reels back slightly and couldn't have looked more shocked if I'd delivered a slap across the face.

'What? Nobody thinks that! We're a close family; I didn't see them all summer because I stayed in London with you! It's not normally that intense, to be honest; it's only that they were excited to meet you. And my mum is just ... a normal mum. She likes it when I go home; she likes to cook a big meal and spoil us all. She's excited that you're going to be part of the family. They were just trying to make you feel welcome.' Sal doesn't look at me, choosing instead to concentrate hard on the road.

I stare out of the passenger window, biting my tongue hard in order not to give rise to the anger that is bubbling away deep inside my belly. I'm not going to be part of the family. *I don't want to be part of the family.* Your mum didn't even seat us together at the dinner table, for Christ's sake. I don't want Sal's sisters and mum poking their noses into our business, knowing everything about us. I want it to just be Sal and me on our own, always. I don't have anything to do with my family, and I'm OK. We don't need Sal's family in our lives, not to that extent. Signalling to take the turn leading to the motorway, I resolve that the less we see of Sal's family, the better.

CHAPTER FIFTEEN

SAL

I take my time clearing up the vegetable patch after you storm back into the house, believing that the longer it takes me to tidy up, the longer it gives you to calm down and see sense. The majority of everything that Maggie and I have grown is completely and utterly ruined, plants and bits of vegetable strewn across the whole fenced-off section of garden. I get to work on clearing the patch, piling everything up in one corner to be burnt next time we have a bonfire. The only items worth salvaging are a few straggly carrots that I put to one side, so I can at least tell Maggie we have something to cook. It's slow, painful work as the fingers on my right hand have started to throb now that the initial hot, sharp pain has subsided and they are already swollen and awkward. I'm ninety per cent sure they're broken. By the time the sun sets and the garden is filled with shadows, I'm done, sweat making my T-shirt cling to the small of my back. I look towards the kitchen in the hope that the room is in darkness and you've already gone upstairs to bed but I see the warm, yellow light spilling from the window and your silhouette cross in front of it, a glass of whisky in your hand. I sigh heavily, but I can't put it off any longer. The night has turned cool despite the heat of the day now that the sun has disappeared below the horizon and I am only wearing a thin T-shirt. I shiver and struggle to my feet, feeling stiff after sitting for so long. Wearily, I trudge my way up the garden path to the kitchen, where I know you will be waiting for me.

You look up from your seat at the kitchen table, hair tousled and eyes bloodshot, when I walk in through the back door. I head straight for the medicine cabinet, screwed to the wall behind the kitchen door, and start rooting through it for strapping and cotton wool.

'You shouldn't have made me do that, Sal.' Your voice is low, and you studiously avoid looking at my poor, broken hand. 'I warned you so many times not to lie to me, but it's like you can't help yourself. It's like you deliberately do it, because you want me to lose my temper and get angry with you. It has to stop, Sal. I've been thinking and I realise that it's been like this right the way through, from the beginning. Since that first time I met your mum and dad and your sisters – I've been thinking about that, how you ignored me that day and put my needs second and you've been doing it every day since. I love you so much, Sal; no one could ever love you like I do.' You get up and move around the table towards me. I brace myself but you just put your arms around me and squeeze me tightly, either not noticing or not caring that my swollen hand is also being squeezed painfully tight as it's trapped between our bodies.

'I'm sorry, Sal. I'm sorry for loving you so much and I'm sorry that you make me do these things. I would die if you left me. I mean it, Sal; if you leave I'll kill myself. You know I mean it.' I nod slowly and look into your eyes, trying surreptitiously to manoeuvre my hand to freedom.

'OK, Charlie. It's all right. I'm not leaving. I'm sorry – it won't happen again, OK? Please, just help strap my fingers up.' I'm tired and I don't want to fight. I hold my hand out to you and you immediately turn away and busy yourself finding the end of the fabric strapping.

'Hold still.' You grab my hand, stuffing the cotton wadding between my fingers and pulling the tape tightly around, squeezing slightly to make sure the end is stuck. I hiss between my teeth as you squeeze and you look up.

'Sorry, is it painful? I think you've learnt your lesson now, haven't you, Sal? And I'm assuming that this now means we won't have any more lying, or disrespecting my things. Just to make sure, I'm confiscating the car keys. You can have them back when you've earned them. It's for your own good, OK?'

You are still gripping my fingers and I have no choice but to nod miserably. For all your talk of how much you love me and how you would die if I left you, it all just boils down to how you can manipulate me into doing what you want. It's all just another stage in the cycle – I can't believe it's taken me this long to realise it. It feels like I'm finally waking up to the fact that it doesn't matter how many good moments, how many perfect afternoons we have together, the cycle is never going to end. You're never going to change – and it's up to me to decide what I'm going to do about it.

'I'm sorry, Charlie. I've said it won't happen again, and it won't.'

'Good. That's what I want to hear. Now, I'm going up to bed, I've got an early start in the morning – just make sure it's all cleared up outside before you come up, all right? I don't want Maggie seeing the mess you've made out there.'

I look after you in disbelief – once again you've turned things around to make them my fault, fear making me keep my mouth shut and accept it.

I decide I'm too tired to eat, and the pain in my fingers is making me feel slightly sick, so I swallow down some painkillers and start to tidy up the dishes you've left in the sink while I was clearing up the destruction in the garden. I think about what you said, about how things started to go wrong from when I first took you home to meet my parents, and I realise that you are probably right.

I am excited that I am finally going to be able to take you to meet my family. I have stayed in London with you throughout the summer break from uni and it feels strange, not having seen them for so many weeks. Now it is October, the weather is turning and we have been seeing each other for five months and living together for two. I still haven't managed to tell my family that we have moved in together, so I am hoping to kill two birds with one stone today. I had suggested going back in the summer, when it was my sister Anna's birthday party, but you had fallen ill with a stomach bug so we had had to cancel. Then I thought we could go for a visit at the end of the summer, for August Bank Holiday, a time when traditionally my whole family would get together and celebrate the summer, all of us being together, and my mum would cook up an amazing meal for us all. But at the last minute you had tripped on the way home from your job at a pub round the corner from our house, spraining your ankle, which meant you didn't really want to travel too far, not with your crutches and everything.

So at long last, after weeks of planning and me making sure you don't fall or eat anything dodgy for the whole week before our trip is scheduled, we make it to my parents' house and I am delighted when Mama throws open the door, gives me one of her huge hugs and tells me that Julia, Paola and Anna are also here to meet you. Mama swoops in for a big bear hug and turns towards you to envelop you in her huge arms, but you already have your hand out in front of you for my mum to shake. Mama pauses for a second, a little unsure. No one shakes hands in our family. We hug, squeeze, kiss both cheeks and go in for another hug, but very rarely do we ever shake hands. I understand, though, why you behave like this. You explained to me in the very beginning that your family are not very tactile – that you don't remember ever seeing your mother and father kiss or hug each other, and that they very rarely showed you any affection growing up. This is something I try my hardest to get my head around, especially when you push me away and tell me to leave you alone.

We head through into the lounge and I'm delighted to see all my sisters are here. I've missed seeing everybody over the summer, and although we've all grown up and moved out, as the youngest I'm still the baby and my sisters love to make a huge fuss of me. Julia, the eldest at twenty-eight, introduces herself to you. Although she's the eldest of us all, she's also the tiniest so makes a huge deal about how she is actually the oldest and therefore in charge of us all, to anyone who will listen. I introduce you to my other sisters and you seem a little quiet, although I understand that being the centre of my huge family's attention is probably quite overwhelming. I squeeze your hand and smile as we head through to the dining room. My mum has done herself proud and has produced a huge tableful of pasta, salad, homemade garlic bread and antipasti. I know how you love Italian food – you always say you can't beat an authentic Italian restaurant – and I'm pleased to be able to show off what Mama can do in the kitchen. You're seated between my mum and Julia, which just goes to show how excited Mama is to meet you. That seat is normally reserved for me, but tonight I sit next to Papa who whispers in my ear as I sit down.

'Hey, Sal, that's a fine one you have there.' He nods his head towards you.

'Thanks, Papa. I hope so. I should tell you something, though … we're kind of living together. I haven't told Mama or Julia yet; I don't want there to be any drama, OK? You know what they're like; they'll have something to say about it and Charlie's a little bit sensitive about stuff. I don't want them upsetting Charlie.'

My dad smiles, his eyes crinkling at the corners. 'It's OK, Sal. You want me to tell your mother when you've gone? I can tell her then, then you can field the phone calls until you're ready to speak to her, but remember it's only because she loves you, right?' My dad always knows the right thing to say.

'I know, Papa.' I smile and squeeze his hand. A giant of a man whose life has been dominated by the whirlwind that is my mother since she waltzed into his life thirty years previously, I wouldn't mind at all if I ended up with a marriage like the one he and my mother share. Turning my attention back to the table, I hear my sisters bombarding you with questions, which you bravely try to answer as my mother shovels spoonfuls of pasta onto your plate. Smiling to myself, I am so pleased we made it here tonight, and so happy that you seem to be fitting perfectly into my loud, crazy family. Julia jumps up from the table and says, 'Come on, Sal, you can help me do the dishes while the others finish quizzing Charlie. You've got out of it all summer.' I pick up on the dig she's making and glance over at you, hoping you didn't pick up on it, too. You're talking to Paola, picking at one last piece of homemade garlic bread, and once again I think how well you fit, how you look like you've always been part of our family. Julia reaches over, pulls me up and drags me towards the kitchen.

Once safely closeted in the kitchen, she turns to me. 'So. Don't think I didn't hear what you were saying to Dad.'

'About what?'

'Come on, Sal, you *know* what. You're seriously living with Charlie? After, what, a few months?'

I roll my eyes. 'Oh, please, Jules, cut it out. You're living with Luca so what's the big deal?'

'Firstly, I am five years older than you, I've finished uni, I have a proper job and Luca and I had been

Lisa Hall

together for a year before we even considered living together. How well do you even know Charlie? Have you met the family?' Julia glares at me, her dark eyes flashing, hands on her hips.

'No, I haven't met Charlie's family yet – but there's a reason for that. They're not like us, Jules. They're not close. I think there was some stuff that went on there when Charlie was growing up.' I pick at the threads on the tea towel I'm holding, while avoiding Julia's eyes, because I kind of know she has a point.

'That's my point, though, Sal – what stuff? You need to find shit like this out before you go moving in together, and what next? Getting married? You haven't even finished uni!'

'No, but Charlie has – Charlie's going to get a job while I finish my degree. I knew you wouldn't understand, Jules; that's why I didn't want to tell you, you or Mama, because you're both as bad as each other!' Julia sighs and runs her hand through her already wild curls.

'Sal. We love you. That's why we nag you about stuff. If you're happy with Charlie, that's fine, we'll accept it; but I just want you to be sure before you commit to serious stuff, like living together, OK? And Charlie doesn't seem like the type I can see you settling down with, that's all.'

I squeeze my big sister hard. 'Thanks, Jules. Thanks for caring, and interfering and poking your nose in;

believe me when I say I really do love you for it, but please ... Just let me be a grown-up – just this once. I really do think I love Charlie and I really do think this could be 'The One'. OK? And if it all fucks up, you can totally pick up the pieces and say "I told you so".'

Julia laughs and flicks the tea towel at me. 'I'd never say that, you idiot. As long as you're sure. Remember you can call me any time, for anything.'

'I know. Now shut up. Mama's coming and Dad already said he's going to tell her after we've left so we don't get the Spanish Inquisition.'

Later that evening, on the drive home, I turn to you to rave about how well the evening has gone and how I'm so pleased you've fitted so well into my family, but you cut me dead. As you rant at me about how I'm spoilt, how I shouldn't think I'm great just because my family do and how, pretty much, you don't think a lot of my family at all, I feel like you've punched me in the guts. It's almost as though we attended completely separate evenings – and my version of the evening went far better than yours.

For the first time in our relationship, I think that maybe Julia is right. Maybe I have made a mistake in moving in with you so quickly, when in actual fact I don't really know you at all. But then, after that night, you never mention how you feel again, not until after we are married anyway. The next evening we go ice skating, falling over each other and laughing till we cry.

Another night full of perfect moments, with the promise of more for the rest of our lives. We go back to our little shared house, falling into bed after a beautiful evening together, and I think maybe I have just imagined the venom in your voice when you spoke about my family. Maybe I have got it wrong.

CHAPTER SIXTEEN

CHARLIE

Anita's voice crackles through the intercom, 'Mr Pavlenco is here for your ten o'clock meeting, Charlie.'

'Thanks, Anita. Get him a coffee and put him in the boardroom. I'll be through in a moment – oh, and can you let Geoff know he's here? He's supposed to be in on this meeting as well.'

'Geoff's not in today, Charlie. He left a message earlier to say he's ill and won't be able to make it in for the meeting today.' And there's the reason why Geoff will never make partner, never amount to anything more than what he is already – and he's only achieved that thanks to his father being an old school friend of Mr Crisp. The guy has no ambition and I'm not even one hundred per cent sure why he bothered to train as a lawyer in the first place, when he can't be bothered to put the hours in. Possibly just to keep his rich old dad happy. I grit my teeth in annoyance before speaking into the intercom again, remembering to smile at the last minute. Apparently you can hear a smile in someone's voice.

'That's not a problem, Anita. I have all the paperwork here and ready. Please make Mr Pavlenco comfortable and I'll be with him shortly.' I lean back in my chair, scrunching my fingers through my hair, and use the ten minutes' grace I've just earned myself to collect my thoughts. Lucian Pavlenco, a Romanian Mr Big and the head of Otex, has arrived early for our meeting this morning, to finalise the last few arrangements before we pitch our buy-out offer to the communications company that's up for grabs. Pavlenco has made a name for himself as a big entrepreneur, headed in the footsteps of the likes of Richard Branson. He just appeared from nowhere one day, it seems, and has spent the last five years buying up small companies, adding them to his existing portfolio and then making a shit load of money out of them. Which is the reason why I'm feeling a little nervous about dealing with him on my own – this is a big deal, and if all goes to plan I'm in with a chance of making partner at Hunter, Crisp and Wilson. *No, not if – I will make damn sure it all goes to plan so that I make partner, even if it means making Geoff look bad.* When I make partner, everything will be perfect. I will be able to keep Sal at home, taking care of the house, and the extra money will make everything a little easier. I won't need to worry any more about Sal making noises about going back to work when Maggie goes to school – if I can earn enough money there'll be no need. Satisfied that I am completely prepared, I grab the files from my desk, smooth down my shirt and hurry down the corridor to the boardroom.

'Mr Pavlenco, good to see you.' I extend my hand and let him grip it in a vice-like handshake.

'Lucian, please. May I call you Charlie?' He smiles a wolfish grin, and gestures towards the chair opposite him. 'Please, sit.'

I sit down, and signal to Anita for more coffee. 'Of course, Lucian. Please do call me Charlie. I apologise that Mr Parker – *Geoff* – can't be here today, but I assure you that I can deal with everything for you in his absence. I have negotiated the draft agreements with the communications company and I have them here for you to look over.' I hand him a slim file containing the agreements. 'You understand, of course, from previous dealings, that the majority of the shareholders must agree.'

Lucian looks up from the file he is reading and gives another sharp grin, pointed teeth gleaming. He reminds me of a wolf stalking its prey. '*Charlie*. Please rest assured that, from my point of view, I have no concerns that the shareholders will not agree to these terms.'

'Of course, Mr Pavlenco.' I can't help slipping back into being formal with him; he gives off an aura that makes me feel slightly nervous. 'But you must understand that another company is also showing an interest in purchasing the communications company you wish to buy out. Therefore, it is in our best interests to ensure that the shareholders will agree to our terms. Legally, the shareholders must, in the majority, be in agreement for you to acquire the company. If this means we need to, shall we say, *amend* our terms to make things slightly more favourable for us, then that is what I suggest we do.'

'As I said, Charlie' – Lucian leans forward towards me across the table – 'I have no fear whatsoever that the shareholders will not agree to the most generous terms that are set out here in our draft agreement.' His voice is low and sends a tiny shiver down the back of my spine. I get the message. I lean back in my chair and busy myself with pouring more coffee.

'Very well, Mr Pavlenco. I shall arrange for …' The intercom buzzes on the boardroom table. 'Apologies, I must answer this. Yes, Anita? I did request that I was not to be disturbed.' I mouth 'sorry' towards Lucian, who shrugs and takes a sip of his coffee, before turning to what I assume is his bodyguard to whisper in his ear.

'I'm sorry, Charlie, but I have a gentleman on line one who is insisting on talking to you. He says he's not going to get off the line until he speaks with you.'

'I'm in a meeting, Anita. I really can't be disturbed. Take a number and tell him I'll call him back in an hour or so.'

'But Charlie …'

'Anita, please. Just do it.' I switch the intercom off to stop any further disruption and turn to Lucian. 'Apologies, Lucian. So you're happy with what we have written up in the draft agreement?'

Lucian stands and once again grabs my hand in his strong, vice-like grip. 'I am satisfied that we will have no problems with this, Charlie. Thank you for meeting with me, and please, do not be worried by the interruptions. Perhaps we can meet for lunch soon? To speak of things other than mergers and buy-outs? Yes?' He gives another wolfish grin and sweeps out of the room, his bodyguard trotting out after him.

I return to my office, catching Anita before she heads out of the door for lunch. 'Jesus, Anita, what was all that about? I told you not to disturb me. Pavlenco is a big deal!'

'Sorry, Charlie, but this guy … he wouldn't get off the phone. He said that he must talk to you, that it was really important. I thought maybe it was something to do with Sal, that something had happened, but he said it wasn't. He said he needs you to call him back urgently. The number's on your desk; his name is Radu Popescu.

Is it OK if I go for lunch? And I'm sorry, Charlie – I wouldn't have bothered you otherwise.'

'It's fine, Anita.' I sigh, trying not to snap. 'Go. I'll call the guy back and see what he wants, although I can't see anything being that urgent.' Glancing at me apologetically, Anita puts her jacket on, smears on another slick of her trademark bright red lipstick and slinks quietly out of the door. I sit at my desk, pondering Lucian's certainty that we won't have any issues with the shareholders' agreement with regard to our terms. With a bit of luck, it'll all come off with no hitches, and I'll be partner by this time next year. Then I'll be able to relax a little bit. I pick up the Post-it note Anita has left on my desk containing the name and number of the crank who called earlier. Screwing it up, I lean over and throw it into the wastepaper basket. If it's that urgent, whoever he is will call back. I have more important things to worry about.

CHAPTER SEVENTEEN

SAL

I buckle up Maggie's sandals as best I can with my broken fingers bandaged up like sausages. They are awkward and bulky, making even the easiest jobs difficult.

'Come on, Mags, give me a hand – can you do this buckle?' The second shoe defeats me, the pain in my hand making my fingers throb like crazy. Maggie tuts, and starts trying to buckle it herself, while I quickly escape to the kitchen to swallow two more ibuprofen before I take Maggie over to visit my mum. The one good side to you getting the job three years ago at Hunter, Crisp and Wilson was that the job came with a significant pay rise, meaning we could leave our grotty old flat in South-East London and move out into Kent. Moving out of London meant our money could go a little further and we could stretch to a three-bedroom house. I argued in favour of Kent knowing that it meant I could be closer to my mum and dad, although I didn't let you know this was my reason – I used my idyllic country childhood as a bargaining tool, stating that it wasn't fair to expect Maggie to grow up in a dirty city when there was a beautiful county of woodlands, countryside and beaches on our doorstep and in our price range. So now, we live in a quiet Kentish village, just a twenty-minute drive away from my parents, but we probably see less of them than we did when we lived in London.

'Quick, then, Mags, or we'll miss the bus.' I finish off the last buckle where Maggie is still fiddling with it, and reach for her chubby little hand. You have taken the car keys to work, as I still haven't earned them back yet, apparently, although I'm not sure how well I could drive with my hand all bandaged up anyway. I tried to put off the visit to my mother today, but when I called to cry off she went to great lengths to tell me how much she had missed Maggie, and how she hadn't seen her since her birthday, so there was no way I was getting out of it. I just need to think up a good excuse to explain away the bandage.

Forty hot and sweaty minutes later, we get off the bus in Little Wealden and start the short walk up the hill to my parents' house. My hand is throbbing and Maggie is whinging – although she likes the idea of taking the bus, the reality is she is bored by the time we leave our village – and I am relieved when we arrive and my mum swings the door open like she's been waiting for us all morning, which in all fairness she probably has.

'Sal! You look frazzled, my love. Come on in and get a cold drink – where's the car? Did you park up the road? Maggie, my beauty, come to Nonna.' She swoops down and scoops Maggie up into her arms.

'No, Mama, we caught the bus. I thought it might make it an adventure.' I smile and, despite feeling the beginnings of a headache, my tension melts away once I am back at my childhood home. 'A drink would be good, though. Come on, Mags, let Nonna back in the door. Papa might be out in the shed.' Maggie squirms out of my mother's arms and races for the back door. There's nothing she loves more than 'helping' my father in his workshop – a shed that he set up in the back garden once he retired to keep him out of my mother's hair.

'I thought that was you.' A voice comes through from the living room, and I enter to see my sister Anna sprawled out in an overstuffed armchair. I lean down to kiss her. 'I didn't know you would be here. How are you feeling?'

'Fat. Hot. Sweaty. Decidedly unattractive. Pissed off and ready for this bun to be cooked. I'm not sure I'll ever forgive Tony for getting me in this mess.' She puffs her fringe away from her forehead and gives a wry laugh. Anna and Tony's baby is due in only eight weeks, and while she may complain about how uncomfortable she is, we all know they are both desperate to meet their baby. It's taken six years of trying and three rounds of fertility treatment for them to get this far.

'Yeah, I don't envy you in this heat,' I say. 'Just put those fat, swollen ankles up and rest while you can – before long you'll be back to your normal skinny self but desperate for five minutes' peace.' Anna laughs, and my mother bustles in carrying a tray containing cold lemon squash and a plate of Mr Kipling's French Fancies. My mother still thinks I'm five years old sometimes, I swear.

'I got your favourites in, Sally. Now, how's Charlie getting on? Still working on that big deal? I hope you're not being too neglected. You need to tell Charlie that life isn't all work, work, work, you know. Family is more important.' My mum eyes me over the top of her glasses.

'Charlie knows that, Mama. It's all OK. Yes, the deal is still on and it's been very busy at work for Charlie, but everything is fine, don't worry.' I smile and reach for a sticky cake, even though in this heat it's the last thing I want. Seeing me reach for the cake, my mum spies my bandaged hand.

'Sal! What did you do? Oh, your poor hand, come here.' Mama makes a grab for my bandaged-up fingers, and I jerk away from her. Shame and embarrassment prickle away at me, my cheeks flushing red, and I think fast for an excuse to offer my mother as to why my fingers are all trussed up like they are.

'No, Mama! Please, it's fine. I caught my fingers in the car door, and they're just bruised. It's fine, nothing to worry about.'

'Well, let me take a look. I was a nurse, you know; when I first met your father, back at home in Vernazza. I met him when he came into the hospital when he sliced open his hand gutting a fish ...' My mum tells us this story every chance she gets and I hope this will steer her away from me and my bandaged fingers.

'Yes, Mama, we know the story. Please, trust me. It's fine. It's just some bruising, and it'll be gone in a day or two.' This seems to satisfy Mama, who takes what I say as gospel, but I see a small frown cross Anna's brow. To turn the attention away from my sore fingers, I bring up the subject of the impending birth of Anna's baby, knowing that this will distract my mother for hours. Sure enough, she's soon on a roll, lecturing Anna about not having her bag packed ('Paola came seven weeks early! *Seven*. Can you imagine it? And I had *nothing* in the hospital. *Nothing*. And then your father turns up with the smallest pair of knickers I owned for me to wear home – could you imagine? After that labour!') and scolding Anna for not having prepared meals for the freezer to 'keep Tony going' while Anna was in the hospital.

'Mama, I'll be in the hospital for, like, a night or something. Tony will live, don't worry.' Anna rolls her eyes at me. Mama turns her attention to me.

'So, Sal, when are we going to get another grandchild from you and Charlie? Maggie starts school in September; you're going to need something to do.'

Mama laughs at herself, while I find it hard to even muster up a smile.

'Sorry, Mama, not going to happen. I'd love to have another one but Charlie says no. Apparently, we can give a better lifestyle to Maggie if she's an only child.'

'Rubbish!' Mama declares. 'So you would have been happier if it was just you? I don't think so, Sally; you're from a big family, you need children around you. You've got to explain to Charlie that it's a decision for both of you to make, not just Charlie.' Anna nods her agreement.

'Just think, Sal, if it was just you growing up,' she says. 'Imagine how boring it would be – and Mags is so sociable she needs other kids around her. Charlie's being kind of selfish, don't you think, if it's not a decision you agree with?' I concede that Anna has a point, but neither of them understands the true nature of our relationship and that's definitely not something I want to start discussing with them.

'I don't really get a say in it, OK? At the end of the day, Charlie doesn't want another baby. Doesn't want a big family full stop and there isn't any discussion about it, so let's just all look forward to Anna's baby and stop worrying about what I'm going to do.' Saying the words out loud is painful; I still haven't really got to grips with the fact that we won't be having any more children. I don't mention the job application sitting in my pocket. I see Anna raise her eyebrows at my mother but neither of them says any more. The discussion turns to Julia and Luca, and the restaurant they are in the process of setting up in Rome, and after a little while I call Maggie in from the shed and tell my mother I'll see her soon.

'I'll see you out.' Anna heaves herself to her feet and follows me through to the front door. 'Are you sure you're OK with the no more kids thing, Sal?' Anna asks quietly, resting her hand lightly on my arm as I go to walk through the door.

'Not really, Anna, to be honest, but what can I do? It's not like I can make a baby on my own, is it? And Charlie is adamant that we shouldn't have any more kids – I'm guessing it's something to do with the family, when Charlie was growing up. Stuff happened that Charlie still hasn't spoken to me about and I don't want to push it. Anyway, between you and me, I'm applying for a job; just keep it quiet. I haven't told Charlie yet.' Anna nods. 'OK, Sal. I'll keep Mama off your back. I'm sure she'll chill out a little bit once this little one arrives.' She pats her enormous belly and I kiss her on both cheeks.

At the bottom of the lane, I pause by the village postbox, fingering the envelope in my pocket that contains my job application for a Year Six teacher in a relatively decent part of South-East London. I take a deep breath and shove the envelope into the postbox.

CHAPTER EIGHTEEN

CHARLIE

Heading back to my desk after a dismal lunch of a soggy Pret sandwich, I bump into Mr Hunter, also walking towards the lifts on his return to his office after, presumably, a more satisfactory lunch than mine. A small man, always dressed in slightly old-fashioned suits, with a pale brown moustache that he is fond of twiddling, Mr Hunter's small stature belies the gravitas he actually exudes within the company.

'Charlie!' he exclaims, holding out a hand for one of his bone-crushing handshakes. For such a small man he has a mighty fine grip. Stella and I are looking forward to your dinner party tonight. I trust everything is still OK?' Oh, God. The dinner party. I had completely forgotten that it was tonight. *Shit. I'd better get upstairs and call Sal, make sure everything is under control.* Confident that Mr Hunter hasn't noticed the panic that flits across my face, I decide the only way forward is to style it out.

'Of course, Mr Hunter. Sal and I are looking forward to welcoming you into our home – there's nothing you don't eat, is there? Sal is a wonderful cook. You won't be disappointed.'

Mr Hunter looks at me, a frown creasing his brow. 'Charlie, I don't eat seafood, I'm afraid. I'm sure I told Anita to let you know when she emailed me with regard to the dinner party in the first place. I'm very allergic. One prawn could be the death of me!' He chortles, a big belly laugh at odds with his small stature, while inside I curse Anita for not passing the message on.

'Of course – I do apologise, Mr Hunter. Anita did tell me but it must have slipped my mind.' *I am going to bloody kill her – I gave her one job, for Christ's sake.* 'No, please rest assured that there won't be any seafood on the menu this evening – everything will be perfect.' I smile reassuringly at him, and he pats my arm as he turns towards the lift and presses the button for the sixth floor – top-floor offices, with stunning views over the river. These are reserved for those who make it to the top of the firm – those who make partner.

'I'm sure it will be, Charlie. And from what I hear, you're doing a fabulous job with the Otex buy-out. Who knows, maybe we'll be having that partner conversation sooner rather than later. I'll see you this evening at eight.' Mr Hunter sweeps into the lift, leaving me open-mouthed and waiting for the next one. *Sooner rather than later. Surely this can mean only one thing? Hunter can only mean that if I pull this whole Pavlenco thing off I will be made partner when Crisp retires in three months' time.* I resist punching the air, but his words put an extra spring in my step, and I bounce my way up the stairs to my third floor office (not in the sixth-floor league, but still not at the bottom). When I reach my office, I give Anita a small scowl as I walk past, as I haven't forgiven her for forgetting to pass the message on to me regarding the seafood allergy. Grabbing the phone, I dial home to remind Sal that the Hunters will be coming for dinner at eight this evening.

After five or six rings Sal finally answers the phone sounding puffed and out of breath.

'Hello?' Sal's voice huffs into my ear, and I feel myself start to get instantly irritated.

'Sal? Why are you out of breath? Where have you been?' I demand. I will be seriously pissed off if Sal's been off gallivanting with Laura and not getting prepared for the dinner party. Especially after the beach incident – I thought I had made myself quite clear how I felt about Sal hanging around with Laura on that occasion. At least this time, I am in possession of the car keys.

'Just out in the garden. Why? What's wrong?' Sal takes a deep breath and I can hear Maggie burbling away in the background.

'Just ringing to remind you that the Hunters are coming for dinner tonight. You didn't forget, did you? They'll be there at eight; they're expecting a full three-course meal. This is important, Sal; it's all part of the whole making-partner package thing. On top of working my arse off for these guys, I have to impress out of work, too.' Sal pauses, and I know, just know, that Sal has fucked up again. It's not just me who has totally forgotten about the dinner party – not that I'll let Sal know that. If there's going to be a cock-up the blame will be laid squarely at Sal's door – I can't be seen by *anyone*, least of all Sal, to have fucked something up this royally.

'Charlie, you never told me about any dinner party. I would remember if you'd told me something as important as that, I swear.'

'*Sal!*' I hiss into the phone. My blood is boiling, but there's no way I want to erupt within earshot of Anita. There's a standard that I have to maintain at work, an impression that people have of me that I can't dispel. 'Are you having a fucking laugh? I told you about *this weeks ago*. Do you seriously mean to tell me that you haven't even got any food in?'

'Charlie, I *swear* you didn't tell me! Of course I would have sorted out a menu if I'd known about it! You can't actually think that I knew about it and did nothing? What good would that do? I *want* you to make partner! I want you to be a success. Jesus, Charlie, what do you think I am?' Sal's breath is coming faster again, and I can tell Sal is getting wound up. Well, guess what? So am I.

'I'll be home at six,' I bark into the phone, as loudly as I dare without Anita hearing me. I don't want her to know that there is potentially a problem. 'Make sure you've sorted dinner out. Make sure the house is presentable and make sure you're presentable. You are *not* going to ruin this, Sal, and if you do there'll be hell to pay. Understand?' I slam the phone down before Sal can respond.

When I walk through the front door, it's closer to seven o'clock than the six o'clock I had told Sal; the house is spotless and Sal is nowhere to be seen. There is, however, the delicious smell of garlic and roasting meat filling the air, and when I head into the kitchen I can see through the glass patio doors that even the garden has been tidied. I check the fridge and am satisfied to see two bottles of Sauvignon Blanc chilling in the fridge and two bottles of Malbec on the kitchen side, one of which has been opened to breathe. Heading upstairs I can smell a mixture of Maggie's bubble bath and Sal's shower gel on the air – it seems as though Sal actually listened to me today when I gave my instructions to be ready on time.

'Sal?' I call out, and Maggie comes barrelling out of her bedroom, wearing a *Frozen* nightie with her still-damp hair pulled back into a messy plait. 'I have to go to bed early,' she pouts, arms up for me to lift her. She smells of baby powder and laundry soap; cosy, homely smells. I carry her back into the bedroom and tuck her into her bed. 'I know, sugar, but it's just for tonight. Maybe tomorrow you can stay up late with Mummy and Daddy? You must behave for us tonight, though, and go straight to sleep.' Maggie nods her head sleepily, seemingly very tired for a kid who's been at home all day. I tuck the duvet tightly around her and kiss her forehead before heading into our bedroom. Sal is fussing in front of the mirror. I take a deep breath and try not to react to the wet towels strewn around the bedroom floor. The Hunters will be here in less than an hour and I really don't have time to reprimand Sal properly right now; it will have to wait.

'You're home. Did you get held up?' Sal peers at me nervously in the mirror, presumably worried that I'm still annoyed. I want to mention the towels but don't, seeing as it won't be long before our guests arrive.

'The train was a bit delayed, that's all – did you get the dinner sorted?' I pull off my jacket and hang it straight up in the wardrobe, where it belongs. Slipping my shoes off, I tuck them into their designated space at the bottom of the wardrobe.

'All sorted.' Sal fusses with one last stray curl and turns to smile at me, and I reach for Sal's hands. Taking them in mine, I give Sal a peck on the lips. All is forgiven, for now. I don't want there to be an atmosphere in front of the Hunters.

'Excellent. I'm going to have a quick shower and get changed. The Hunters will be here in forty-five minutes and I need you to be downstairs ready to let them in.'

'OK. I'm ready now anyway; the meat is in and the wine is chilling in the fridge. Everything is all ready.' Sal smiles, apparently relieved there is no fallout from our conversation this afternoon. I nod and pick up my clean, dry towel, ready to hit the shower.

An hour later the Hunters have arrived and pre-dinner drinks have been served. Sal seems to have taken on board everything I said earlier and is behaving impeccably. Maggie has stayed in her room and Mrs Hunter has been very complimentary about the décor in the house. Mr Hunter has requested that I call him Stan. So far, so good. It's when we get to the table that things go rapidly downhill.

We are all seated around our six-seater, scrubbed-wood dining table. Sal has gone all out and provided a linen tablecloth, a small vase of flowers acts as a centrepiece, and even the silver cutlery set has been dragged down from the loft and polished. We are sipping our wine and making small talk when Sal bustles in with the starters. The starters, which are made up of angels on horseback. *Oysters. For the guest with the seafood allergy.*

Mr Hunter, *Stan*, opens his mouth to say something. I jump in quickly. 'Sal? Did you not remember what I told you about Mr Hunter's, sorry *Stan's*, allergy?'

Sal looks confused and slightly hot and sweaty from leaning over the oven.

'Sorry, Charlie, what allergy? I don't know anything about an allergy.' I feel a wash of hot rage sweep over me. *I don't believe this.*

'I called you earlier, to remind you. *Remember?*' Sal's face flushes red, and before I can speak again Stan pipes up. 'Charlie? It's fine, honestly; I know Anita didn't give you the message. I'm happy to go without; the main course smells delicious.' I bestow a gracious smile on him and grip Sal by the elbow.

'It's no problem, Stan. I'm sure Sal can whip you something else up. Seafood free, of course.' Stan gives a little chuckle and I steer Sal into the kitchen.

'Jesus Christ, Sal, are you doing this on purpose? Just when I think you're taking stuff on board and actually listening to what I say, you pull a stunt like this.' I keep my voice low, so as not to disturb Stan and Stella in the next room. My hands are shaking with rage and I feel like I need to take a deep breath. Sal won't look at me, making me even more furious.

'Honestly, Charlie, I didn't know – but I can fix it, OK? I can make him something else, something better. Please, Charlie, please don't be angry.' I tug my arm away from Sal's outstretched hand.

'Don't think that I'm letting this one go; I'll deal with you later. I suggest you sort something out for Stan to eat, and stop being such a fucking loser.' Leaving

Sal standing forlornly next to the steaming hot oven, looking *pathetic*, I storm out of the kitchen, pasting my false smile on before reaching Stan and Stella, who are talking between themselves and sipping at their wine. Please, God, don't let them be talking about what a shit time they're having. 'My apologies again, Stan. I don't know what Sal was thinking.' I pick up the bottle of red and top them both up. Maybe if they're a bit pissed they won't realise what an actual fuck-up this whole dinner party is.

Sal returns ten minutes later with the starters and a baked Camembert for Stan. The rest of the dinner party goes off without a hitch – I am witty and charming, entertaining and intelligent. Stan has laughed at all my jokes and I am hopeful that Sal hasn't ruined my chances of a promotion. In the hallway, Stan is shrugging his jacket back on while Sal retrieves Stella's from the bedroom. He turns to me, straightening his collar as he says, 'Charlie – about the Otex deal. It's not too much for you, is it? I know it's putting a lot of pressure on you.'

'What? Goodness me, no. It's all fine. Honestly, I am one hundred per cent certain I can pull this off without a hitch.' Sweat prickles in my armpit – I have to be one hundred per cent confident I can pull this off. It's imperative to me that I make partner, that I am a success. There is no room for failure when you're Charlie Trevetti. I'll have the perfect job, the perfect home, the perfect family – everything will slot into place.

As we close the door on the Hunters, Stella a bit pissed and waving madly from the back of the taxi, I feel Sal's hand creep quietly into mine.

'Really, Sal? I don't think so.' I snatch my hand violently away. 'You nearly fucked this whole evening up for me entirely. Are you completely stupid? Who serves oysters to a man with a seafood allergy?' I feel a flicker of triumph when I see Sal's head bow. 'You know what, Sal? You're lucky to have me – because I can tell you this now: there's no one else out there who would want someone as stupid as you. And if you carry on the way you are doing, even I won't want you any more and nor will Maggie.'

CHAPTER NINETEEN

SAL

I can hear the telephone ringing as I fumble to get my key in the front door. Maggie is tugging on the hem of my T-shirt, whinging and whining due to being hot and tired after the bus journey back from my mum's. I know it can only be you calling me on the landline, which makes me fumble even more in my haste to get to the phone before you ring off and I have to call you back and explain myself.

'Hello?' I puff into the phone, trying my hardest to make it sound like I'm not out of breath. Maggie lets me go and stomps off into the living room, muttering under her breath.

'Sal? Why are you out of breath? Where have you been?' I can hear the sharp edge of irritation in your voice in that one sentence. *Please, Maggie, don't shout out anything about Nonna or Aunty Anna.* I take a deep breath and try to calm my breathing.

'Just in the garden. Why? What's wrong?' My heart sinks as you begin to whisper into the phone something about Mr and Mrs Hunter coming for a dinner party. Funnily enough, my first thought is that Anita must be in your office or there's no way you would be keeping it together this much. Then realisation dawns as I take in what you're actually telling me. Your boss, and his wife, are coming *tonight* at eight o'clock and will be expecting me to serve up a full-on, three-course dinner. In a spotless house. And your chances of making partner rest not only on completing this deal with Pav-whatever and Otex, but also on the outcome of this dinner party. Which I am sure I have never heard of before this conversation. *Shit.* Looking around while you hiss menacingly into my ear, I take in the toys Maggie has strewn around the living room, the shoes jumbled at the bottom of the stairs, and I know that I haven't finished tidying the kitchen from breakfast this morning. I thought at the time I'd have a good few hours when I got home from visiting my parents to deal with it all.

I try to tell you that I didn't know about the dinner party, that I am sure, one hundred per cent sure, that you never told me about it, but as you launch into another tirade about how useless I am, how you told me about it weeks ago, etcetera, I feel myself getting riled. *I know you never told me about it. I'm sure you didn't. Did you?* Beginning to doubt myself, I hold my tongue and you bark into the phone that you'll be home at six. That gives me just four hours to get the bus back into town, pick up the groceries, clean the house and make myself look presentable.

'Mags, get your shoes back on,' I call through to Maggie, who starts to grumble at the thought of going back out again.

As we walk down the front path, Laura pokes her head out from next door.

'All right, Sal? I thought I just saw you get back – are you off out again?' She smiles and flicks her red hair away from her face. As usual baby Fred is winding his way around her legs.

'Hi, Laura. We're just popping up to town – Charlie's boss is coming for dinner tonight and I … kind of forgot. I have to go and pick up the dinner.' I smile at her, sheepishly.

'So … are you not taking the car?' Eagle-eyed, Laura has noticed that Maggie and I have reached the gate and are leaving without wheels. Smile fading, I pause for a minute, unsure of what to tell her. I don't want to have to explain why I'm going all the way into town, but not bothering to take the car. Thinking fast I say, 'It needs a service. Charlie doesn't want to use it until it's sorted, in case it's dangerous, you know? So we're going on a bus adventure.'

'Right.' Laura nods slowly, her eyes fixed on mine. 'Well, don't drag Mags up to town; she can stay here and play with Lucy, if you want?' On hearing this, Maggie starts dancing around me, clasping her hands under her chin and whispering '*pleeeease*'. It would make things easier for me, doing the shop without Maggie whinging that she's hot and tired and wants to go home.

'OK. If you're sure? It really would help me out a lot.' I smile at Laura and bend down to kiss Maggie goodbye. 'Be good. I won't be long.'

'Take your time. And don't worry – I won't mention it to Charlie.' Laura gives me a small smile in return and, taking Maggie's hand, heads back indoors. I look after her retreating back, unsure of exactly what it is that I'm feeling.

An hour and a half later, I make my way back up the garden path with four bags of shopping and fingers that are turning blue where the supermarket bags have cut off my circulation. Packing the shopping away, I turn my attention to the rest of the house. I know that I am already in the dog house for not knowing or remembering about the dinner party (even I am not sure which it is now – you were so convinced on the phone that I *did* know about it, now I am even doubting myself), so it's vitally important that the house is up to scratch by the time everyone gets here. I spend another hour and a half scrubbing, tidying, emptying bins and polishing surfaces. I even get up in the loft and drag down the solid silver cutlery set we were given as a wedding present by my parents, and give it a good polish. I lay the table with a fresh white tablecloth and the freshly polished knives and forks, and am just stepping back to survey my handiwork when Laura's face appears at the kitchen window. Smiling at her, I go to the back door to let her in.

'Tah-dahhh! What do you think?' I sweep my arms wide, displaying the laid table. 'Does it look OK? I'm rubbish at this sort of stuff.'

'Impressive. There's something missing, though. Hang on.' She disappears back down the path and returns two minutes later holding a bunch of pink and white alstroemeria, mixed with tiny pale pink rose buds. Judging by the water dripping from the ends, she's pinched them from her own vase.

'Perfect,' she sighs, popping them into a vase and placing them in the middle as a centrepiece. I have to admit it does finish the table off perfectly.

'Brilliant. You're a genius – but tell me, who's been buying you flowers?' I tease, and she blushes.

'Don't be daft, Sal. I bought them for myself. Nobody's bought me flowers since Jed left, and even before then it didn't happen that often!' She gives a sad chuckle. 'Anyway, of course it looks perfect. Sometimes you just need a woman's touch.'

'Well, it looks brilliant. Charlie will be so impressed – oh, and thanks for looking after Maggie today. I really appreciate it, and I would also appreciate it if we don't tell Charlie. It's just less hassle, you know?' I'm embarrassed to even say it, but I have to. I don't want a row caused by one off-the-cuff remark. A look crosses Laura's face, one that I'm not sure how to interpret.

'Of course, Sal. No problem. Enjoy the dinner party, OK?' Laura reaches up to kiss my cheek, and sweeps out of the back door. I stand there for a moment, before calling Maggie in and heading upstairs to get ready.

You arrive home later than expected, which is good in a way, as it means I am ready in plenty of time. I bathe Maggie and get her into her pyjamas before jumping in the shower and getting changed. You seem to have calmed down by the time the working day is done, so I go with it and don't mention the fact that I wasn't told about the dinner party again. The Hunters arrive on time and you are invited to call Mr Hunter Stan, a good sign if ever I saw one. I pour pre-dinner drinks and eventually we make our way to the table.

'Starters are served!' I push my way backwards through the kitchen door to the table, carrying the hot plates containing my starter of angels on horseback. All three faces at the table drop, and I stand there, unsure as to what exactly I have done wrong.

'Sal? Did you not remember what I told you about Mr Hunter's, sorry *Stan's*, allergy?' Your face is

like thunder. I feel a look of confusion cross my
face. You definitely didn't tell me anything about a
seafood allergy. Definitely. Mr Hunter is trying to say
something, but I burble out something about how I
didn't realise. I feel an ugly flush creep up from my
neckline and my face feels hot with embarrassment.
You grab my elbow and steer me roughly towards
the kitchen, making noises to the Hunters over your
shoulder about how I will fix something else for Mr
Hunter to eat. Once in the kitchen, you grab the plates
out of my hand and hit me hard on the arm.

'Jesus Christ, Sal, are you doing this on purpose?
Just when I think you're taking stuff on board and
actually listening to what I say you pull a stunt like
this.' You whisper urgently at me, keeping quiet so that
the Hunters don't overhear you. I can't look at you –
I know you never told me about any allergies but it's
pointless to try and tell you that. This is going to be my
fault; it always is. I rub at the spot on my arm where
you hit me. Reaching towards you, I try to reassure you
I can fix it, make him something else, but you yank
yourself away and point your finger in my face.

'Don't think that I'm letting this one go; I'll deal
with you later. I suggest you sort something out for
Stan to eat, and stop being such a fucking loser.' With
that, you storm out of the kitchen and leave me open-
mouthed, gaping after you. *How did things between us
get this bad?* There was a time when you would never

have spoken to me that way, never have been so angry and hateful towards me, but now it seems everything is my fault. There was a time, before, when, if you had spoken to me like that I would have retaliated, told you that you were out of order. I know you never told me about the seafood allergy, but it's not worth even trying to stick up for myself any more; it's almost like I'm too exhausted to fight back. In your eyes you told me, and I went against what you had said deliberately, to try and sabotage your evening. Sighing, I splash my hot cheeks with cold water and try to figure out what exactly I can rustle up for Stan to eat that won't kill him, hoping against hope that they don't think I'm a complete moron.

For me, the rest of the evening doesn't get any better. I try and make conversation with the Hunters but you seem determined to put me down at every turn. When discussing careers, before I get a chance to tell them how I was a teacher before we had Maggie, how I'm just taking a small career break as we both agreed it was more important for someone to be home to take care of the baby than to have a dual-income household, you tell them that I *don't work*.

'No, Sal doesn't work. Stays at home all day, lounging around watching soaps like some sort of kept woman, while I go out and earn a crust.' You and Mr Hunter chuckle together, but I see Mrs Hunter glance sadly towards me, before turning back to her roasted duck.

Talk turns to families and once again you don't let me speak for myself, deciding to tell the Hunters how my family are 'overbearing and slightly interfering. We find we can manage perfectly well on our own, so we don't see a lot of them.' I want to say that actually I do, but I have to sneak over there when you're not around in order to be able to see them without your snipes and cruel comments. I bite my tongue repeatedly throughout the meal, when my housekeeping skills are criticised by you, my dress sense, my chronic shyness and inability to hold a conversation with people I don't know. You've had too much to drink and seem to be under the impression that you are witty and amusing, instead of just cruel. I am relieved when, after you seem to run out of steam, you turn to Mr Hunter and start talking shop, leaving me with Mrs Hunter, *Stella*, a woman with whom I have nothing in common. I manage to make it through the evening, my only struggle coming at the end when Stella, slightly pissed, grabs my hand as she leaves and tells me, 'Don't ever let them get you down; you're doing the hardest of all jobs and I admire you greatly.' This is almost enough to bring me to tears.

You, however, will not bring me to tears. This evening has shown me that I am worth much more than you give me credit for and I resolve to no longer let you treat me this way, especially when you tell me, after the Hunters have staggered their way to their waiting cab, that I'm so stupid no one else will ever want me, and that, one day, this might even include you. Not even the all-too-rare perfect moments, those times when everything seems like it's going to work out OK in the end, are enough for me any more.

CHAPTER TWENTY

CHARLIE

I wake up early the next morning, still not too sure how the dinner party went. It seemed like after Sal's idiotic mix-up with the starters everything seemed to go fairly well, so I am hopeful that Mr Hunter isn't going to hold it against me when it becomes time to make his decision regarding who will be made partner when Mr Crisp retires.

I rub a hand across my face, yawning, and decide to get up. Sal is still snoring softly away next to me, but I can hear the chatter of early morning cartoons, which means that Maggie couldn't sleep in this morning either. I can't lie and listen to Sal's irritating little puffs of breath in and out without feeling my temper rise, not this morning when I still feel so disappointed in Sal's efforts for the dinner party, so I get up and make my way downstairs. The kitchen and dining room is spotless – the array of empty glasses, wine bottles and the bottle of single malt Stan and I sampled with our after-dinner coffee has all been cleared away. Likewise, the linen tablecloth has been removed and the silver cutlery set is washed, dried and back in its box. Only the small vase of flowers still stands on the table, heads now wilted and crinkled. Sal must have made an effort to make sure everything was tidy before coming up to bed last night, after I stormed out of the kitchen in a fog of disappointment. The disappointment still lingers, despite Sal's best efforts, and I think back to the time I first realised Sal was going to need to be kept in check if we were going to stay together. *The first time I realised Sal wasn't aware of the rules.*

It is not long after Sal has graduated from university, after completing a PGCE. Sal wants to become a primary school teacher and has a placement lined up at a primary in South-East London, not the most salubrious of areas, but it is OK – there are a lot worse places out there. The placement is due to start at the beginning of September, and I know Sal is excited about it, despite the fact that I am not really keen at all. There is a mix of male and female teachers at the school, something I am not especially happy about, and the idea of not being able to contact Sal during lesson time is also something that puts me off. However, we are in the process of buying our first flat together and we need to have two incomes coming in. I have just been offered a position at Hunter, Crisp and Wilson, also due to start in the first week of September, so it seems as though everything is coming together at last, exactly as I want it.

We decide to celebrate the fact that everything is going well with a cheap, last-minute holiday. Sal browses online and eventually finds a week in Egypt – Sharm el-Sheikh, to be exact. It looks like a little piece of paradise, and the dates coincide with Sal's family's annual Bank Holiday summer get-together, another excellent reason for us to go on holiday and avoid having to make excuses as to why we can't attend. (I am fast running out of excuses, to be perfectly honest, what with the faked sprained ankle and numerous 'stomach bugs', but at least we have managed to avoid seeing Sal's parents the last three times they had invited us over.)

I pack for us both, Sal sorts out the taxi to Gatwick (although I did have to step in and do some negotiation regarding the fare – Sal is completely useless at bargaining), and some hours later we get off the plane to scorching sunshine and smiley little men with brown teeth all desperate to carry our bags for us.

'Isn't this gorgeous?' Sal pulls me in close for a hug, as we wait for our coach transfer to our hotel. 'I'm shattered, but just think, we've got a whole week to recharge our batteries, just you and me.' Dark, purple circles underscore Sal's eyes, a sure sign of the fatigue that comes with finishing three years at uni followed by a year-long PGCE. I squeeze back. Yes, it was just what the doctor ordered, just Sal and me, on our own, with no one around to interfere. It should have been the perfect week.

The week does start out perfectly – we are staying in an all-inclusive hotel, which could have meant shitty food and poor service, but in fact it is the opposite. The staff are friendly, the hotel is clean and the food is good. Being right on the beach means that there is no struggle to get down there in time to get a sunlounger and Sal and I spend our evenings out late, and our mornings in bed.

On the third morning I wake up alone. Calling out to Sal and getting no response, I slip out through the sheer curtains to our hotel balcony and peer out over the beach. The sky is a beautiful, clear, deep blue, the sun a scorching, white-hot ball above us and I can already see the heat shimmering above the sand. Standing not too far from the shoreline, I see a mop of dark curls and realise it is Sal, distinctive red swimming towel slung over one shoulder. Sal is talking to a woman, about thirty years old, with long, dirty-blonde hair that is tangled and lifting in the sea breeze, gesturing towards the pier that branches out from the sand several metres out into the sea. I rush back into our room and grab an overlong T-shirt and a pair of beach shorts. Hooking a beach towel with my fingertips as I race towards the door, I snatch up the hotel key by the fob and run down the stairs into the lobby. As I approach the seafront I see the woman turn and start walking back down the beach, Sal calling something out after her that I can't catch as the wind takes the words and blows them away from me towards the woman.

'Who was that?' I gasp as I bend over at the waist, trying to catch my breath. It was a long jog from hotel room to beach.

'Morning, sleepyhead,' Sal kisses me and starts trying to lay out the beach towels, the sea breeze whisking them up and making it an impossible task.

'Sal? I said, *who was that?* Who was that woman you were talking to?' I straighten up and glare at Sal.

'Oh, her. That was Amaryllis. Can you believe that name? It's brilliant. I think we should name our first daughter *Amaryllis.*' Curly hair whipping in the breeze, Sal snakes an arm around my waist, trying to pull me close.

'Sal. Fuck off. Who was she and why were you talking to her? This week is supposed to be about me and you, not some old slag you picked up on the beach. She looked like a right old hippy.' I pull away, folding my arms across my chest in a gesture that states *don't come near me.*

'*Charlie.* Bloody hell, I was just being friendly, all right? She's here with her boyfriend – Matt, I think his name is – and she was asking me about the pier. I was just chatting to her, not about anything specific. And that's a bit harsh, calling her a slag. I barely spoke to her. She seems really nice.' Sal mimics my arms-crossed-stay-back posture, but I'm not sure if it's unintentional or to take the piss out of me.

'Well, don't. OK? I want this week to be about you and me, not collecting random strangers on the beach.

I'll never see you when we get back; you'll be off doing all sorts of teacher-y type stuff, while I'm going to be working ridiculous hours at the new office. I don't want to spend this week hanging around with weirdos. Don't just leave me in the hotel room; wake me up, for God's sake.' I grab the other end of the towel that Sal is trying and failing to lay out properly. 'And give me that end, for fuck's sake. You can't even do that right, can you?' Sal stares at me, seemingly a bit lost for words.

'Sorry, Charlie. I didn't think. I just assumed you would want to sleep in. Of course, this week is about you and me. I won't speak to Amaryllis or her boyfriend again, if that's what you really want?'

'Good. You know I'm only saying this because I love you so much, Sal. I don't want to share you, not for this week.' I finish with the towel, satisfied that it's as straight as it's going to get, and pull Sal towards me.

My words must have had some sort of effect on Sal, as we spend a brilliant day together snorkelling under the pier again. Sal goes into the little hotel shop to buy an underwater camera and we use up the film on shots of the angelfish under the pier, and take photos of ourselves pulling ridiculous mugshots under the water. That evening, as we are sitting at our table after dinner, waiting for the cabaret to start (not my usual idea of a great way to spend the evening, but it's all the hotel can offer), Amaryllis and her boyfriend enter the room.

Spying us, she makes a move towards our table but Sal avoids her eye and gets up to leave.

'I'm going to get a drink – do you want one?' Sal whispers urgently and I shake my head. I still have a full glass of wine in front of me, as does Sal, but I'm not going to stop Sal from leaving the table. Sal squeezes behind my chair and heads for the bar. Amaryllis (I mean really? Hippy parents? Or maybe she changed her name? She's probably called Sandra) reaches our table and holds out her hand for me to shake.

'Hi – Charlie, right? I'm Amaryllis. I met Sal on the beach earlier – Sal is very knowledgeable about the snorkelling round here; you guys must have done loads since you arrived?' She grins inanely at me, flicking her dirty-blonde hair back over her shoulder. It doesn't look in any better state than it did down on the beach.

'Not really,' I say dismissively. 'Not to be rude, but Sal and I are a bit busy. Maybe we'll see you around.' With that I pick up my mobile phone, making it clear that I don't want anything more to do with her.

'Right. OK. Nice to meet you.' Amaryllis pulls her hand back and, raising her eyebrows at the tall, dark-haired man behind her (who I presume must be Matt), she saunters off, but not without letting me hear her comment under her breath: '*God. Rude or what?*' I shrug my shoulders. I couldn't give a toss what some old beach hippy thinks about me. I don't think we'll have any more bother from her again.

We decide to spend our final evening of the holiday going for a romantic walk along the beach. We are both conscious of the fact that it's back to normal tomorrow, and then a few days later we'll both be thrown head first into the next stage of our lives. We walk for what feels like miles, the stars bright and clear in the sky overhead. A soft breeze wafts over us, warm like silk, and we hear a few notes of Arabian music floating over to us on the breeze. Following the music brings us to an 'authentic' Bedouin tent set up on the edge of the beach, and a funny little Egyptian guy comes out to greet us. Despite us protesting that, 'No, no, it's fine, we were just passing, we really don't want tea,' he brings us a teapot full of some awful herbal tea and a shisha pipe. Sal can't stop laughing at the awfulness we've become swept up in, whereas I am not finding it quite so funny. I'm not good with spontaneity – I'm a planner. I want to know exactly what I'm doing, keeping everything under my control at all times.

'Come on, Charlie, just go with it. It's all part of the experience!' Sal laughs, pouring me another cup of godawful tea. It tastes like how I imagine camel piss would taste and now, thanks to Sal, the teapot is empty and the little guy brings us another one. A troupe of 'authentic' dancers now joins us in the 'authentic' tent, and Sal's eyes are out on stalks. This really is it now; I have had enough. It's bad enough that Sal has spent the entire time on our *last evening* laughing and talking with the dirty little man who seems to be in charge of the tent; to now have to watch Sal sit and gawp at semi-naked dancers is enough for me.

'That's it, we're leaving,' I announce, grabbing Sal's hand.

'Oh, Charlie, come on. Let's just watch the dancing for a bit, eh? It's all part of …'

'*Yes, I know,*' I hiss at Sal. 'All part of the experience. Well, I'm not here for this experience, Sal. OK? I'm here to spend time with my *partner*. Not watch you throw yourself at other people the entire time.' Sal stands reluctantly and gestures some sort of goodbye to the tent guy.

I storm on ahead all the way back to the hotel. For fuck's sake, Sal has to ruin everything. Sal scurries along behind me trying to keep up, making excuses about this evening, but I'm not in the mood to listen. Once back at the hotel, I head for the bar and order myself a double single malt. Two minutes later Sal lopes into the hotel, sweating and out of breath.

'Charlie, please listen. I just wanted to watch the dancing – what's wrong with that? Why are you being such a …. a fucking psycho?' Sal demands, pulling on my arm to turn me away from the bar.

'Seriously, Sal? All you've done all holiday is behave like an old tart! All you want to do is spend time with anyone except me! And I'm the only one you're actually here with, remember? I'm the only one who actually wants you.' I turn back to the bar and take a huge, fiery gulp of my whisky.

'Charlie, please. Keep your voice down. You're embarrassing me.'

'I'm embarrassing *you*? Now you know what it's like! You've done nothing but embarrass yourself since we got here.' Sal face crumples a little and I spy that little bitch Amaryllis sitting on one of the hotel bar couches. She's whispering into the ear of her boyfriend, all the while keeping her eyes on Sal and I. I grab Sal's arm and march us towards the lifts.

'I'm not going to tolerate this, Sal. Are you with me or not?'

'Of course I'm with you, Charlie. You know that. I don't understand what all this is about.' Sal looks bewildered and I feel myself soften slightly as I look into those dark chocolate eyes.

'It's about you and me. It's about you and me, against the world. I am the only one who will always be here for you, the one who loves you the most, right? I just wanted you all to myself this week, before we both start work, that's all.'

Sal nods slowly. We enter the hotel room and Sal gets straight into bed, seemingly falling asleep straight away. I wait up for a while, sipping the last of my whisky on the balcony. I don't speak to Sal at all on the flight home.

CHAPTER TWENTY-ONE

SAL

I hear you wake up early the morning after the dinner party. I lie still, making sure my breathing sounds like I'm still sleeping, in order to not have to face you just yet. I'm not sure what kind of mood you are going to be in today – you spent plenty of time last night telling me how useless and stupid I am, but this time you didn't really get physical with me, so now I don't know if I've escaped it altogether or whether you're still angry and just biding your time. It's funny how a single punch on the arm feels like a lucky escape for me, whereas for other people in relationships, I imagine it would be a reason to leave immediately. I hear you yawn and feel the duvet pull back as you go to get up and leave the bedroom. There is a click as the door closes behind you and I let out a small sigh of relief. The air lightens the minute you leave the room. Hopefully by the time I get up and come downstairs, you will have noticed that I have cleaned up all the debris from the party last night before coming to bed, and that will go some way towards appeasing you.

Things weren't always like this – in the beginning it seemed like the perfect relationship. You were always attentive, complimentary, and although I knew you weren't keen on spending time with my family I could understand it. You come from a family that consists only of your mum and dad, and although I'm not entirely sure of all the details, even after all this time, I know that you don't get on. So, I can understand that it might have been pretty overwhelming the first time you met my family, with everyone talking over each other and hugging and kissing every five minutes. I thought you would soon get used to it, maybe even enjoy being part of a large family, but you soon showed me that that would never happen, although for different reasons than I had originally thought.

Lying in bed listening to you move around downstairs, I think back to the first time you showed me the other side to you. The first time you showed me you weren't entirely charming all the time. I'd seen a glimpse previously on our first trip to visit my mum and dad, but this was the first time you had properly shown me your true colours.

We book a holiday to Egypt after I finish my PGCE. You have been offered the job at Hunter, Crisp and Wilson and, as we are both going to be starting our new jobs in September, we decide this is the best time to take our first holiday together. We arrive at Sharm el-Sheikh International Airport and step off the plane into gorgeous bright sunshine, clear blue skies and a faint whiff of tobacco on the air. I can't help it – I squeeze you close, I'm so excited. Growing up we had very few holidays and the holidays we did enjoy usually involved tents set up in fields in places like Cornwall (once – Dad never wanted to do that drive again), Weymouth (also once – Dad didn't realise it was *quite* that far) and Margate (often – Dad didn't mind driving an hour from home; it was close enough to go back when everyone got tired of each other whinging about being cold and tired, or missing home). This is my first-ever holiday abroad and I'm excited to be sharing it with you. We've been together for two years now and it's mostly been amazing all the way through. I mean, we have our ups and downs, and you can be a bit snappy with me occasionally, but you constantly surprise me with your thoughtfulness. Little things like leaving me a mug with a teabag in it next to a full kettle on the mornings when you leave the house before me, or bringing home a Chinese takeaway on a Friday night when you know I'll be too tired to cook. This year has been a brilliant success for us so far – I've finished my PGCE and landed a job, you've got your dream job, we are saving to buy a house and it feels like everything is meant to be. We've spent every weekend together, getting to know each other inside and out, making the most of our free time before we really have to settle into what can only be described as the 'real world'.

Our hotel is pretty much perfect. The room is spacious, with a huge king-sized bed and a balcony, accessed through a set of sheer curtains, which looks out over the sea. You are very impressed – I had booked allocation on arrival so we are extremely lucky; it could have all gone terribly wrong and we could have ended up in a proper shit-hole. It's a hundred times nicer than our first weekend away together, last year, when I took you to a music festival – it poured with rain and there was mud everywhere, and you weren't too impressed at sleeping in a tent for the weekend, but we had the most amazing time. Dancing, singing, laughing all weekend, it felt like there was nowhere else on earth that I would have rather been. Apart from here, now – the view is breathtaking. There is a pier that stretches out from the beach far into the sea, and we decide on our first morning to go and explore. The water is like glass, perfectly clear and warm like bath water. It's paradise. Jumping off the pier into the warm water, you call up to me: 'Sal! There's fish! Come and look!' I jump off the pier and join you in the shallow water – it's only waist-high, but you are right; there are dozens of tiny fish swimming under the pier. We head up towards the hotel shop and invest in a snorkel each and spend the rest of the day snorkelling under the pier, pointing out different types of fish to each other. It's a perfect day, one that now, when I think back to it, sums up the first couple of years of our relationship perfectly. We didn't need material things, or to 'prove' how much we meant to each other; we were just happy existing alongside each other, comfortable in our own relationship. Thinking back to that perfect day makes it even harder for me to understand how we came to be in the place we are now. That evening we hit the hotel bar and their 'cabaret' entertainment – the only entertainment they have, but there is the novelty of being able to stay out late, drink as much as we want and know we don't have to get up at the crack of dawn tomorrow. Everything is completely perfect.

Things take a slightly less perfect turn on our third day, and I begin to get a glimpse into the other side of you. You freak out at me for talking to someone on the beach, and I'm knocked sideways by the force of your rage – why are you angry with me? I'm pretty sure I haven't done anything wrong. I tell you I just met the woman walking along the beach, that I barely really spoke to her; surely there's nothing wrong with speaking to someone? I pull you close, wanting to give you a squeeze, but you push me roughly away and start shouting about how you don't want to spend any time with other people, that this holiday should just be about you and me and no one else. I'm confused – I didn't realise that spending time together on holiday meant I'm not allowed to even speak to anyone else. You are furious, and when you throw into the mix that I should have woken you up, I decide the best thing to do is be contrite and apologise. I'm not keen on confrontation at the best of times and I don't want our first holiday to be spoilt by a huge row. I apologise, and promise not to speak to Amaryllis or her boyfriend in future.

This seems to appease you, even though a tiny part of me thinks your attitude is wrong, but when you go on to tell me how much you love me, and how it's you and me against the world, I feel bad for feeling some animosity towards you. It must have been hard growing up in the environment you did and maybe I should cut you some slack – I know you do love me and perhaps I should feel flattered that you're a bit jealous of my spending time with someone who isn't you, even if it is just a two-minute exchange with someone on a beach. You don't have anyone else important in your life; maybe I should feel flattered that you feel as strongly about me as you do.

Things go smoothly for the rest of the day. We snorkel, taking pictures with an underwater camera, but I am forever conscious of your temper, bubbling away under the surface, and think before I speak, something I've never felt I had to do with anyone before.

You are back to your normal self for the rest of the holiday: attentive and happy, making me crack up laughing at your ridiculous jokes. It's as if you never freaked out at me, as if you never lost your temper as I've never seen you lose it before. I start to feel like maybe I was making a big deal about nothing – after all, everybody argues, don't they? We do some more snorkelling, hire a speedboat, ride camels, and although I would have loved just a few days lying on a sunlounger reading, the exhilarating whirlwind of it all thrills me, draws me in and feeds my addiction to being with you. For the rest of the holiday this is, until our last night, when once again something sets you off and I am made to feel like a small child that has been disciplined. I make my way up to our room and get straight into bed, faking falling asleep immediately while you stand on the balcony and finish your drink so I don't have to talk to you any further, your reasoning behind your outburst and the flimsy apology that followed not really cutting it. I lie there, eyes closed, thinking hard about what to do and feeling desperately unhappy. By the time we get back home, after a flight during which you don't say a word to me, I am more or less convinced that the only option I have is to leave.

But of course I didn't. Things reverted back to normal, you behaved as you always had before and, again, I thought it was a one-off. You were funny and affectionate, thoughtful and kind, and I let that push away the memories of how you treated me on holiday. I didn't think it would become part of the cycle. I didn't realise that that was the turning point, the first time I ever let you get away with speaking to me like that, the first time I didn't call you out on it – the beginning of the cycle that we find ourselves trapped in now. The cycle I'm starting to think I need to escape from.

CHAPTER TWENTY-TWO

CHARLIE

I battle my way into work early on Monday morning. The tube is packed, dense with hot, sweaty bodies even this early in the morning. The heatwave that currently has Britain in its clutches is probably enjoyable to everybody else, all those people who don't have to take the tube to work, but for those of us that do, it makes life unbearable. After spending the best part of an hour with my face crushed against someone's armpit, by the time I reach the office I am not in the best of moods. This is not helped by the fact that, when I get to my office, after grabbing a quick coffee from the temperamental coffee machine outside the lifts (it claims to offer latte, macchiato, cappuccino, the works. It's just a shame that whichever option you choose turns out to be the same dark-brown sludge, completely unrecognisable as the option selected. And that's on the days when it actually works), Geoff is sitting at my desk, swivelling backwards and forwards on my chair and poking through my in-tray. I sigh, throwing my laptop bag onto the desk.

'Morning, Geoff. To what do I owe the pleasure?'

'Little bird tells me you had Hunter and his missus over for dinner Friday night. How did that go?' Geoff is incurably nosey, and while he has no inclination to further his own career, I'm not always sure he's happy to see me trying to further mine.

'It went fine, Geoff. Nothing to report.' I take a sip of my scalding coffee sludge and pointedly nod towards my chair. Geoff makes no effort to move.

'So, Sal didn't try and kill off old Hunter with a delicious seafood starter then?' Geoff laughs a rumbling, deep laugh, made slightly breathless by the sheer number of cigarettes he smokes. 'I knew you were ambitious, Charlie, but I didn't think you'd resort to that to get your own way.' Geoff quite plainly thinks that he is hilarious, and his big old belly heaves up and down as he chortles. *I am going to kill Sal for this.* I take a deep breath, in order to stop myself from launching across the desk and smacking Geoff in his big, wet mouth. Instead, I focus on the splotch of egg that stains Geoff's tie and smile calmly, hoping that Geoff doesn't realise my belly is swooping with butterflies and my pulse is thundering in my ears. *Please, God, don't let everything be ruined.*

'Just a slight misunderstanding, Geoff. Sal pulled it back with an excellent baked Camembert, so no harm done. How did you find out anyway?' I can't resist asking, although I am dreading his response. I'll be mortified if the entire office knows what happened on Friday night. I push at his arm, gesturing for him to move. He heaves his bulk out of my chair, and stands to one side to allow me to squeeze past him into my seat.

'Saw Hunter this morning, so I asked him how it went, didn't I? He said Sal tried to kill him.' Geoff wheezes out another croaky laugh. I swear, if the guy doesn't change his lifestyle soon he'll be a goner.

'What? Did he actually say that?' I am alarmed, thinking to myself that if Mr Hunter really is pissed off about the whole dinner party thing, then it doesn't matter whether I complete this buy-out successfully for Pavlenco or not, as I won't be making partner anyway. Everything will have gone up in flames before it's even started.

'No, Charlie, of course he didn't. He said it all went well, apart from Sal having to make him a different starter to everyone else. I heard him complimenting your house, your whisky and the fact that Sal does a grand job looking after the house and the baby.' Geoff looks sheepish, and I narrow my eyes at him.

'Geoff, did you even speak to Mr Hunter yourself?' I am suspicious – I can't see Stan making conversation like this with Geoff. While he's always friendly and likes to remind us all in meetings that we are a 'family' firm, he's not known for chatting about his personal life to the staff.

'Errr … no. Not exactly. I was passing the kitchen and I heard Crisp ask him how it went, so I just waited for a bit … round the corner, you know. I just wanted to hear what he said, to see if it all went OK. I know what you think about me, Charlie, but I do want to see you do well.' Geoff fiddles with his tie. I am strangely touched by this. Geoff is an idiot, ninety per cent of the time. He's a good lawyer, but personally, he's just not my cup of tea; the lack of ambition and 'do just enough' attitude is the complete opposite to mine. I smile at him, feeling a bit guilty for being annoyed with him.

'Thanks, Geoff. I do appreciate it, you know. And you're a good guy, even if you're not up to my standards.' We both laugh, and Geoff holds out a hand for me to shake.

'I hope you remember that Charlie, once the firm is Hunter, Trevetti and Wilson.'

When Geoff leaves my office, I sit back in my chair and heave a sigh of relief. It looks like Sal hasn't totally scuppered my chances of achieving what I've set out to do. I decide to ring home before Anita gets in.

'Hello?' Sal's voice sounds husky, and I realise I must have woken the household up; if Maggie was awake she'd make sure Sal was, too. It's not even 7.30am yet.

'Sal, it's me. Did I wake you? Sorry.' I am feeling gracious now, knowing that Stan thinks the dinner party went well. I can afford to apologise to Sal for waking the entire house this early now I know things are going my way.

'A bit. It's OK. Is something wrong?' Now more awake, Sal's voice has a hint of urgency to it.

'No, nothing's wrong. Just the opposite, in fact. Geoff has just been in here; he overheard Hunter and Crisp talking in the kitchen. Stan was telling Crisp how well the dinner party went and how you pulled off an excellent meal. Sal, do you know what this means? It means that if the Pavlenco deal comes off, I've done it! It'll be my name on the letterhead.'

'That's … brilliant, Charlie. Really brilliant. I'm so pleased. Everything is just falling into place, isn't it?' I can hear Maggie start shouting in the background, and Sal murmurs to her.

'Listen, I just wanted to tell you, that's all. I knew you'd be pleased; I'd better let you go and see to Maggie. I'll be home late tonight, I expect. I really need to pull out all the stops on the Pavlenco deal, but at the weekend we'll celebrate, yeah? Do something nice, all of us together, like at the river the other weekend. We all enjoyed that, didn't we?'

'OK. Whatever you want to do, Charlie, it's all fine with me.' Sal still sounds tired, but I don't want to get into a big conversation about how Sal isn't sleeping properly, or how Maggie keeps getting up (I know Maggie keeps getting up – I can hear her. I just don't think, if I've got to go to work in the morning, that it's my place to get up with her), so I don't ask, hanging up before the conversation can start. I can't stop the huge grin that spreads across my face as I lean back in my chair with my hands behind my head. I am totally going to nail this deal – and then everything will be spot on. Everything will be perfect.

I have already spent an hour or so pulling together different aspects of the Pavlenco deal when Anita lets herself into the office. Within a few minutes of arriving she's refreshed my coffee (with coffee from the percolator that she keeps behind her desk; none of that machine muck once Anita gets in), and then she comes in and takes a seat on the other side of the desk.

'Charlie, we need to go through these emails that came through on Friday after you left, and there are several phone messages for you – a couple from the gentleman who called you last week.' Anita shuffles through her notepad and I frown, trying to remember exactly whom she's talking about.

'Who, Anita? What's the guy called? I can't remember everyone who leaves me a phone message.' As I say it, something clicks in my memory and I have a sneaking suspicion it's the guy who called wanting to talk about Lucian Pavlenco.

'His name is Radu Popescu; he called before, wanting to talk to you – remember? He said he wouldn't get off the phone until he spoke to you and I managed to fob him off the first time. He called again on Friday, same thing. He refused to get off the line until he spoke to you. I tried to tell him you had already left for the day, but he wasn't having any of it, I'm sorry, Charlie. I had no choice.'

'What do you mean, *you had no choice*?' I raise my voice slightly, feeling a prickle of alarm – I really hope Anita hasn't done anything stupid, like giving this guy my mobile number.

'Don't panic, I didn't give him your mobile number.' Anita knows me well; she must have seen the look of panic cross my face. 'But I did have to give him your email address. He was insistent that it's a matter of life or death he speaks to you. I can't imagine what he's got to say; it was all terribly dramatic.' Anita looks at me from over the top of her glasses. She has this real knack of pulling a mother hen act on me, while all the time maintaining her high level of professionalism. If I get made partner, *when* (I feel so much more confident saying that this morning), I'll make it a condition that Anita comes with me, instead of my PA being one of the girls from the partners' offices.

'I have no idea, Anita, believe me. Don't worry, I'll check my emails and see what's been sent through. Pavlenco is a highly respected businessman; I doubt it can be anything that bad.' Anita runs through the other phone messages and emails that have come in since I left on Friday afternoon. Now I remember why I stay late in the office. The amount of stuff I have to go through every time I leave before 8pm makes the early finish a complete waste of time.

When Anita has finished and goes back to her desk, ready to type up the letters I have dictated to her, I turn my attention to my emails. My curiosity is piqued by this Radu Popescu and his insistence on talking to me. His name has never come up in any of the conversations I have had with Lucian, so I'm completely in the dark as to what he might want from me. Surely it can't be anything that could jeopardise the deal, or Pavlenco would have told me about him. I am wading through email after email, forwarding relevant information over to Anita for printing, or to add to the ever-growing pile of things I have to respond to, when Mr Hunter, *Stan*, pokes his head through the door.

'Good morning, Charlie. How are you today?' His moustache is wiggling above his smile, and I can see where he has twiddled the ends, something I've noticed he does a lot. Some sort of compulsive habit, maybe?

'Very well, thank you, Mr Hunter.' I give him a confident smile, all shining white teeth, and stand to shake his hand.

'Good, good. Please, Charlie, when it's just us, do call me Stan. I wanted to thank you for a very pleasant evening on Friday, and to send my regards to Sal. It was very kind to rustle up another starter for me on Friday evening; I'm just sorry that Sal wasn't made aware before.'

'Honestly, Stan, it was no trouble. We are just so glad that you and Stella enjoyed yourselves.' I want to grab hold of him and plead with him to tell me if I'm going to make it or not, whether he has decided if I make the grade.

'I'd like to invite you and Sal to dinner, Charlie. When do you think you'll have the Pavlenco buy-out wrapped up?'

'Not long. A few weeks, maybe? There are just a few last-minute things to be agreed. Once I've got them all signed off, the final paperwork will be ready to be prepared.' I smile at him, hoping he can't hear my heart pounding.

'Excellent. Let's say the Friday after you've wrapped up. Say, the twenty-eighth of next month?' He peers at my desk calendar over the top of his glasses.

'That sounds perfect, Stan. I'll get Sal to put it in the diary.' He nods briskly and strides off back to his office. I have to sit on my hands to resist the urge to punch the air. *YES. It is all finally coming together.*

The encounter with Mr Hunter keeps me on a high for the rest of the morning, and I forget all about Radu Popescu and his phone calls until Anita pokes her head in a couple of hours later.

'Charlie, that Popescu guy has been on the phone again. I told him you were in a meeting and couldn't be disturbed but I had to tell him you were discussing Pavlenco to get him off the phone. He said to let you know he's sent you an email and it's important you check it as soon as possible.'

'Thanks, Anita,' I sigh. He's persistent, if nothing else. Something to be admired, I suppose. 'Leave it with me. I promise I'll deal with him today.' She disappears back to her desk, littered with an ever-growing number of photos of grandchildren, all with the same green eyes and red hair that Anita has. I click on my email icon and scroll through. This guy is clearly not going to leave me alone until I at least respond to him in one form or another and I have to hand it to him: he knows persistence works. Finally, I come across an email with 'LUCIAN PAVLENCO' in the title.

To: c.trevetti@huntercrispwilson.co.uk
From: radu.p@hotmail.com
Monday 22nd June 2015 8.59am
Subject: LUCIAN PAVLENCO

Dear C Trevetti,
My name is Radu Popescu. I am trying to speak with you about Lucian Pavlenco. I have highly important things to tell you and I think you need to listen to me. Lucian Pavlenco is not who you think he is. He is not

what you think he is. I have tried to call you but you won't speak to me. Please contact me – this is very urgent. I hope I do not have to call you again; you need to know these things that I must tell you.

Regards,

Radu Popescu

I read and reread the email several times. Although the English is good, I can tell it is written by someone who doesn't speak English as his or her first language. This ties in with what Anita was saying about him having an accent. Could this possibly be someone who knew Lucian before he came to Britain? Maybe someone who holds a grudge against him? In all honesty, the guy sounds like a bit of a crackpot, and I can't see what he has to tell me about Lucian that most people don't already know. Lucian is a high-profile businessman who has had his fair share of lurid tales told about him, all of which have come to nothing. I decide to send one email to Radu Popescu, in the hope that once he has a formal response from me he'll get the message and back off.

To: radu.p@hotmail.com

From: c.trevetti@huntercrispwilson.co.uk

Monday 22nd June 2015 10.13am

Re: LUCIAN PAVLENCO

Dear Mr Popescu,

I apologise for my delay in responding to you. Unfortunately, I deal only with Mr Pavlenco as regards business matters; therefore, I do not think your information will be relevant to myself, or my company. Please refer any information you may have regarding Mr Pavlenco to Mr Pavlenco's office address directly.
Yours sincerely,
C Trevetti

Ignoring the niggle of unease burrowing away at the back of my mind, I hit the send button, and forward a copy over to Anita's email address. I breathe a sigh of relief, and hope that this will be the end of Mr Radu Popescu and his 'highly important' information.

CHAPTER TWENTY-THREE

SAL

After the way you spoke about me in front of Mr and Mrs Hunter at the dinner party on Friday night, and the way you sulked like a little child all weekend, I am not feeling too gracious, especially not when I am woken by a telephone call from you, babbling about how the dinner party turned out to be a success in the end. Add into the mix that you can apologise for a little thing like waking me up, but not for accusing me of ruining your career – when, if anything, I've done you a favour – it's little wonder I feel ungracious. Why do you do that? If you apologise to me when you're wrong, do you think I then have some sort of power over you? That you're losing your control over me? Whatever it is, I don't think I'll ever understand it. It's like someone flips a coin and, whatever side it lands on, that's the mood I get treated to, and I just seem to find it more and more difficult to keep up with the switches from good to bad – it's not easy any more to just write it off when you've accused me of all sorts, told me how useless I am and how I don't deserve you, and then the next minute everything is rosy, like nothing ever happened. Eventually, you hang up and I lie back down on the fluffy pillows, just for two more minutes. I can't sleep at the moment – it seems that every time we reach this phase in the never-ending, exhausting cycle we are trapped in, the insomnia returns for another bout, each one sharper than the last. I can't get excited for you about Mr Hunter being a fan of the dinner party, however hard I try. You spoke about me like I was nothing to you, like I was a piece of dirt on your shoe in front of other people, and each time this happens I am finding it harder and harder to forgive you. Especially when there are other people around me, telling me I'm not as useless and pathetic as you would have me believe.

Pulling myself together, I get out of bed and look for Maggie. I can hear her in the dining room, high, childish tones singing the *Dora the Explorer* theme tune. I poke my head around the door, and there she is, sitting under the dining room table, singing, with a large teddy bear playing the part of Swiper the Fox. She runs over to me and squeezes my legs, and I wish she would never get any older.

'Morning, chipmunk.' I scoop her up and kiss her baby-soft curls, so like mine, inhaling the sleepy scent of her.

'Good morning,' she says in a very serious tone, planting squidgy kisses on my cheek. I carry her through into the kitchen, even though she is too old to be carried really, and set about making some breakfast while Maggie sits at the table still humming the Dora song. I think about before, when we returned home from Egypt and I had more or less decided I was leaving. How differently things might have turned out if I had left then.

On our return home from Egypt, you don't say a word to me on the flight, despite my repeated attempts at starting a conversation. I have apologised again and again for whatever slight you think I made towards you in the Bedouin tent that evening, and I have made sure to avoid Amaryllis and her boyfriend for the rest of the holiday. Now, on the flight home, I refrain from making eye contact with anyone who looks like they might be up for having a conversation with a stranger, so there is no chance of you going off on one again. I am pretty much decided that when we get home I will speak to you – tell you that, while I love you very much, there is no way I want to continue like this – it's not how I thought our relationship would be. I'll move back in with my parents; it will mean a long commute to my new job, but it's for the best. Things don't happen that way, though. When we get in through the front door at our tiny new flat, it's like someone has flicked a switch – you can't do enough for me, and you actually apologise.

'I'm sorry, Sal, for how I was on holiday. It's just – there was a whole new side to you. One I didn't know

existed before.' You twine your fingers up into my hair. 'I
got jealous – I mean, look at you, Sal – you're gorgeous,
and I don't want anyone else to ruin what we've got.
It's special. I just got worried that you didn't want me
any more.' I weaken, beginning to think that maybe the
problem is me – maybe I shouldn't have spent my holiday
talking to other people, when it was all supposed to be
about you and me, spending quality time together before
our jobs started. Maybe I didn't pay you enough attention.

'It's OK, Charlie. I understand – maybe all the stuff
that happened when you were growing up made you a
bit insecure?' I hint at your past, hoping that for once
you might actually open up to me, instead of keeping it
all locked away like you usually do.

'Maybe.' You brush it away, sweeping it under the
carpet again. 'I just don't want to have that for us, you
understand? I want us to have the perfect relationship.
It's you and me, Sal, always you and me, and I was
thinking … now that we've got the flat, and we've both
got proper jobs … we should get married.'

'Is this a proposal? Are you serious?'

'Deadly. Do you love me?'

'Yes, Charlie, of course I do. It's just … do you really
want to? Get married?'

'Yes, you idiot. I wouldn't have said it otherwise,
would I?'

'Then bloody hell, Charlie, yes. Let's get married!' We
laugh, each seemingly a little shocked by how easy that

was, and you start making plans to go ring shopping. I am so happy – swept up in the idea of getting married, starting our own little family. It is everything I have ever wanted. I can see us getting old together, taking care of our children, then our grandchildren. I know it's not all going to be plain sailing, that there are bound to be little blips like we had on holiday, but if I can give you the kind of life that my parents have given each other, as opposed to whatever happened in your family between your parents when you were growing up, then I'll be happy. Egypt seems like a distant memory already. It's almost as though I have already chosen to forget the arguments and cold-shoulder behaviour, and to focus instead on remembering the brilliant sunshine, the warmth of the sun on my back, the tiny fish swimming beneath the pier.

We start to make plans for a small, simple wedding. You don't have anyone in your family you want to invite, and when I ask you about inviting your mum you bite my head off.

'Jesus, Sal. Leave it. You've got no idea what went on, and you've got no idea what kind of a person she is, so drop it, OK? I just don't want her there.'

I don't push it as I don't want to cause any arguments, but when it turns out you don't even really want anyone from my family there either, I am upset and hurt. I can't leave it and have to say something, and eventually, you realise that, if you don't give in, you'll be completely outnumbered.

'Charlie, it's my mum and dad, my sisters. I have to have them there.'

'It's supposed to be about you and me. The start of our new life together, not the start of our lives together with your mum and dad.'

I want to ask you: what kind of weirdo gets married without their parents there? Their family? But given that you have invited a couple of people you work with and that's it, I can't say a word. You concede begrudgingly in the end that there will be invitations sent out to my parents, Julia and Luca, Anna and Paola. You don't want to invite any of our old friends from uni, and none of the embarrassingly few friends we have picked up since we moved into our little flat and new jobs. I'm gutted that some of my old uni friends aren't invited, but I don't push it, just in case you decide you want to retract the invitations to my family.

The day goes off without a hitch. You are polite to my family, despite not wanting them there. When the registrar pronounces us 'Mr and Mrs Trevetti', amidst the sound of the cheers, you whisper into my ear, 'Together, for ever.' The sun disappears behind a cloud, casting a dark shadow across the day and I shiver.

Things do not go swimmingly as we embark on married life together. You tell me that, now we are married, I don't need to have contact with my family, that you are my family now. At first I fight hard against you, telling you that just because you don't get along with your family doesn't mean we should have to be without mine. I try to explain how our family behaved when we were growing up and how I want you to be a part of it all. You are stubborn and won't budge, telling me that maybe, if they are more important to me, then perhaps we shouldn't have got married at all? Perhaps we should call it a day now, before we get too settled. I can go back to living with my parents and you can find someone else, someone who will really appreciate all that you do for them, instead of being ungrateful and fighting against you all the time. As much as I hate being told what to do and whom to see, especially if it means little contact with my family, the thought of you being with someone else, someone who is not me, makes me feel sick. So, I agree to reduce the contact with my family down to one phone call a week to my mum, the minimum I can get away with without causing fuss, without my mum turning up on the doorstep to see what's wrong. In reality, I just wait until you're working late before giving her a quick ring before you get home, or I pop over there for an hour when it's half-term and I am at home for the week.

I find that, once you have your own way, life is a lot more settled. If I do as I am told and don't question you, there are no rows, no shouting, no accusations. Until we find out that we are going to have a baby.

The day we find out for certain that Maggie is on the way you are furious.

'How the fuck could you let this happen, Sal?' Your lips are a thin line of fury, anger blazing in your eyes. The positive pregnancy test sits on the coffee table between us, neither of us willing to look at it.

'Me? It takes two, Charlie. It's both of our faults. This doesn't have to be a bad thing – we were always going to start a family; it just means that it's going to happen sooner rather than later.'

'Were we, Sal? I don't remember having any agreement about having children. I never wanted to have kids, after all I went through growing up! And you know what? I don't think I want to have this one.' Your words are like a punch in the guts to me. No, we never officially had the conversation in which we agreed that we would have children, but I thought you wanted the same as me – to build a family together.

'Don't say that, Charlie. Please. We can work around this, find a way to make it work for both of us. Charlie, you know this is all I ever wanted.'

'And you must have known that this is all I *never* wanted, Sal. You have no idea what it was like for me, growing up. I don't want children. It was supposed to just be you and me.' My heart breaks at the thought of getting rid of our baby.

'It'll make us stronger together, Charlie. Think about it – it'll be you, the baby and me, together against the world. We'll be tied together for ever through our baby.'

This seems to give you pause for thought and, after weeks of to-ing and fro-ing, it's decided that we will keep the baby, much to my relief. It's agreed that, once he or she is born, I will stay home and raise the baby while you go out to work – you've already impressed the partners at Hunter, Crisp and Wilson. I am ecstatic, and when I make one of my secret phone calls home, my mum is over the moon too. The only person who doesn't seem to be too happy is Julia. She calls one evening, luckily at a time when you are working late.

'Sal? It's me. Have you got something you want to tell me?'

'Julia! Oh, God, you spoke to Mum, didn't you? I knew she wouldn't be able to keep it a secret – I wanted to wait until we'd had the first scan before I told you.'

'Well, congratulations.' Julia sounds a little *off*.

'Jules? What's the matter? Aren't you pleased for us?'

'I'm pleased for you, Sal. As long as you're happy, I'm pleased for you.' A prickle of annoyance tickles the back of my throat.

'Julia, if you've got something to say, I'd rather you just said it.'

'I just … Are you sure, that's all? I mean, Charlie is pretty …' She heaves a huge sigh. 'No one hears from you, Sal. Since you two got married, it's like Charlie's got you chained up in a dungeon or something. You missed Anna's birthday party again this year; you missed Mum and Dad's wedding-anniversary dinner. You never call. It's like you can't do anything unless Charlie says so.'

'Don't be ridiculous. I'm just busy, that's all. You know what it was like when you and Luca got married – it's completely hectic for weeks after. The class I'm teaching are a handful and I have reams of paperwork to do every night. Charlie has nothing to do with it.' Julia assures me that she believes me, even though I can tell by her tone that she doesn't, and I hang up before one of us says something we'll regret. I don't want to admit that she does have a point, that since we got married the few friends I did have, have fallen by the wayside and I don't see much of anyone any more.

After a long, lonely pregnancy, in which you carry on as normal but I am expected to prepare the house for the baby ('You've got more time than me, Sal.') and fend off any visits from my family – you are not even happy that I told anyone in my family in the first place, but I have managed to make you realise that that is just weird – Maggie is born at home on a cool October evening. Any worries I have harboured throughout the pregnancy about you not bonding with Maggie go out the window the minute you turn to me, Maggie a tiny, red-faced bundle in your arms and say, 'Look Sal, look what we made. We did this. Together for ever.' Now, my heart gives a little squeeze as I think back to that moment, the way your hair stood out on end, the dark, tired circles under your eyes and the pure love that radiated out from your every pore. I had hoped this would mean things would be a little easier from now on, that you would calm down and not be so angry all the time. I couldn't have been more wrong.

Things escalate with the first visit from my parents. They are desperate to meet their new granddaughter, and so they arrive the day after she is born, following a furtive phone call from me in the early hours of the morning, once I have settled Maggie and you are asleep.

'What the fuck are they doing here?' you hiss, as you come downstairs from a shower to see them standing in the hallway, removing their coats, laden with pink-wrapped gifts. We are in the kitchen, under the pretence of making coffee.

'Charlie, they are her grandparents; they want to meet her.' I turn to the kettle, flicking the switch and busy myself getting down coffee mugs from the cupboard and a plate for biscuits.

'I say when they can meet her – they don't just fucking turn up. Although I suppose you rang them, didn't you? Running to Mummy and Daddy again, just like usual. I don't want them here, Sal. If I wanted them here I would have invited them. You fucking idiot.' Your face is ugly, contorted with rage.

'Charlie, please. Be reasonable. I'm sorry I called them; I thought I should get it out of the way. Then it's over and done with, see?'

'God, you're stupid. You're lucky I married you, because no one else with half a brain would want you. They'll be here all the fucking time now, now you've invited them. They'll think they can pop round whenever they want.' The kettle is boiling merrily, the steam hitting the ceiling, and you grab my hand and hold it hard against the burning metal. I yelp, and try to pull my hand away, but you just hold it tighter and harder.

'Charlie, fuck, please. OK, I'll get rid of them, please, please. Please let me go.' Hot tears are spurting into my eyes and the pain makes me feel sick. You let go and I rush to the cold tap, holding my hand under to ease the pain. *Fuck. What the hell was that?* I hear you push the door open into the lounge, apologising.

'Giovanni, Maria, I'm sorry. Sal's just had a little accident. I think it's best if you go.' I hear my mother protesting, fussing that she should come into the kitchen and help me, but you wave her away.

'It's fine – just a little burn from the kettle. Clumsy old Sal wasn't paying attention. It'll be fine. I think it's the tiredness, you know? Sal's completely worn out at the moment. New baby and all that.' I hear the rustle of coats and realise you are shepherding them out of the door, before they've even had a chance to see

Maggie. I want to run after them, to tell them it wasn't an accident, that you hurt me on purpose, but fear and shame keep me rooted to the spot. *What kind of person lets their partner burn them on a hot kettle and does nothing about it?* A terrified one, that's who. The front door slams and you appear in the kitchen doorway.

'I'm sorry I had to do that, Sal. Don't put me in a situation where I have to do this stuff, OK? Get ice on that hand.' Ice-cold and emotionless, you turn on your heel and leave me gaping open-mouthed after you, shaking with shock.

A few days later, there is another incident. It's almost as though Maggie being born has given you a licence to go from simply abusing me verbally to physically hurting me. When I ask you to just double-check the number of scoops of formula in the bottles you are making up (it's the first time you have done it, we are both exhausted, and the midwife was very clear on the dangers of under or overscooping the formula), you turn on me, lightning quick, shoving me backwards into the fridge-freezer. As I stand there winded, you pick up an empty bottle and throw it at me, hitting me on the head. Then you throw another and another, until every bottle on the counter has hit me somewhere. 'You fucking do it then,' you scream in my face, and slam out of the kitchen, leaving me to pick up the bottles and sweep up the formula that's spilled all across the kitchen floor. Later that evening, you come up to bed and see the black eye that has formed after a bottle hit me square in the face. You kiss it, making me flinch.

'I'm sorry, Sal. It won't happen again, I promise. I'm just so tired. I guess we never realised just how exhausting looking after a newborn baby was going to be, did we? Do you still love me?' You stroke my hair away from my face, and kiss a blue-purple bruise that has appeared like a dark smudge on my forehead.

'Of course, we're both tired.' I think about saying: *no, it's not OK. We are not OK*. But I'm worried about how you will react, sure that anything I say will set you off again, so I just let you get away with it, taking the easy way out and unwittingly spurring the cycle on to the next phase. 'Let's sleep now, while she's sleeping. We've got an hour or so until the next feed. Don't worry – I'll get up to her.' I'll just put your behaviour down to exhaustion, surely that's it? You smile, roll over and fall asleep within minutes. I lie awake until Maggie starts squalling for her next bottle.

Even though you promise it won't happen again, it does. When I come home from the supermarket with the wrong brand of nappies, so tired I am unable to see straight, let alone see which brand of nappies I'm picking up, you hit me hard in the kidneys, leaving me feeling winded and sick. By this point, you have already burnt me, pushed me, and kicked me hard in the shins. The full force of a punch to the kidneys doesn't come as a surprise. Then, one evening you decide to put Maggie to bed. I jump at the chance. You rarely offer to do anything like this, and I don't like to ask, given that you are at work all day and I am home with Maggie. All those little things like feeding her, bathing her, putting her to bed, feel like they are my jobs to do. You disappear upstairs and I switch on the television. There's nothing in particular I want to watch but it's just a novelty to be able to sit and watch something, even for ten minutes. I feel like I haven't had a chance to catch my breath since Maggie arrived. I am sitting quietly on the couch, watching the BBC News when, bam! A blow to the side of the head and an excruciating pain knocks my world off kilter.

'*What? Charlie?*' I sit up, one hand clamped to my ear, spots dancing in front of my eyes. The pain is unreal, and I swallow hard in order not to vomit.

'Don't you *ever* make that much noise when I'm putting the baby to bed again, you hear me?' Your face swims into focus, leaning over me as I lie back down on the couch. 'You fucking imbecile. I try to do you a favour and that's how you repay me. Well, you can fuck off, I won't be helping you again.' You stalk out and I lie still on the couch. With the force of your blow to my head, I suspect you have perforated my eardrum. The next morning, you apologise and say it will never happen again. You tell me you love me.

CHAPTER TWENTY-FOUR

CHARLIE

I don't hear anything in response to my email, so after a few days have passed, it feels safe to assume we have seen the last of Radu Popescu. He is obviously just another troublemaker trying to stir things up for Lucian, a man who has worked hard to get where he is today. Things are quiet at home, Sal is behaving properly and I am feeling on top of the world – it seems I am finally getting everything that I have worked for, everything that I deserve. The phone on my desk buzzes, startling me out of my reverie and I hit the answer button.

'Anita?'

'I've got Alex Hoskins for you.' *Shit.* I forgot all about returning Alex's call from days ago; the Radu Popescu thing must have preoccupied me more than I thought.

'OK, fine. Hello, Alex?'

'Charlie! I thought you were ignoring me – you didn't return my call. Not avoiding me, are you?' Alex's husky voice pours into my ear, warm and comforting like honey.

'Of course not, Alex. How are you? It's been years.' Alex was at university with Sal and I. We had a bit of a thing going on, but then Sal came along and it was like I couldn't see Alex properly any more. Sal dazzled me. And truth be told, Alex was just a little too feisty for my liking, not as easy-going and happy to fall in as Sal is.

'Very well, Charlie, very well. I hear you're doing great things over at Hunter, Crisp and Wilson. You're working on the Otex buy-out, aren't you?'

'Yes, I am. I don't know who's told you great things, but I'll take it.' We both laugh, and it feels like the years have been stripped back and we are in our twenties again.

'Listen. I won't lie. My company are direct rivals in the Otex deal. I'm working on behalf of Vygen, and I'll be honest with you – they are very interested in getting their hands on this company. Your name came up in our discussions and it seemed like an omen to get back in contact. It's been a long time, Charlie. All water under the bridge.' Alex wasn't this gracious at the end of our time together, and I feel a slight pang of guilt at how I behaved at the end of our relationship. 'We should meet up, have dinner or something. Obviously, we can't discuss our cases but it would be nice to catch up. I heard you married Sal and you have a little girl together?'

'That's right. Dinner would be good, and I'll be happy to talk about anything except the buy-out.'

Alex laughs and we make an arrangement to meet for dinner in a couple of weeks' time. I can tell Sal I'm working late. I'm not sure why, but I don't think it will be a good idea for Sal to know I'm meeting Alex, and I definitely don't want Geoff or Stan to find out. Not until I know if I can squeeze any secrets out of Alex over dinner. If I can find out any bits of juicy gossip or information that may work in our favour from Alex after a few drinks, it'll make the sneaking around worthwhile.

The rest of the morning passes in a busy blur, aided by the slight high left by Alex's phone call, and when lunchtime rolls around, I decide to head out somewhere to grab a bite to eat. The heatwave still has Britain in its grip, and I feel like today I shouldn't be eating at my desk wasting the day. Who knows how long the sunny weather will last? I grab some cash from my desk drawer and shout through to Anita that I'm going out. As I step outside into brilliant, warm sunshine the pavement is teeming with people – office workers, mums with pushchairs, teenagers slouching their way up the street. Jackets are slung over shoulders, pasty white legs peep out from short hems and shorts, everybody enjoying the novelty that is the great British summertime. There is a faint smell of hot tarmac and exhaust fumes on the air – the delicious smell of London in the summer. I smile, and start walking up towards the bakery at the end of the street; a proper baker's run by a mad Portuguese man that sells filled baguettes and those tiny little Portuguese custard tarts. I decide to buy a bag of custard tarts to take back to Anita – anything to keep her sweet – when someone grabs my arm.

'Charlie Trevetti?' I whirl round to see a small, thin man with dark hair gripping my forearm. Sweat forms a sheen on his face and his clothes look like they've seen better days. Grime sits in the beds of his fingernails.

'Who are you? Get off!' I yank my arm away and feel for the cash and my phone in my pocket. Still there.

'I am Radu Popescu.' I stop, staring at him. Small, slight, with a swarthy complexion, this is not how I imagined Radu Popescu to look. I also thought I had seen the last of him after my email. This can only mean trouble ahead.

'Look, Mr Popescu, did you get my email? I already told you, there is nothing relevant to my work that you can tell me. If you have a problem, or if you need to speak with Mr Pavlenco, you need to contact his office directly. I'm terribly sorry but I can't help you, and accosting me on the street is not going to do you any favours.' I smooth down my shirtsleeve, as if to wipe his handprints off me.

'You don't understand. I have to speak with you, but not here. It has to be private. What I have to say to you is very important. I have tried to speak with Lucian but with no success. Please, you are the only one who can help me.' His dark eyes look at me beseechingly, and I start to feel ever so slightly nervous under his intense gaze. A bead of sweat rolls down his temple, leaving a shining trail in its wake, and I swallow in distaste.

'I'm sorry, Mr Popescu, I really can't help.' I move to the left as if to swerve around him, and he sidesteps, blocking the pavement.

'Mr Popescu, move out of my way immediately. This is harassment and I am within my rights to have you arrested.' I move to the left again and once again he sidesteps and blocks my way. A prickle of alarm snakes up my spine and my palms start to sweat. There is something not right; he is too insistent, and I am starting to feel extremely on edge.

'Charlie Trevetti, my name is not Radu Popescu. My name is Lucian Pavlenco.'

I go cold, a shiver running down my body. *Is he serious?* My mouth falls open and I find myself gaping at Popescu, or Pavlenco, or whatever he wants to call himself.

'I beg your pardon?'

'I said, my name is Lucian Pavlenco.' He stares at me and I stare back, completely lost for words.

'Yes, I thought that was what you said. I'm sorry, but I really do think you need to explain yourself.' I don't believe him – of course I don't believe him –

but something needs to be explained. The man is delusional, schizophrenic or something; that's the only answer. There is no possible way this can be the truth – no possible way at all. He must be a lunatic.

'Like I told you before, I have to speak with you in private. I can't tell you anything where he might be able to find out what I am saying.' Radu peers over his own shoulder, as if Lucian Pavlenco is about to pop out from behind a parked car at any moment. Definitely delusional. It seems as though I have no option but to go along with his idea to see him privately, so I agree to meet him later on that afternoon.

I head back to the office, minus the lunch that I stepped out to get. I seem to have lost my appetite this afternoon. I tell Anita to clear my diary; that I have an urgent meeting that has arisen unexpectedly and I am not sure what time it will finish. Closing my office door, I lift the telephone receiver and dial Lucian Pavlenco's direct line.

'Pavlenco.'

'Mr Pavlenco, it's Charlie Trevetti.'

'Ahhh, Charlie. So good to hear from you. I told you, call me Lucian. Now, what can I do for you?' His voice is like thick syrup, soothing, and it's easy to see how he has managed to win over so many people, and come so far in business.

I explain to him that I have met a man named Radu Popescu, who says he has urgent information for me, and that he has told me his name is actually Lucian Pavlenco.

'What does this man look like?' There is a sharp edge to Lucian's voice now, no longer soft and syrupy. His voice is hard, telling me he hasn't come so far in business by simply winning people over. I describe Popescu, and Lucian lets out a little laugh.

'I have never heard of this man, Popescu. From your description he sounds like nobody I would ever deal with. Charlie, do not be fooled. This man is nobody relevant to either me or to the deal we are about to undertake. Do you hear me? He is *nobody*.' I breathe a sigh of relief, a little shaken at how relieved I am, actually – I must have been more worried about this guy than I thought. I knew that Lucian would either know him, and I could deal with it, or he wouldn't know him and it would be exactly as I thought – another bloody crackpot trying to cash in on someone else's fortune. I hang up, apologising to Lucian despite his being very understanding about the whole thing, and decide to skip the meeting with Popescu. I have a lot to do, preparing for Lucian's deal, and I don't need to waste time with a crackpot loony.

When I leave the office at eight o'clock that evening there is a familiar face waiting for me.

'You said you would meet me this afternoon. I waited and waited and you didn't turn up. Why?' Popescu is standing right outside the entrance to the Hunter, Crisp and Wilson offices, still looking slightly sweaty and with a pretty pissed-off expression on his weasel-like features. I sigh, heaving my laptop bag more firmly onto my shoulder and shuffle him over to one side, out of sight of the doors. The last thing I need is for Stan or one of the other partners to get wind of this – I need to get it dealt with, and fast.

'Listen, Mr Popescu, I spoke with Mr Pavlenco today. I told him I saw you and that you wanted to meet and he said he's never heard of you in his life. Explain that, if you can.' His face pales, and the only way I can describe the look that crosses his face is pure fear.

'You spoke to Lucian? Oh, no. Oh, no, this is terrible. You've made a terrible mistake.' He wipes a shaking hand across his sweaty forehead.

'No, Mr Popescu, you have made a terrible mistake. Please, just leave. Go on and get on with your life and stop meddling in Lucian Pavlenco's.' I step past him, intent on making my way towards the train station when he grabs the arm of my jacket.

'You don't understand. Lucian Pavlenco's life *is* my life.'

That's it. I have no choice but to sit down with this crazy, sweaty lunatic and get to the bottom of exactly what it is he wants to say. I'm afraid I have no chance of getting rid of him until I at least hear him out.

'OK,' I hear myself saying, 'Half an hour, all right? You can have half an hour, and if I still can't do anything to help you, then you leave me alone. Yes?' He nods enthusiastically and we walk a little way up the road, where I know there is a half-decent bar where we won't be disturbed.

I get us both drinks and we sit in a small, dark booth at the back of the room hidden away from the door. The booth is chosen by Popescu, and it occurs to me that he is either very eccentric or very, very frightened.

'So ...' I take a large sip of my cider, a taste that always takes me straight back to my first summer with Sal. 'Tell me what you've got to say.' Popescu takes a deep breath, sips his Coke and stills his slightly shaking hands on the table.

'It's true, what I said to you. My name is not Radu Popescu. My name is Lucian Pavlenco. I came to this country many years ago, to try and make a life for my family. I travelled over here and a few months later my best friend followed. We had known each other for years in Romania. We grew up together in our tiny village. Our parents were friends. His family was my family and my family, his. We went through a lot together.' He takes another small sip of his drink and tears glisten in the corners of his eyes. While this is all very emotional, I am still failing to see what it has to do with Lucian Pavlenco.

'I travelled here legally, with papers,' he goes on, 'but my friend, he couldn't. So, he came here illegally.

I didn't care about that; I was just so happy to have him here with me. I said I would help him to get a job, cash in hand, something to keep him going until we could get his papers sorted out, and I did. I found him work washing dishes in a small restaurant. Just like I am now.' He pauses, looking at me as if checking to see if I am still listening.

'Go on,' I urge. 'Then what happened? Did he get caught? Was he sent back to Romania?'

'No,' he states simply. 'He found that he had a bit of a gift for buying and selling. If someone had something to sell, he would buy it from them, and then somehow end up selling it at a profit. He started to actually make money from it. The problem came when he decided that was what he wanted to do; he wanted to build a business, but he couldn't because he was illegal. He was making some money from buying and selling, but not enough. He was sending money back to Romania, we both were, but he wanted more and more.' I am starting to feel nervous, a sick feeling beginning to churn low down in my stomach, hoping against hope that Radu is not trying to tell me what I think he's trying to tell me.

'So, he had an idea. I was working legally, for a car workshop. Back home in Romania, I worked in the best garage in town; I was a very good mechanic, but there is no money there. The garage was going to close and I had no choice but to come to England and try to make a better life for my family.' His voice is becoming hoarse, and he takes another small sip of his drink, while my nausea intensifies.

'My friend told me he had a plan. If I would lend him my identity, as a legal migrant, his business idea would grow. He already had the contacts he needed to make it successful; all he needed was his papers to make it legal. He promised me that, if I would give him my identity and become Radu Popescu, he would pay me a 60/40 split of the profits. He did all his sums, and showed me I wouldn't need to work; the profits from the business would give me a comfortable enough life. I would be able to watch my children grow up, instead of working all hours to ensure there was enough food on the table. Like a fool, I agreed.' A single tear tracks a silvery line down his rough, stubbled cheek. I feel as though I want to vomit, my mouth watering and my stomach churning like a washing machine on a spin cycle – I do think Radu is trying to tell me something that I really, *really*, don't want to know.

'Are you trying to tell me that your friend, the one who came over as an illegal and used your identity, is Lucian Pavlenco?' I rest my hand lightly on top of his. He nods, slowly, staring into the depths of his drink and I close my eyes. *This is a fucking disaster.*

'He did pay me, in the beginning. A payment would come into my bank and I would be able to feed my family, to buy my children new shoes for school. I gave him my passport and all my papers and he took them to someone he knew. When I got them back, it was still my picture, but it said Radu Popescu instead of Lucian Pavlenco. He was me, and I was him. It was that easy. But then, after a few months, the money stopped. He was in the newspapers, shouting about companies he was buying and then selling on at a huge profit, and my family were sitting there with nothing to eat. I am working now, cash in hand. I am washing dishes, just as he did all those years ago. I tried to contact him, to ask him why he had stopped paying me, why he would leave my family with nothing. He threatened me, told me he knew people who could shut me up. He told me he would have me deported; leave my family hungry and alone with no one to take care of them. There is nothing left of the boy I grew up with.'

Shit. This had better not be true. Everything I've worked for is going to go up in flames if this is really what happened. If Lucian Pavlenco is an illegal immigrant.

'Listen, Radu. I'm going to need some proof, OK. I can't just take your word for it.' Thinking about it, I am pretty confident there won't be any proof. Lucian Pavlenco is absolutely not an illegal immigrant; he can't be. And even if he is, I'll bet he's made damn sure there's no proof. Radu nods. 'I can send you proof. I can do that. My best friend has betrayed me. All I wanted was a new life for my family and now I have come to you because I am desperate.' He bows his head, and I pat his hand quickly, before he can draw attention to us with more tears.

'I will try and help you, OK. But you must not speak to anyone about this. If you do, there will be nothing I can do for you, understand?' I speak sharply to him, as if he is a small child. I have to sort this mess once and for all and no one must ever find out. *Fuck. This sweaty, weasel-faced little man could ruin everything.* There is no way I can let this take down my entire career, and I have already decided I will get rid of Radu Popescu one way or the other.

CHAPTER TWENTY-FIVE

SAL

You have been nothing but sweetness and light since Mr Hunter told you how much he enjoyed the dinner party, but I am struggling to shake off the dark clouds that seem to constantly hang over my head. I am not sleeping terribly well, tossing and turning all night long – this insomnia seeming to hold me in its vice-like grip every time we argue. It's almost like my brain wants me to lie awake at night going over everything I said, everything I did, wondering what particular comment or action set you off. Wondering what I need to remember to lessen the chances of it happening again, the list growing longer every time.

It takes more and more time for me to get over it and return to a normal sleep pattern. Just when it seems as though everything is settled, when you are being kind and decent, making up for what has gone on before and I can once again sleep through the night, something else happens. I say the wrong thing, do the wrong thing, you

get angry – lash out – and then the whole cycle begins
again. I feel like I'm forever walking on eggshells. I'm
constantly living on a knife-edge, and it's exhausting. I
have no other option, though, it seems – if I retaliate or
tell you you're wrong, the consequences are so hideous,
it's no longer worth trying to stick up for myself, and
if I tell you it's over you'll do what you did last time,
and hide away in the bathroom with razors, screaming
at me through the bathroom door that 'this time' you
really mean it; you'll kill yourself and it will all be my
fault. I can't put Maggie through that, so I just soldier
on, trying not to offend you in any way.

You've gone off to work early this morning as usual,
and although I am awake when you leave I fake sleep,
once again, in order to avoid you. I seem to be doing it
more and more these days, the effort it takes to sustain
a conversation with you getting harder and harder.
You have been a different person these past few days,
since Stan told you the dinner party was a success.
You've been a *nicer* person, making an effort with
Maggie, doing the dishes so I can put my feet up, all
the little things that give me a tiny glimpse into how
our lives could be all the time. The only trouble is,
now I recognise it for what it is – a tiny glimpse and
no more – I don't find myself thinking that maybe
you've changed this time, that maybe the tiny glimpse
will become the norm and, it frightens me a little bit. It
frightens me that maybe I've recognised you for what

you are, that maybe I'm realising I'm not as worthless as you make out.

That evening, although you seemed a little preoccupied, as though there is something else on your mind, you come home with a takeaway, so I don't have to cook, and a bottle of wine.

'Here.' You thrust the carrier bag at me as you walk in the front door. 'I got us a curry. I didn't think you'd want to cook after I woke you up this morning.' You kiss me, and scoop up Maggie, who has run to the front door to welcome you. 'Look at this, my perfect little family.' You smile at me, a tiny dimple appearing in your cheek, which tells me it is a genuine smile and I manage to raise a smile back. We go through into the kitchen and I start to serve the food up onto plates. Maggie has eaten, so it will be just you and me at the table. Bringing out a bar of chocolate from your jacket pocket, you wave it at Maggie and laugh as she squeals and makes a grab for it.

'Nicely!' You laugh, before handing it to her. She runs off to the living room to eat it and I lay the cutlery out for our meal.

'Listen, Sal, I was thinking. It's been a busy few months – we should go away. Just for the weekend. Somewhere by the sea. We could even let Maggie stay with your mum.' I turn to you, open-mouthed. You never, *never*, let Maggie stay with anyone else.

'Really? You would do that?'

'Why not? I know I haven't before but I think we need a break, Sal. Just think, walks along the beach, fishing on the pier, we can go to the pub for dinner. It'll be nice.' I nod, agreeing with you, but not getting too excited, as I know the offer could be retracted at any moment.

'OK,' I say. 'That would be nice, just you and me. Maybe once you're done with the Otex thing and you're a partner.' You beam at me, and I know I have said the right thing this time. I resolve not to ask my mum to have Maggie just yet, not until something is booked. I don't want to disappoint her, or Maggie, if you decide to change your mind. It's been known before – almost as though you dangle a carrot to get your own way, only to withdraw it at the last minute.

Stretching, I yawn and close my eyes. Despite feeling so tired, I know I won't be able to go back to sleep. Maggie is beginning to stir next door, little shuffling noises coming from her room as she fidgets in bed, and it won't be long before she is up and ready for another day. My eyes fly open at the thud of the post hitting the mat downstairs, so I pull on some pyjama bottoms and make my way downstairs. If I'm really quiet I can maybe sneak in a quick coffee before Maggie gets up and starts her daily demands. Much as I love looking after Maggie, love being at home with her, sometimes it is just exhausting and I'll take a little snippet, a little moment here and there, just to be by myself whenever I can. I pad silently downstairs, the house already warm from the sun streaming in through the patio doors to the garden. It's going to be another scorcher of a day, no sign of the heatwave abating. I should try and enjoy it; goodness knows when we'll ever have a summer like this again. Scooping up the post from the mat, I head into the kitchen and switch on the coffee machine. I normally just have time to grab a quick cup of instant, but while Maggie is sleeping I'll take the time to make a proper pot of coffee. I flick through the post while I wait for the pot to warm. Mostly junk mail, a couple of bills and then, finally, a smooth white envelope addressed to me. The envelope is handwritten and postmarked South-East London. As I move to open it, the gurgling of the pot alerts me that my coffee is ready. Discarding the envelope, I pour a cup, just as Maggie enters the kitchen.

'Hey, Mags. Good sleep?' I lean down and ruffle her crazy dark curls. She looks adorable, all mussed-up bed hair, her chubby face lined with sleep.

'Yep. Got Coco Pops?' she asks, climbing up onto a kitchen chair to sit at the table. So much for my quiet cup of morning coffee. I pour Maggie a bowl of cereal, and the envelope lies forgotten on the kitchen counter as I run around after her, making sure she cleans her teeth and brushing the wild tangles out of her hair. It's a few hours later and headed towards lunchtime before I remember about the letter.

With slightly shaking hands, I ease open the envelope and slide out the letter. Unfolding the paper, I feel my breath hitch as I recognise the emblem for St Martin's. Quickly, I skim the letter, before going back and reading properly. And then rereading, before rereading again. *Shit.* My hands are properly shaking now and a smile creeps across my face. Following on from my application, Mrs Prideaux, head teacher at St Martin's C of E Primary School, would like to invite me to attend an interview on Wednesday 8th July. This will be an all-day interview and will include the opportunity to show my teaching skills.

Fuuuuuck. I can't believe it. I actually can't believe it. I honestly thought I would get a letter back, saying thanks but no thanks. I haven't taught in so long, having been home with Maggie all this time, that I really didn't think I would have any chance of even getting to interview stage in the first place. I take a deep breath and look for my phone.

Although my first instinct is always to call you and tell you when something happens, I can't in this case. I still haven't confessed that I even applied for a job, and I don't want to tell you anything until, *unless*, I actually get it. I don't honestly believe you would be terribly supportive; in fact, I think the shit will hit the fan big-time, but I also think that if I actually have a job offer, it'll make my case for taking up the job stronger. *And*, a tiny voice pipes up inside my head, *if you do end up having to make a big decision regarding you and Charlie, you're going to need a job.*

I decide to text Laura – she knows about the application and I hope she'll be home with the children. I also know, without a doubt, that she'll be excited for me. I pick up my phone to text her, but my phone is dead. Typical. There are only two places a phone charger might be. I look in the top kitchen drawer – no charger. There are keys for locks that we don't even have any more, old birthday candles and a roll of clingfilm, but no phone charger. Checking that Maggie is still happy playing Barbies in the front hallway (where else is there but the front hallway to play Barbies?), I run lightly up the stairs to our bedroom, my good news making me feel altogether lighter all over. I look next to the bed, my side and yours, but still no phone charger. That's weird. These are the only places the phone charger is ever left – you are extreme in your demands that things have a certain place, and they must always be left *in the correct spot*. That way, nothing ever gets lost. Only, this time, it is lost. I recheck next to the bed, looking underneath and in the bedside drawers. I go back to the kitchen, checking the usual drawer and both drawers underneath. Still no charger. I ask Mags if she has seen it; she says she hasn't. I even check her toy box. There is no sign at all of the phone charger. Sighing, there's only one thing I can do. I'll have to go and buy a new charger to replace the one that's gone missing, before you get home tonight and want to charge your phone up. There is no doubt in my mind that if you get home and it's not here, I will be the one who gets the blame, regardless of whether I have used it or not.

'Come on, Mags.' I slip her sandals on her chubby little feet and we head out the front door, straight up the path next door to Laura's. Laura opens the door before we reach it, having obviously seen us on our way up the path.

'Hey, you two, what can I do for you?' She grins, pushing her red hair out of her eyes with a pale, slim hand.

'I have *news*.' I widen my eyes at her, and she gets the hint. 'But first, I need to go into town and get a new phone charger. Fancy a trip on the bus? We can get a coffee at that new place, and I can tell you *all about it*.' I waggle my eyebrows at her and she laughs, a deep, throaty laugh.

'How could I resist? One thing, though – we're going in my car. There's no way I'm taking these two on the bus!' She calls through to Lucy and Fred and I help her with shoes, cardigans and the pushchair.

An hour later, we are strolling through the town centre, a new phone charger swinging from the small carrier bag in my hand. Mags and Lucy are holding hands and walking in front of us, pretending they are shopping on their own. They have persuaded us they *need* a *Frozen* top each, one they have seen displayed in Primark's front window as we walk past, so both are swinging their own little carrier bags.

Laura turns to me. 'Coffee, then? I could murder a latte.' We reach the swanky new coffee shop, and as we enter the aroma of roasted coffee and buttery pastry hits me, making my stomach growl, and I remember that I never did get to drink that coffee earlier. We get our order and find a booth with big, squishy couches. There is a tiny play area in one corner of the room, so Maggie, Fred and Lucy all hit the miniature ball-pit and we are free to talk in peace.

'So, come on then, *spill*. I want to hear the *news*.' Laura waggles her eyebrows at me, in much the same fashion as I had at her earlier.

'I got an interview,' I say, and Laura squeals and pulls me into a bear hug.

'Shit, Sal. That's amazing. Fucking hell, I knew you could do it!' I grin at her, unable to hold it in.

'Steady on, I only got an interview. I didn't get the job!'

'*Yet*, Sal. You didn't get the job *yet*. I've every faith in you.' Laura takes a bite of her lemon and poppy seed muffin, neat white teeth taking neat little bites.

'Thanks, Laur, for being so supportive. I still haven't told Charlie yet. I think I should just see how it goes, you know? I don't want to cause a row if it's not even going to come to anything.' I sip my latte, disappointment tugging at me. Surely it's not right to feel this way?

'Listen, Sal. You've got to remember you're still your own person. You're still *you*. What are you going to do when Mags goes to school if you haven't got a job? You'll go bat shit staying indoors all day with nothing to do. Charlie has to understand that.'

'Easier said than done.'

'Is everything OK with you two? It's just … sometimes things don't always seem balanced between you. I mean … you know you can always talk to me, right?' Sighing, Laura puts her hand on top of mine and I subtly pull away.

'It's fine, honestly. Charlie just has a stressful job and not a lot of time to deal with the family stuff. Things can get a bit tense, that's all. There's nothing wrong.' Laura nods slowly, and I avoid her eyes. I wish I could tell her everything, but the last time I tried to talk to anyone about what went on at home it backfired on me hugely, and I am loath to ever try to discuss it with anyone again. The excitement of earlier has firmly abated, and we decide to make a move towards home.

I leave Laura at her door and take Maggie inside. It's swelteringly hot outside again, and so I get the hosepipe and sprinkler out for Maggie after dousing her in sun cream. I plug my phone in with the new charger, dispose of the bag at the bottom of the bin, and start emptying pockets in order to put a load of laundry on.

When you arrive home, a little later than the other nights this week, your good mood seems to have broken. You are tense, moody, more than a little snappy. I decide to keep out of your way for a little while, while you relax with a cold beer. *Maybe it's just the heat getting to you?* I'm pretty sure I haven't said or done anything that could have set you off, but to be on the safe side, I go out into the garden, intent on getting Maggie dry and dressed before dinner.

'SAL!' My heart sinks as I hear you roar from the kitchen. Obviously, our time of peace is over and it's back to being a war. Another exhausting, bloody battle in which there is only every one victor and it's never me. Closing my eyes, I stop for a second, before leaving Maggie to carry on her solo water fight and trudging back up the garden to the kitchen. You are standing against the counter, a small white slip of paper in your hand.

'What the fuck is this?' You wave it at me, and my throat constricts in terror as, at first, my eyes somehow see the letter from St Martin's. Then I realise it is just the receipt for the phone charger I bought earlier.

'It's a receipt, Charlie.' I stretch out to take it from you.

'I can see that, you fucking idiot. What the hell have you been buying from EE? A new SIM card, is that it?

One I don't know about, so you can ring people behind my back?' I stare at you incredulously. I honestly don't understand the way your mind works.

'What? No! I couldn't find the phone charger this morning, and my phone was almost dead. I was worried that you wouldn't be able to get hold of me, so I thought the best thing to do would be to go and get a new one. I didn't want you to not be able to charge your phone when you got in.'

'No phone charger? What the fuck is this, then?' I look on in horror as you violently pull the kitchen drawer open to reveal the charger, sitting snugly in its usual place. I know it wasn't there this morning, I checked *over and over* and it definitely wasn't there.

'You're a liar, Sal,' you sing-song at me, 'a fucking liar. Nothing ever changes, does it? Maybe you need to be taught a lesson?' A tight smile flits across your face as I back away from you, feeling sick. You pick up the boiling hot cup of tea you must have poured while I was out in the garden with Maggie.

'Charlie, please. I'm not lying – let's not ruin what has been a lovely week. Come on, Charlie?' I say, my voice trickling out in a thin moan, backing up to the kitchen counter as far as I can, trying to get as far away from you as possible. You seem to stumble as the boiling liquid arcs out of the mug, over my bare arm, and I look up to see Laura's horrified face gazing in through the kitchen window.

CHAPTER TWENTY-SIX

CHARLIE

I spy the receipt on the kitchen worktop immediately, as I'm putting the phone charger back in the kitchen drawer. Lying there, snug among the safety pins, old keys, and other bits of tat that seem to collect in this drawer, is a brand-new, shiny white phone charger, the plastic seal still wrapped around the lead. I know what has happened straight away – Sal couldn't find the phone charger and so has rushed out to buy another one. I don't know why I can't just accept it, just leave things alone and get on with having a pleasant evening with my family, and a part of me *does* want to just forget about it, but it suddenly strikes me that this is the perfect opportunity. This is the perfect time to really question Sal about something that I know won't be lied about – giving me the chance to make it easier for me to tell when Sal is actually lying.

I lean out of the kitchen window and roar at Sal to come in, waving the white slip of paper high over my head, all the time watching Sal's body language for clues. As I scream and make my accusations, Sal plays right into my hands, denying everything I toss out and telling me what I already know. I watch carefully, absorbing every fleeting expression that crosses Sal's face, every muscle twitch, feeling the weight of those chocolate-dark eyes staring into mine as Sal *begs* me to believe what I'm being told. I close my eyes briefly, a perfect snapshot of Sal's face imprinted into my memory bank, to be brought out at a later date to prove to me whether Sal is lying or telling the truth.

Now I have what I want, I can't bear to listen to Sal bleating on any more – today's meeting with Radu Popescu has already pushed me to my limits. I am feeling frazzled and stressed. I am damned if I know how I am going to sort this problem out, and given that it's Sal's fault I am working on this case – let's face it, I am fighting to make partner so Sal can stay at home and keep house, stay home under my control because Sal can't be trusted out in the real world – unfortunately, this means Sal is going to get the brunt of it. If I can't completely control the outcome of the Pavlenco deal, I can at least control what goes on in my own home. Now, as I scream and shout and wave things around, I am too far gone to stop myself. Of course Sal bought a new charger if the old one was missing – even I would have done the same thing. But, irrationally, even though I know Sal is telling the truth, I have convinced myself

Sal is trying to make me look like a fool. I can't back down now and say, 'Oh, sorry, Sal, my mistake.' I'd look like a right idiot, and the fact that Sal has made me feel this way means the only course of action is to carry on. Anger is still coursing through me, and I can't help it. I feel nothing but contempt for Sal, for all those people who won't stand up for themselves properly. Before I even realise what I'm doing, I snatch at the boiling cup of tea and the hot liquid lands directly on Sal's arm.

Slamming out of the house, I make my way up the hill to the park, a short distance from our house. A huge green space, dotted with oak and birch trees and surrounded by a circular footpath, it's the perfect place to escape and get away from everything. I find an empty bench and throw myself down, breathing heavily. It's not my fault, I tell myself. If Sal didn't do these things, didn't wind me up all the time, none of this stuff would ever have to happen. Sal knows I have a temper, but does everything possible to make me lose it. Why not just tell me the phone charger was lost, instead of sneaking it into the house like it's forbidden contraband – am I that awful? Why lie about stuff all the time? *Did my dad think like this?* In all honesty, I called him Dad but he wasn't my father. My real father died when I was six, a lump that turned out not to be harmless taking him away from me and my mother for ever within eight short months. I didn't really understand at the time what was happening, and my mother obviously didn't feel the need to explain properly. I barely remember him; it's like I came home from school one day and he was gone.

Within a few short weeks, my new 'dad' arrived. Looking back, I think he must have been hovering in the background for a while, but who knows? My mother is not the kind of woman who can be on her own. He was all very charming and polite, until he got his feet under the table and somehow persuaded her to marry him. Before my real dad had been gone six months, they were married and I was told I wasn't to call him Clive any more, but must call him 'Dad'. I rebelled against it, crying and begging my mum not to make me – I already had a dad, he just wasn't there – but all it got me was a mighty slap to the side of the head and an evening locked alone in my bedroom. That was just the beginning. Clive ruled our house with an iron fist, (in my head, he was always Clive, although I never made the mistake of calling him that to his face again). He was clearly resentful of my being there, preferring whenever he could to get my mother alone. I didn't understand why he had chosen us – surely he must have realised I existed, that I came with my mother as part of a package? As I grew up, I realised he probably hadn't known about me in the beginning. I was doubtful my mother had ever said anything about me until it was too late, so that she didn't lose him and end up on her own.

My father had left a small amount of money to my mother when he died, along with a small legacy for me, apparently to help me get through university. Once Clive had that ring on my mother's finger he also got access to the money. He burnt through it in less than a year, and we went from a family that was doing OK, to a family that was pretty much permanently skint. I went from having the latest trainers and being able to go on all the school trips, to being the kid that had second-hand clothes (right down to my shoes), and who could only go on the school trips if the school had enough put by to pay for those kids who couldn't afford the 'voluntary contribution'. Clive, however, still managed to spend an inordinate amount of time on the golf course and still enjoyed his bottle of Bushmills most evenings.

The more Bushmills sunk of an evening, the higher the number of slaps dished out. I prayed so hard some nights for a brother or sister, someone who could take a share of the blows. In the beginning I had been defiant, telling Clive he wasn't my dad and couldn't tell me what to do, but after feeling the back of his hand repeatedly, it was just easier to shut up and put up with it all. My mother went from a bright, intelligent woman, not afraid to speak her mind or throw back her head in laughter, to an empty shell. A woman who was there but not really there at the same time. We tiptoed around Clive, always unsure every evening what kind of mood he would be in, knowing that if the front gate slammed shut, rather than quietly clicked, we were in for a stormy evening.

The final straw comes just before I turn eighteen. I have just finished my A-levels and am planning to go into town to meet some friends to celebrate.

As I make my way down the stairs, Clive is waiting at the bottom, glass in hand, alcohol fumes pouring off him in waves.

'Where d'you think you're going?' He shoves his meaty face right in mine, breathing his toxic breath all over me. He stands at the bottom of the stairs, blocking my way.

'Just to town. I've finished my last exams today; I'm meeting a couple of people to celebrate. Excuse me, please.' I move forward in an attempt to get past him.

'I don't think so.' He raises a hand and pushes me back slightly. 'Your mother says your room is a shit-hole. I suggest you get back up there and sort it out – you're going nowhere.'

I can't help it. Just who does he think he is?

'Sorry, what? No, *Clive*, I am not a child – I am going out to meet my friends and celebrate the end of my exams. I'm sick to death of your bullying. You're not my dad – in fact, you're nothing to me – so why don't you just fuck off?' I go to push past him again, my heart hammering in my chest so hard it hurts. I haven't stood up to him since I was a child. Slowly, deliberately, he places his whisky glass on the telephone table.

'Just who the hell do you think you are?' he hisses in my face.

'I am *not your child*,' I hiss back, gasping as he grabs my wrists, pulling them up high and throwing me back against the wall. Pinning me to the wall by my wrists, he screams into my face. I turn my face away, spittle landing on my cheek, his whisky-infused breath hot and sour in my face. He clasps a fistful of my hair, pulling me down the stairs before grabbing my head and slamming it against the wall. 'That's for giving me cheek, you little fucker. You and your mother would be nothing without me. Get the fuck out of my sight.'

I lie, dazed, at the bottom of the stairs for a few minutes, before turning and slowly crawling up them, my wrists and head throbbing with every step. Climbing into bed, I pull the covers high, my head sore and tender where it meets the pillow. A little while later, I hear the bedroom door open and my mother enters. She places a cold glass of water and a packet of paracetamol on the bedside table, and then lays a cool hand on my forehead.

'How are you feeling?'

'Mum. Are you joking? I'm not *ill*.' I push her hand away and struggle to sit up.

'No darling, I know, I … look, I've bought you a glass of water and some tablets.' She gestures to the table.

'Jesus. Seriously, Mum, did you see what he did to me? Aren't you going to speak to him, tell him it's not on? He's lucky I'm not going to press charges – it's assault, for Christ's sake. I'm not a kid, Mum. He can't treat me like that.' I stare hard at her, willing her for once, just this once, to be on my side. To defend me over him.

'Well, darling, you did provoke him. You didn't have to say those things, you know. He has provided for us since your father left.'

'For fuck's sake, Mum! He didn't *leave* – he fucking *died*. It's not like he chose to leave us!' I can't believe what I'm hearing, her words making me feel just as sick as my bruises. 'I provoked him, did I? Have I been provoking him for the past twelve years? He's a bully, Mum, and you just let him get away with it. I'm your *child*; I should come before anyone.' She turns her head away and starts fussing with the duvet cover.

'Charlie, you don't understand what it's like, to be a mother on your own, with a child. You don't know how difficult it was for me to cope after your father died. Clive saved me.' Tears fill her eyes, and I start to feel even sicker than I did before.

'What are you saying, Mum? That it's OK for Clive to do these things? Are you saying you'll always support Clive over me?' She bows her head, tears making damp marks like tiny clouds on the duvet. She won't make eye contact with me.

'Fine, OK.' I grab the tablets and swill three down with a huge gulp of water. I push the covers back and pull my jeans back on, a wave of dizziness making me stagger.

'Charlie, wait ... what are you doing?' My mother grasps my arm and I shake her off, pulling an old holdall out of the wardrobe. I begin stuffing clothes and toiletries into it, refusing to look at her.

'What does it look like, Mum? I'm leaving. You've made your decision; I'll let you get on with it. You're on your own.' Zipping up the holdall, I throw it over my shoulder and head downstairs. 'And don't come crying to me when he starts on you.'

'Charlie, please. Just think about it. Don't be hasty.' She tries once more to grab my arm but I'm out the front door before she can reach me.

I haven't been back since. I spent a few weeks sleeping on various friends' couches, before heading to London, university and my new life. I didn't go back for Clive's funeral a few years later, and although I call my mum at Christmas, it's more just to check she's still alive; a duty call, if you like. I'm past caring whether she's happy. She made her decision all those years ago and I can never forgive her for choosing that man over her own child.

The sun is going down and it's starting to get chilly sitting on my lonely park bench. I feel calmer now, ready to go back and sort things out with Sal. The red mist that descends more strongly with each row has lifted and I suppose I should go back and check Sal's arm is OK. If only Sal didn't wind me up so much, this would never happen. Sometimes I worry I'm no better than Clive, that I'm just as much of an animal as he was. But then I think, *No*. He didn't have the kind of high-powered, stressful job that I have. He wasn't responsible for thousands and thousands of pounds at work every day; he worked in a fucking factory, for God's sake. And no matter how angry I get, no matter how strongly the red mist has me in its grip, I would never hurt a child; I would never hurt Maggie. Clive was a sad, sadistic bully who was only happy when he was making others miserable. That's not me – I am in no way anything like Clive – in fact, you could say I'm just the opposite. Yeah, sure, I lose my temper, but not because I want to make my family miserable. I want us to be *happy*. I want us to be strong, a team, a family that is going to be together for ever. Sal just needs to learn to rein it in a bit. If Sal would just learn to do what I ask, to do what I want to make us all happy, then none of this would ever happen, would it?

CHAPTER TWENTY-SEVEN

SAL

I cry out in pain as the scalding liquid hits my arm, splashing down onto the kitchen counter where it forms a steaming pool. As I raise my eyes to yours, I see something from the corner of my eye – Laura's face, framed with a red halo where the sun streams in behind her, eyes wide with horror. You don't notice; you're too busy looking at me in disgust before you turn abruptly and stalk out of the kitchen. A few seconds later I hear the front door slam.

Wiping away the tears that leak soundlessly from my eyes, I switch on the kitchen tap and try to hold my burnt arm underneath the cooling stream, a hot flush of shame staining my cheeks. Laura lets herself in, fumbling with the door handle in her haste to get to me.

'Fuck, Sal, are you OK? God, no, stupid question. Here …' She rolls my sleeve right up out of the way to avoid it getting soaked. I hiss between my teeth as the cold water runs over the burn.

'Keep it there. I know it hurts, but you must keep it there. It'll help, I promise.' Laura's voice is calm and soothing, and I remember how she used to be a nurse, before Lucy and Fred, before Jed left her a single mother with no support and no way of going back to work. I smile shakily at her, and reach my good hand under the stream of water, reaching back to splash it over my hot face. Laura hands me a clean tea towel and when I fumble and drop it, my hands still shaking with shock, she picks it up and gently wipes my face.

'Thank you.' I don't know what else to say to her. I'm in pain and feeling sick, my stomach turning over and over. I am embarrassed that she has witnessed your true nature. Stumble or not, I am sure you meant for the hot tea to hit my arm. Laura smiles in response, but doesn't speak, and after a little while has passed, she tells me I can remove my arm from the cold water.

'You should really get this looked at, Sal. By a proper doctor.'

'*No.* Laura, please, I don't want to see a doctor or go to hospital. It's just a little burn.' We both look down at my arm, at the red, blistered skin. It's not just a little burn, it's a bloody big one, but I really don't want to go to hospital and have to answer any questions. It'll only make you angrier, if nothing else. Laura gives a slight shake of her head, but doesn't argue.

'Well, have you got a first-aid box? I've got one next door – Jed's mum is there to see the kids. I can run back and get it, if not.'

'There's one up there.' I point to the very top cupboard next to the oven – it came in the back of the new car when we picked it up, and so far we haven't had to use it. Laura reaches up and grabs it, and begins searching through for gauze and bandages.

'Sal, we have to talk about this.' She doesn't look at me, but carries on digging through the packets, searching for everything she needs to dress my arm.

'There's nothing to talk about, Laur. It was an accident, that's all. Charlie tripped.'

'I'm not stupid, Sal. I saw the whole thing. I was coming over to give you this.' She leans down and picks up the little carrier bag containing Maggie's new *Frozen* top. 'Mags left it in my car. I thought she might want it.'

'It's not how it looked, Laura. Charlie can't help it … it was my fault,' I stutter, trying to explain it away as nothing; but looking into Laura's clear, green eyes, I know I'm fooling nobody.

'Sal. I saw everything with my own eyes, and I've not told you this before but I've been in your situation. Before Jed, there was a guy. We went out for a while, but he seemed to get more and more controlling the longer we were together. He didn't want me to see any of my friends; he decided what I would wear, where I would go. Then one day, he hit me. I left immediately, never went back. It took me a long time to get over it but, Sal, there are people out there who can help you.' She looks at me steadily, as she smooths antiseptic cream onto the burn on my arm.

'It's not that simple, Laura. I know you think you understand, but you really don't. Charlie doesn't beat me or anything; it's not like that. It was just a misunderstanding today. I did something stupid and Charlie got a bit cross and tripped. That's all.' If I say it enough times maybe Laura will believe me, but I still can't bring myself to meet her gaze.

'What about your fingers, Sal? A couple of weeks ago, when your hand was bandaged up – what happened then? Did Charlie do that to you as well?'

'No. Of course not. I told you at the time that I caught my hand in the door; it slammed shut and took my fingers with it. Don't see things that aren't there, Laura.' Laura gently places the gauze on the burn and begins to wind the bandage around to secure it.

'OK, Sal. Have it your way.'

I know she doesn't believe me, but who else is going to believe the truth? I tried before, to get help, to tell someone, and it was a disaster. I'd made friends with a woman at the baby group I went to after Maggie was born. We got friendly with her and her husband, like you do when you have a new baby, taking it in turns to host dinners at each other's homes. You actually quite liked her, and I was 'allowed' to see her, but only when you were around. One day, after a particularly vicious row, she popped over unannounced while you were at work. You had let me have it, both barrels, before you left that morning and I was struggling. At the time, you liked a good punch to the kidneys to make me uncomfortable for the whole day and that day I was in a lot of pain. Sian, the woman I had befriended, came over and noticed that I was awkward and stiff in my movements. I don't know what came over me, but I told her everything. I'll never forget the look on her face when she heard what I had to say. She looked at me as though I was weak, a liar; as though I was making things up as an excuse to seek attention. She looked at me the way you look at me. It turned out she was friendlier with you than I had realised, and she told you everything, clearly of the mind that I didn't deserve any loyalty from her, that I was lying about it all. You made sure, after that, that I never felt the urge to tell anyone again – the consequences too much to make it worth it – and I never felt able to trust anyone again, not with this.

Laura gets up, and pours us both a glass of wine. 'I am here, though, Sal, whenever you need me. You might not want to talk now, but if you change your mind you know I'm just next door.' I smile gratefully at her.

'I know, Laur. You're a good friend, but please, just leave it, OK? Charlie's got a temper, I agree, but it's nothing I can't handle. Today was just a fluke, I promise. Just, please, don't say anything to anyone. Especially not to Charlie.' We drink our wine in relative silence – both of us unsure of what to say next. I feel ashamed and embarrassed that Laura has witnessed what happened today, angry at myself that I'm not brave enough to talk to her about it, not brave enough to trust her, but I still can't bring myself to admit what really goes on in our relationship. After a short while, after checking that I feel OK and that my bandage isn't too tight, Laura leaves and goes back next door to her mother-in-law and children. Maggie has tired of her water fight and is slumped in front of the television. I feed her, bathe her – awkwardly, as Laura has advised me not to get the burn wet – and tuck her into bed.

Some time later, I am curled up on the couch, watching something mind-numbing on the television when I hear the gentle click of the front door latching closed. You appear in the doorway, looking tired and rumpled, your eyes flicking to the white bandage on my arm. I struggle into a sitting position, trying not to nudge the bandage on my arm and set off the white-hot sparks of pain again.

'Sal, I'm sorry, OK? I lost my temper.' You sit on the couch next to me, your thigh laid along the length of mine, and I resist the urge to shuffle away. 'You just make me so mad – why do you have to lie all the time? It's as though you deliberately try to antagonise me.' You stroke the bandage gently, and I freeze ever so slightly. It is still so painful and I am nervous that you will press too hard and hurt me. Your words make me flinch – I never lied, I know I never lied. The phone charger wasn't in the drawer, and I never bought a new SIM card. I don't want to anger you so I just shrug.

'I don't know, Charlie. I'm sorry. It won't happen again.'

'You say that, Sal, but it always does, doesn't it? Does your arm hurt terribly?'

'No, it's not so bad.' You lift my arm, inspecting the bandaging.

'This is good bandaging, Sal, considering you must have done it with one hand.' *Shit.* I think fast. I'll have to tell you the truth, after all your ranting about how I lie all the time. What could you do to me today that's worse than what you've already done?

'I had to get Laura to do it.' A frown creases your brow. 'It's OK. I just ran next door and told her I dropped the kettle; after all, that's what happened, isn't it?' A puzzled look crosses your face, before a small smile appears. I have said the right thing – by rewriting what actually happened, we can pretend you had nothing to do with this. That it was not your fault.

'Absolutely. I'll get you some painkillers. You stay there and relax – did you eat? Let me make you something.' Before I can tell you I'm not hungry, that funnily enough my appetite disappeared when you threw boiling water over me, you bustle off into the kitchen. I lean back into the sofa cushions and let out a deep sigh. Any more trouble seems to have been averted for now, and without a doubt we will enter that phase in the cycle in which you can't do enough for me. I'm no longer sure which is more terrifying – your rage and all that ensues, or the smothering, intense phase that follows.

You enter the living room, balancing a plate of cheese on toast in one hand and a mug of tea in the other. I can't help it – I shrink back from the hot mug, worried in case it spills on me. Catching the small movement, you place the mug on the floor, and sit next to me.

'Sal, don't be silly. It was a stupid accident. It's not going to happen again.' You smooth my hair down, and take my hand in yours. 'Let's just agree to forget about it now, OK? Remember, I love you, Sal. More than anything, and more than anyone else ever will. As soon as I've finished this case, we can take a holiday, a weekend away together, just us. We can spend the whole weekend on our own with no one to disturb us, just you and me. How does that sound?'

I smile weakly at you, your intense gaze boring into me, almost defying me to say no.

'It sounds perfect, Charlie. Just perfect.'

The rest of the week passes without any further incidents. You make a couple of references to 'issues' at work, and I realise that that is what must have made you flip out in the kitchen, the day you threw the water over me. You cook for me, despite getting home late, and put Maggie to bed so I can have a rest in the evenings and actually sit down before nine o'clock, and I even wake up to my mug, all prepared ready for a cup of tea in the mornings, just like you used to, even though I switched to coffee after Maggie was born to help cope with the sleepless nights. You cut the grass, front garden and back garden, at the weekend, a task usually reserved for me,

('You have more time, Sal. I don't want to spend the weekend mowing the bloody grass. I need to relax, for Christ's sake.') It's a little reminder of how life used to be, before you got so angry all the time.

Laura keeps her distance, and although at first I worry she's angry I lied to her, I begin to realise that maybe it's just because you are around; maybe it's actually you she is avoiding. I resolve to go over there, once you are at work and things are back to normal. There is always an intense phase after a row in which you hover over me, unable to do enough to 'make it up' to me, but this wanes after a few days.

Your behaviour, for now, is impeccable. It's like nothing happened; like the water incident, the lasagne incident, the allotment incident – none of that stuff ever happened. Anyone looking at our life from the outside would think we have it all. They would think we lead the perfect life.

CHAPTER TWENTY-EIGHT

CHARLIE

Following on from Sal's accident with the kettle (Clumsy Sal), life pretty much gets back to normal. I find myself taking care of Sal, cooking, dealing with Maggie; I even cut the grass. I always find that after we have argued I need to show Sal exactly how perfect our life is, how lucky Sal is to have me. I know then that Sal can never leave me, not while I can show how perfect our life actually is most of the time, little blips and arguments aside. Everyone argues now and again, don't they? I don't hear anything from Radu Popescu and, after a few days, once again, I begin to think he has disappeared, realising his ludicrous tale is exactly that – a story that no one wants to hear, that no one believes. After all, I asked him for proof and nothing has been forthcoming so far.

My relief is short-lived, however, and on Tuesday morning an email lands in my inbox. Checking my door is closed (I do not want Anita to see any correspondence between Popescu and myself), I open it. To my dismay, a long-winded email is completed with two attachments. Opening them, I realise that one is the original birth certificate for Lucian Pavlenco. The other is a Romanian driving licence, also in the name of Lucian Pavlenco, but bearing a photograph of Radu Popescu. The driving licence looks old, authentic; there seems to be no way this can be a fake. There are also photos. Photos of two boys who can only be Radu Popescu and Lucian Pavlenco as children, proof that they did indeed grow up together. *Shit. Maybe Popescu is telling the truth – which means I have to rectify this immediately, before anyone else can find out. What the hell am I going to do?* I drum my fingers on the table, thinking hard. There is only one answer. I am going to have to meet with Lucian Pavlenco and get to the bottom of this, once and for all.

'Anita?' I open my door and shout through to my ever-efficient secretary. She appears, a freshly brewed pot of coffee in hand.

'Charlie! I thought you might need this.' She pours a cup and hands it to me.

'Thanks, Anita, you're a gem. Listen, I need you to get me Lucian Pavlenco on the phone. It's urgent. Tell his secretary it's regarding the issues we discussed in our last conversation.' That should get him on the line; he's notoriously difficult to get hold of, but knowing what our last conversation consisted of, I'm pretty confident he'll want to speak to me.

Ten minutes later, my telephone buzzes with the internal ring.

'Anita? Where's Pavlenco?'

'I tried, Charlie, I really did. I spoke to his secretary and told her what it was regarding. She came back and said Mr Pavlenco had a message for you – he said to tell you he has nothing further to say on that matter; as far as he is concerned that subject was dealt with in your previous conversation and he sees no reason to revisit it.' A burst of anger washes over me. *Damn that man. Doesn't he realise this could jeopardise everything for both of us?* Taking a deep breath, I try to regain my composure. It wouldn't do to lose my temper in front of Anita.

'Fine. Thank you, Anita.' I hang up and lay my head in my hands. I feel the beginnings of a headache coming on and I reach for the painkillers in my top drawer. This is a bloody nightmare. If what Popescu is saying is true, this could destroy everything I've worked so hard for and I'll have no chance at making partner here. I'll lose everything. It seems I have no alternative. I'm going to have to do what Radu Popescu did to me; I'm going to have to go directly to Pavlenco's offices and refuse to leave until he sees me.

I shout out to Anita that I'm going out for a while and to hold all my calls, grab my jacket and stride towards the tube station. While still warm, the heatwave that seems to have been suffocating London is lighter today. A short spell of warm rain yesterday evening has broken the oppressive air that crackled with static electricity and today almost feels fresh in comparison. The Tube station, however, is not. Still sticky, grimy and ridiculously humid, I am sweating by the time I jump off the train three stops down. Outside Pavlenco's offices, I take a moment to calm down. I fold my jacket carefully over my arm and smooth my hair, which has a tendency to stick up of its own accord in the humidity. Feeling more collected and confident, I march into the reception area. A cool blonde with a disinterested air about her looks up eventually and asks if she can help me.

'Charlie Trevetti to see Lucian Pavlenco.' She places a call and, after an interminable wait, eventually, Pavlenco's secretary arrives. She doesn't seem best pleased to see me, and I imagine Pavlenco is not too happy either. She marches me up to his office and after another short wait, the secretary announces, 'Mr Pavlenco will see you now.'

The door to Pavlenco's office swings open and I see Lucian sitting behind a huge walnut desk. He raises an eyebrow at me as I enter, no wolfish smile this time, and a swarm of butterflies beat their wings frantically in my stomach. He is a formidable character at the best of times, more so when he is displeased.

'Charlie. I wish I could say I was delighted to see you but I don't believe we had an appointment.' He steeples his fingers and stares hard at me.

'Mr Pavlenco. Lucian. I did try to contact you earlier. I have a very urgent matter that I need to discuss with you, one that will affect the outcome of the deal if we are not very careful.'

'And I believe I already gave you a message that I had nothing further to say on this matter. Was there something not clear about my message, something that perhaps you did not understand?' His face is passive and I sigh heavily, trying to calm my shaking nerves. There is no way I am leaving here today without discussing Radu Popescu.

'I have met with a gentleman named Radu Popescu. You may remember I asked you previously if you knew him? And you told me you had never heard of him, that he was *nobody*.'

'And that is the case.' Lucian leans back in his chair, studying me hard as if he is defying me to carry on.

'I don't believe that is the case, Mr Pavlenco. If you wish me to act for you in this buy-out, I think it is vitally important that we have an honest relationship, don't you?'

'Why, of course, Charlie. Do you not think that is how it is?'

'I need to know, Lucian. I need to know exactly who Radu Popescu is and why exactly he thinks he is Lucian

Pavlenco. I have met with him and he claims you are Radu Popescu. That you used his identity to set up your business because Radu Popescu came here as an illegal immigrant.' I sit back and watch his face, holding my breath in anticipation. There is the slightest flicker in one eyelid, but no other emotion crosses his face at all. I have to admit – either this guy is an accomplished liar or Popescu is lying and Lucian is innocent.

'And you believe this man? Charlie, I thought we had built a relationship together; I thought we trusted one another.' He finally smiles, his usual wolfish smile, ever so mildly threatening. I sit up straighter in my chair, nerves making the sweat prickle under my armpits. *God, it's hot in here.*

'Lucian, he emailed me proof. He sent me copies of his birth certificate, with the name Lucian Pavlenco. He sent me a Romanian driving licence, in the name of Lucian Pavlenco, but with his photo on it, not yours. And he sent me photos. Photos of two small boys, who can only be you and Popescu as children. So, now tell me you don't know him, that he's lying. That he is *nobody.*' Lucian's face pales slightly and he swallows hard.

'Photos? Photos of us as children? I thought they were all gone.' His voice is barely above a whisper and I gape at him, wondering if I heard him correctly. Popescu really was telling the truth? I realise that I never honestly believed there would be any truth in what he was saying. There is a sad gleam in Lucian's eye, before it is swiftly replaced by his usual steely manner.

'OK, Charlie, I will tell you, but I must warn you – if this gets out, I will ruin you. You will never work again, not as a lawyer, not even as a fucking *garbage collector*. I will come after you and I will come after your family. *I will destroy you.* And I don't care how you do it, but you will make this go away. Do you understand me?' I gulp; Pavlenco doesn't have a ruthless reputation for nothing. Pausing for just a moment, I make my decision.

'Understood, Lucian. We can work together on this, I'm sure.' There goes my last chance to walk away from the whole thing. Now I am trapped – I have to see this thing through to the end, and *successfully*, if I don't want Pavlenco to destroy everything I hold dear.

'Very well. Everything that Radu has told you is true. He came here many years ago, with his papers and got a job in a garage. He is a talented mechanic. He started to build a life for his family. He said he would send for me, and I waited until I couldn't wait any more; it was taking longer than I ever thought possible, so I came of my own accord, you understand? I worked hard when I arrived, and I made some contacts. Business contacts that I could use to set up something successful – but I didn't have the papers to back it all up. That's where Radu comes in. He was Lucian, at the time, but I promised him that if I became Lucian, I would take care of him and his family. He wouldn't need to work such long hours any more, he wouldn't need to work at all – I would have told him anything; I just needed to get my hands on his papers.' He shrugs, and takes a sip of the coffee in front of him, seemingly nonplussed that he has just confessed to identity theft and fraud.

'So how did it all go so wrong?' I ask, intrigued as to how this man's mind works, how he can possibly believe he can get away with all of this. How he has managed to get away with it for so long already.

'I paid him every month at first, but then I didn't see why I needed to. I didn't need him any more, so why should I give him my hard-earned money? I had built up a strong profile as Lucian Pavlenco, international businessman. Who would believe a Romanian car mechanic, one who wasn't even here legally by the looks of it? He had no papers to confirm he was legal; I could have reported him at any time. It's a dog-eat-dog world out there, Charlie. I'm sure you know the saying?' He smiles another wolfish grin and I am shocked at the coldness radiating from him. It's like his entire history with Radu has been erased, an entire childhood forgotten. What had Radu said? *His family was mine, and my family was his.* I thought I was ruthless – Lucian makes me look like a pussycat. I push aside any personal feelings I may have, although knowing what I know now about Lucian I am not sure whether to be impressed by his cold-hearted business acumen, or horrified that he could treat his childhood best friend in this way. I switch back to impersonal lawyer mode.

'Right. OK. So, how are we going to deal with this?' I ask. 'You know Radu is not going to go away, don't you? He can barely afford to feed his family and the only work he can get is cash in hand at minimum wage – sometimes below minimum wage. He's not going to just sit back and watch you turning over millions of pounds, when he firmly believes it's him that has put you here.'

'Of course he won't,' Lucian concedes. 'But you are the lawyer, Charlie. How do you propose we deal with this situation? It is your responsibility now to make sure this doesn't affect anything. It's your job to make this go away.' Lucian throws the ball firmly back in my court, presumably so that if things do all go wrong, it'll be me that takes the blame. Unfortunately, I have no other option. In agreeing to hear his side of the story I have tied myself to him until all of this is resolved. I have trapped myself like a fly in the big, bad spider's web of deceit that Lucian has created.

'I think you should pay him off. You said that in the beginning you paid him a small amount of money – why not just pay him a lump sum and get rid of him? How much would work? Fifty grand?' I raise my eyebrows at Lucian – fifty grand to him is like fifty quid to us mere mortals.

'And if he comes back and says he wants more?' Lucian questions.

'Then we get him deported. Report him to the authorities and get him sent back to Romania – if he no longer has proof of who he once was there won't be a problem. Job done.' Satisfied with my solution I lean back in my chair and regard Lucian coolly. He's not the only one who can be cold-hearted and ruthless.

'I like it, Charlie Trevetti. I was not sure about you, but I think you really do have balls of steel. I will be putting a good word in for you, in time for your promotion.' He winks at me, and I smile back, breathing a silent sigh of relief. It seems Mr Pavlenco has a finger in every pie.

It is agreed that Lucian will write out a cheque for fifty thousand pounds, instructing his accountant to find a way to write it off so there is no trace of where it has actually gone. I will arrange to meet Radu Popescu with the cheque, making clear that this is a one-time offer and any further contact will result in the Home Office being informed that Popescu is here illegally. A condition of the fifty thousand pounds is that all original paperwork that Radu has relating to the real Lucian Pavlenco, including photographs, must be passed on to me so I can arrange for it to be destroyed. I am confident that this will neutralise the threat over our heads from Popescu and that everything will be OK. It has to be OK – I'm too deep into it now for it not to be. Lucian stands to shake my hand, and we agree that I will contact him only once more with regard to the matter, to inform him that his offer has been accepted.

'And in payment to you, Charlie, I will ensure you get what you deserve – you will be made partner.' I leave his office, ten times lighter than when I entered, a huge cheque sitting in my briefcase.

Stepping out into the warm sunshine, I decide to walk back the office. It's not far, and despite feeling relieved that a conclusion has been reached regarding Radu Popescu, I feel as though I need to shake off the oppressive darkness that seems to surround everything that Lucian Pavlenco touches. I can only hope this doesn't backfire and we can all come out of this unscathed. That the darkness doesn't come to settle around me.

CHAPTER TWENTY-NINE

SAL

Today is the day. Finally, the day has arrived for my interview with Mrs Prideaux at St Martin's Primary. You have left earlier than usual for the office, which is a godsend, as I wouldn't want to have to explain to you why I was dropping Maggie off with Laura at this hour of the morning and heading into town. I did wonder briefly, when I woke, if there was something more to this particular deal than you are actually telling me. You have always been a bit of a workaholic but you seem more preoccupied than usual. Maybe it's just because this is apparently *the* deal, the one that's going to get you exactly where you want to be. I don't ask. I don't want to give a window of opportunity for you to tell me I'm wrong, or stupid, or to mind my own business, as you do so often these days, constantly pushing me away while at the same time complaining that I don't take enough of an interest in you.

I shower and dress carefully. The storm that raged last night, with huge cracks of lightning illuminating the whole room and low rumbles of thunder that went on for so long I was convinced Maggie would wake up at any minute, has cleared the air. The heatwave seems to have finally broken, and while today has dawned sunny and clear-skied, there is a pleasant breeze and an altogether more breathable quality to the air. Flicking through the clothes in my wardrobe, I settle on a long-sleeved white shirt – despite the fact that, although the weather has broken, it is still warm outside, I need to wear something to cover my arms. The burn is starting to heal, but I still need to cover it with a bandage for now and I don't want to draw attention to it. I am ironing my shirt when Maggie appears in the kitchen doorway.

'Morning, baby.' I smile at her. 'Did you dress yourself by any chance today?'

She is wearing a long, floaty 'Princess' dress, a present from Anna last Christmas that is now far too small for her, knee-length stripy socks and a pair of dressing-up heels.

'This is what I'm wearing today.' She beams at me, twirling around to show me how her dress flies out.

'You're going to Laura's today, remember?' I switch the iron off at the wall and crouch down to look into Maggie's eyes. She pouts, tears brimming at the corners of her big, dark eyes – another legacy of mine, to go with the typically Mediterranean curls.

'Don't want to. I want to come with you.' The tears threaten to spill over onto her cheeks.

'Please, Mags. It's just for today – you can play dress-up with Lucy. And I bet Laura will make some biscuits with you, if you ask her nicely.'

God, this is just one day. *Am I making the right decision? If I get this job, I'll have to leave her every day.* I squeeze her in close to me, terrified in case I am making the wrong choice. *No, I have to do this. I have to find Sal the person again, instead of Sal the partner, Sal the parent. I have to be brave. I have to make sure I'm ready, just in case.* My last thought jolts something deep inside me, something that seems to have been awakened by recent events, and it makes my stomach churn a little with nerves and anticipation. The mention of biscuits seems to have dried up the tears and Maggie smiles. I'm not so sure Laura will be smiling when she realises what I've roped her into – the last time Mags and Lucy made biscuits together it was like a bomb had gone off in a flour factory.

'Come on, baby, let's go.' Maggie lets me buckle her shoes, not noticing when she leans on my burnt arm for balance, making me give a quick hiss through my teeth.

Laura is waiting on the doorstep as we walk up the path to next door. She looks relaxed and casual, dressed in yoga pants and a soft T-shirt, nothing on her feet. She looks the complete opposite to how I feel right now.

'Jesus, Sal, it's an interview, not the firing squad.' Laura laughs, showing her even, white teeth and holding out a hand to Maggie.

'God, do I look that terrified? I was going for casually shitting myself.' I reach up and try to smooth my wayward curls down. Laura throws back her head and laughs.

'If you can charm the old girl like that, you'll walk it!' She squeezes my arm, taking care not to touch my forearm, where the bandage sits hot and sticky under my shirtsleeve. 'Seriously, good luck. Not that you'll need it; you're an obviously good person, inside and out. An asset to any team.' I smile at her, pleased that any lingering awkwardness after our conversation in the kitchen the other evening seems to have disappeared. I kiss her on the cheek, suddenly overwhelmed at how much support Laura does provide, whether she realises it or not.

'Thanks, Laur. Let's hope so, eh? And thanks for having Maggie today. I do really appreciate it.' I kiss Maggie goodbye and start to walk up the garden path, before turning back to say, 'Oh, and I may have told Maggie that you would make biscuits with her and Lucy today …'

'That's it,' Laura calls back, grinning, her cheeks flushed a gentle shade of pink. 'You're off the team!' Smiling, I wave and make my way in the direction of the train station.

By the time my train pulls in, nerves are making my stomach flutter as if it has been filled with a million tiny butterflies. It's been a long time since I made the morning commute and even longer since I've attended a job interview. Walking up towards the school, it is early, a little before eight o'clock, but the roads are still busy with people making their way to work. A few parents are standing outside the school gates, presumably waiting to drop their children off for breakfast club before their own morning commute. I press the buzzer on the gate, and wait for a moment before a disembodied voice comes back to me: 'Yes?'

'Sal Trevetti here, to see Mrs Prideaux. I have an interview today.' I see a few parents glance at me curiously out of the corners of their eyes, no doubt wondering whether I will be the one to teach their child in September. The buzzer squawks, and the gate opens. I follow the signs to the reception office and am greeted by a slim, dark-haired woman who smiles a heartbreaking grin as I walk in.

'Sal? I'm Aurelie Jones, school receptionist. Mrs Prideaux is just tied up at the moment but can I get you a coffee?'

'I'd love one, thank you.' Aurelie bustles away into what I presume is the staffroom. I take a moment, just to steady my nerves and take a look around. Aurelie seems friendly enough, although maybe slightly disorganised for a school receptionist. Her desk contains a huge in-tray, which is swarming with loose sheets of paper. She re-enters the room, carrying a tray, and spots me eyeing up her desk.

'Oh, gosh, don't look at that!' She laughs. 'The other receptionist is off sick at the moment, so I'm doubling up on her work as well. Trust me, it's not usually as messy as this!' She laughs again and hands me a cup of steaming hot coffee. I breathe in deeply, the aroma steadying my nerves, and this, alongside Aurelie's relaxed manner, means I begin to feel a lot calmer. We make conversation for a little while, then a neat, grey head appears around the door to the right of Aurelie's desk.

'Sal Trevetti?' The grey head peers round, and a small bird-like woman steps out into the main office area. 'I'm Lana Prideaux, head teacher here. Nice to meet you.' She holds out a small-boned hand and I grasp it – she gives a surprisingly strong handshake. Lana Prideaux ushers me through into her inner sanctum, the complete opposite of the chaos of Aurelie's desk outside. She beckons to me to sit, and I realise that a stout gentleman is sitting in the chair on the other side of the desk, perched on the end like he's going to up and leave any minute.

'This is Mr Benetti – Chair of Governors here at St Martin's.' I lean forward and he gives me a cold, flabby handshake.

'Trevetti, eh?' Mr Benetti looks at me over his glasses. 'Italian?'

'Yes,' I nod, taking a sip of my now tepid coffee. 'My parents moved here back in the eighties. They live in Kent now.' Benetti nods his approval, and Mrs Prideaux jumps in.

'Mr Benetti has been Chair here for many years, Sal, starting when his own son began his education with us, so I hope you don't mind if he joins in with our initial interview today. He will have a few questions for you.' I nod my assent, surreptitiously wiping my damp palms on my trousers, and the formal interview begins.

An hour and a half later, I am feeling more than a little worn out, but confident. I have answered every question that Mrs Prideaux and Mr Benetti have fired at me, questions that range from 'How do you deal with a disruptive child?' through to 'What *exactly* do you believe you can bring to St Martin's, that no other candidate can?' I thank my lucky stars I read up on practice interview questions on the train before arriving this morning; I really don't think I could have come any more prepared than I did. Mrs Prideaux informs me that it's now playtime for the children, and I am more than welcome to go out onto the playground and observe; however, she will require me to go to the Year One classroom at ten-thirty to meet Annabel Green, the Year One teacher whose class I will be teaching for the rest of the morning. I smile my thanks, shake hands with both of them and walk out into the sunshine.

The rest of the day flies by – I spend the morning with Year One as agreed, Annabel Green taking a back seat and using the time to plan her lessons, while I teach some maths skills under the watchful eye of Mrs Prideaux. Lunch is spent in the staffroom and Aurelie kindly introduces me to the other members of staff, explaining that I am here on an all-day interview. Apparently, I am the third person to have been interviewed so far for the position, Miss Green lets slip, and I am not too sure how that makes me feel. The afternoon is spent with possibly my favourite year group, Year Six. I taught Year Six previously, and this is the position I am applying for. The bunch of kids at St Martin's are a joy – noisy but not rowdy, curious but not rude. They want to know all about me and I agree to tell them, as long as they each tell me about themselves. Before I know it, it's ten to three and Mrs Prideaux is telling me it's time to wrap things up. The children scrape their chairs back noisily, and make a grab for bags and jumpers all hanging on pegs at the back of the room. When the last child is gone, I let out a long breath and look up at Mrs Prideaux, who is waiting at the back of the room.

'Well done, Sal. I would never have guessed you've been away from teaching for so long. You're a natural.' I smile at her, relieved that she didn't think I was total crap.

'Thank you for the opportunity, Mrs Prideaux. I've had a really enjoyable day.' She shakes my hand in her strong grip one last time, and I pick up my bag to leave. 'Oh, Sal,' Mrs Prideaux calls. 'We'll be in touch.'

I am pretty much on cloud nine on the train home, despite feeling completely exhausted. Even if I don't get the job, I know I can still teach. I know I can still teach and, more importantly, *enjoy it*. I don't want to get my hopes up too far, but I can't help feeling I did OK today. It's going to be worth it, I decide. If I get the job, it's going to be worth all the tears and recriminations that are bound to follow once you find out. I realise I almost feel as though I don't care any more – yes, if I go back to work you will be angry, you will be annoyed that you can't get hold of me all day long as and when you please, but for the first time in a long time I'm not bothered. I'm not frightened. This job is what I want, what I need, and I am confident that no matter how angry you are about it, I can ride it out. The old Sal, the Sal who enjoyed life and had the confidence to try and achieve the best it had to offer, is there, shimmering below the surface, ready to make a bid for freedom.

Laura has the door open before I even set foot on her front path, leaning against the door frame with an anxious look on her face.

'Well?' she demands, hair up in a messy topknot, flour dusting her cheek.

'You baked, then?' I ask, brushing the flour away. 'Aren't you going to let me in?' She moves to one side and I enter the blissfully cool hallway – the train was packed despite it not being rush hour and I am hot and sweaty in my long sleeves.

'What? Oh, those girls. They thought it was the *Great British Bake Off* or something.' She blushes slightly and gives a little laugh. 'Are you going to tell me how it went?'

'Oh Laur, it was *brilliant*. I honestly forgot how much I love teaching. I mean, don't get me wrong, I love staying home with Maggie, but I'm ready, you know? I want to go back. And it went really well – at least I think it did, anyway.' I can hear the girls shrieking and laughing in the back garden, as Laura pours me a glass of crisp, cold white wine.

'Here.' She passes it to me. 'I thought you might need this.' I take a large sip, feeling the icy liquid make its way down my neck.

'You thought right. Honestly, Laur, they fired a ton of questions at me, and I answered them well, I'm sure of it. The head said she would be in touch, so it's just a question of waiting now.' We sip at the rest of the bottle, while I tell Laura all about the rest of the day and how much I loved being back in the classroom. It's so nice to be able to just sit and talk, without worrying about saying the wrong thing, or causing a row unintentionally. It would be so nice if you could be this supportive, if you could just sit and listen and encourage me instead of always thinking I'm fighting against you. When the wine is gone I thank Laura, grab Maggie and head next door. You are late home tonight, very late, and I go to bed alone, hugging the day to me like a secret, wishing and hoping that today will mark the start of a new beginning.

CHAPTER THIRTY

CHARLIE

After my meeting with Lucian, I try to contact Radu
Popescu to get the deal done as soon as possible, but it
seems that whereas if you don't want him around, you
can't get rid of him, when you do need to contact him,
he's nowhere to be found. I put my dinner with Alex on
hold until I get this sorted, making excuses about the
weight of my workload, and spend what seems like
every spare minute trying to get hold of the guy.

Anita gives me the contact telephone number that
he left, but it just goes straight to voicemail and every
email that I send him remains unanswered. I debate
whether to just leave it, give Lucian his cheque back
and let myself believe Popescu has decided it's not
worth it, especially when I find myself going home
later and later every evening. Then I remember the
desperation in his eyes when he talked about feeding
his family, and decide there must be some other
reason.

After a full week of no contact, I decide to track him down myself. Lucian calls me that morning, his usual cold-hearted self. 'Charlie, he obviously realises the mistake he is making. Tear up the cheque and leave it. We have much work to do before this new company is mine.'

'You don't understand, Lucian – if we leave it, he could pop up at any moment. We need to make sure we eliminate anything that could destroy this for us, especially with the Vygen people getting involved. If you want to make this deal without any hitches, you need to be squeaky clean.' I feel sick at the thought of Radu appearing from nowhere and telling the world the truth about Lucian, the fear of it keeping me awake at night. Eventually, Lucian concedes that I am right, and I make the decision to hunt down Radu Popescu myself.

In the end, it is surprisingly easy to find him. He mentioned when we spoke that he was washing dishes on a cash-in-hand basis near the South Bank. I loiter around several different restaurants, before approaching the managers and asking for Radu Popescu. Several of them quite clearly have never heard of him, but one looks shifty and tries to deny he knows him until I explain that I am nothing to do with the police or Immigration. He then confesses that Radu does work there, but that he was only trying to do a favour for a friend.

'Yes, OK, whatever. I'm really not interested in his legal status,' I snap, relief making me impatient. 'What time does he start? It's vital that I speak to him – don't let him leave until I get here.' I hand the guy my mobile number and head over to the Greek restaurant further downriver to grab a bite to eat and wait to hear from him. Radu is due into work at one o'clock, slightly later than usual, so that gives me time to eat lunch and prepare what I'm going to say to him.

True to his word, the restaurant manager calls me at ten minutes to one and says Radu has arrived. 'You can have five minutes with him,' he tells me with a somewhat bullish attitude. 'He's coming in late today as it is.' I remind the manager that, *actually*, I'll take as long as I please, especially seeing as Radu isn't an employee – he's working illegally, cash in hand. I make my way back up to the restaurant and, as I follow the path round to the back, I see Radu waiting, hunched over a roll-up cigarette, looking even thinner than he did a few weeks ago.

'Radu? It's me, Charlie Trevetti. I've been trying to get hold of you.' He looks at me warily, and then peers behind me as if expecting someone else to also be there.

'Are you alone?' he asks, and I nod. 'Ahh, I see. Lucian sends you to do his dirty work.' He takes a deep drag on his roll-up and I bristle at his words.

'Mr Popescu, I can assure you that Mr Pavlenco does not send me to do his *dirty* work. Mr Pavlenco has sent me, *as his lawyer*, to make you an offer, but if you are not interested, despite being the one to contact me in the first place, I am more than happy to leave now.' I turn on my heel as if to leave.

'Wait.' He takes one final puff and throws his butt on the ground, crushing it underfoot. 'What does he want to say to me?' I turn back, looking him up and down.

'He has a proposition for you. I've been trying to get hold of you for some time now, in order to let you know. You're a hard man to reach when you want to be.'

'I have no money. I have no money to feed my family, let alone pay for my mobile phone. I ran out of credit and couldn't top up, and I didn't even have a spare fiver to pay for an Internet café so I could email you.' It sounds strange to hear the word 'fiver' uttered in his deep Eastern European accent.

'Well, Mr Popescu, your troubles may be over for a time. Mr Pavlenco has a very generous offer for you.'

'Please, I cannot discuss it here; my manager will hear and I will lose my job. He knows I am illegal, but I have to be so careful.' His fingers worry at his sleeves and he refuses to meet my eyes. Realising he is ashamed of his situation, I agree to return at the end of his shift.

After an afternoon in the office, in which I try to tie up any other loose ends with this godforsaken buy-out, Popescu is never far from my mind. I can only hope that the fifty grand will do the trick and get rid of him, at least until the deal is complete, and I am made partner and have nothing more to do with Lucian Pavlenco. In fact, if it weren't for the chance to be made partner, I'd be wishing I'd never been the one to deal with Pavlenco in the first place. The pressure of this case is mounting and I am struggling to sleep at night, worry that everything will blow up in my face keeping me awake. It doesn't help that Sal is completely oblivious to any strain I am under, wafting around day to day as usual, with no regard for what I might be going through.

I meet Radu that evening, in the same pub we visited before. He is sitting, small and hunched, in the same booth tucked away at the back of the room and I get the impression he doesn't want to be seen with me any more than I want to be seen with him.

'Radu. Can I get you a drink?' He nods, pushing away the glass in front of him.

'Yes, please. The barman was not pleased with my order of tap water.' He gives a rueful smile and I fetch him a pint. Tucking myself into the booth alongside him, I jump straight in feet first.

'So, Radu. I met with Lucian. While he doesn't necessarily support your claims, he is happy to make you an offer. A one-time-only offer. By accepting it, you will also accept that you have no further claim on the name Lucian Pavlenco. Nor will you persist in contacting Mr Pavlenco. That will be it, Radu. No contact with Lucian ever again. Trust me, I think it's the best thing for both of you, especially for you. You know yourself he is a very powerful man, one who always gets what he wants.' I watch him closely and see the slight flinch he gives when I tell him it means there will be no more contact. Ever.

'I thought it would come to this. He is changed, Charlie. He is not the boy I grew up with. He has become hard, poisoned against all those who loved him once and love him still. Do you know, he hasn't been home to see his family even once?' Radu takes a sip of his drink and gazes ahead, lost in the memories of some other time. 'His mother got sick, you know. A long time ago, when he was barely a teenager. His father was long gone, and he had no one. We sheltered him from it, made sure that he never knew how ill she really was. We took him in, my family and I, even though he was in a bad way, struggling to cope with the responsibilities of caring for his family. My mother took care of him as if he were her own. She loved him as if he were her own son.'

'People change, Radu. Things happen; people have different experiences that change the way they look at the world. Sometimes you just have to accept that there's nothing you can do. Sometimes friendships just naturally come to an end.'

Radu bangs his fist on the table, fury raging in his eyes. 'A natural end? This man stole *my life*. There is nothing *natural* about that,' he hisses at me, cheeks suffused with anger. 'I gave him *everything*, Charlie, everything. I shared all I had with him and this is how he repays me.' Shaking, he takes a deep breath.

'Radu, calm down. I have an offer from Lucian for you – a very generous offer, one that could potentially make everything OK for you.' Now that Radu is calmer, I think it's best to just get the offer on the table, and get out of there.

'Go on, I'm listening' is all he says.

I outline the offer from Lucian – a fifty-thousand-pound cheque, right now, for him to cash immediately. In return for the cheque, he will disappear, out of Lucian's life for ever. The original documents that he sent over to me will be destroyed, and he will have no further contact, either with Pavlenco, or with me. I reiterate the importance of the fact that he is to stay away from Lucian's office, family, and friends. No further contact, ever. At these words Radu looks a little shell-shocked and I realise that, despite his bravado and all his gesturing, he never really believed Lucian would cut him off completely.

'Give me a minute, please,' he says, and I walk over to the bar to order another pint. A text buzzes on my phone – it's Lucian, and simply says, 'WELL?' I tap out a quick reply. 'In meeting now. Will update as soon as I can.' As I carry the fresh drinks over to the table, Radu looks up at me.

'I have no choice,' he says, pulling a pint towards him. 'This money will save my family. My mother is still in Romania, and she is dying, Charlie. She has cancer and until now I have not been able to afford the treatment, but with this money I might be able to save her.' Tears threaten to spill down over his shirt. 'I earn £3.90 an hour, Charlie. When you're illegal there is no minimum wage. There are no rights; you have to take what you can get and be grateful for it. If I had known this was how it was going to be, I never would have said yes. If I had known that trying to help my oldest friend would mean I lost everything, I would never have done it. I still cannot believe that he has done this to me.' The tears do fall now, and I glance about anxiously, worried that other patrons in the bar will see. That's the last thing I need – for someone to spot me with Radu and remember us at a later date.

'Radu, please. Pull yourself together. I'm sorry this has all gone so wrong for you, really I am, but you must see that Lucian is giving you a lifeline. You said yourself your mother is dying – this can help her, maybe save her life.' I cringe inwardly a little at this. I know I am ruthless but referencing his dying mother is a little harsh, even for me. Even so, I need him to take the cheque and sign the contract I've drawn up, stating all the clauses he has agreed to. I need this to be over. I need to get a decent night's sleep and finally get my life back. Radu wipes his eyes, and takes a shaky breath.

'Yes. I understand this. I have no choice, although signing this will break my heart. You can tell Lucian I bear him no ill will. Everything that he deserves, he will get.' Pulling the contract towards him, he takes the pen I hold out to him and signs his name with a flourish. I can't help but feel a tiny sense of foreboding at his last words. *Everything he deserves, he will get.*

When Radu leaves the pub, taking his fifty-grand cheque with him, I send Lucian a text. Three words only: 'It is done.' His response is immediate, and I instantly feel better. Radu is just a small blip on the way to greatness, and now the threat of him has been eradicated I can focus on getting this deal done and dusted, with no time for any sentimentality. Pavlenco didn't get where he is today by being sentimental, did he? Feeling a little high on my success, I text Alex, rearranging our dinner date for the following week. Hopefully, Alex will accidentally drop some nuggets of information over the course of our meal, things that I will be able to use with Otex to make sure we acquire the new company, not Vygen. Wiping the memory of the look on Radu's face when I told him the contract meant no contact ever again with Lucian from my mind, I stuff the contract in my laptop bag and head for home.

CHAPTER THIRTY-ONE

SAL

Whatever has been playing on your mind for the past week seems to have cleared, as you come home late on Friday night in a much better mood than you have been. For the most part, this week with you has been unbearable. You haven't been physical – I've made sure I've kept out of your way enough that even you couldn't justify it – but every time I speak to you, you snap, telling me I have no idea what you go through every day, the stress you are under, the things you have to do to get where you want to be, to give me what I allegedly demand from you. When I ask you about it, you tell me I'm too stupid to understand and turn your back on me, choosing instead to freeze me out. You would think I wouldn't mind that, you freezing me out and ignoring me; it has to be preferable to your screaming in my face and hitting me. But it hurts just as much. It makes me feel just as ashamed and weak, just as inconsequential. Lying in bed on Friday evening, I try again but, as usual, you don't seem to want to talk about it when I ask, turning the conversation instead to the weekend.

'We should do something, all of us together. I know I've been preoccupied at work lately but everything seems to be coming together more now. Let's go somewhere, take Mags out for the day. It's been a long time since we spent time together as a family.' You twine your fingers through mine, squeezing my hand tight. I feel almost content, lying next to you hand in hand – it reminds me of when we first got together and would spend hours in bed talking, holding hands and drinking wine. It reminds me of an altogether calmer time, one that I have missed, and it has been a long time since we did anything as a family. It seems that, lately, either you are working, or something has happened between us that means you don't want to spend time with me, or I don't feel up to going out after you've lost your temper with me. Jumping on the chance to have an enjoyable weekend with Maggie, I suggest all of us spending the day at Legoland. Maggie has been dying to go, the weather is still good and it seems the ideal family day out.

'Sounds perfect,' you say, kissing my cheek before settling down for sleep.

The next morning dawns bright and early, with Maggie almost doing cartwheels of excitement when she hears where we are off to. I am looking forward to it, too, and am just packing a backpack with snacks while you are in the shower when the telephone rings.

'Sal?' A gruff voice comes down the phone and it takes me a moment to place it.

'Tony? Is Anna OK?' Realising it is my brother-in-law on the end of the line makes my heart race – Tony never, ever calls here. You and he had a bit of a spat right back at the beginning when we first moved in together, and although Tony tried to make it up with you, apologising and letting bygones be bygones, you refused to accept his apology and haven't spoken to him since.

'She went into labour last night. He's here, but, oh, God, Sal, he's so tiny. It's too early.' I hear a hitch in his voice and realise how hard he is trying to hold it together. 'He's in an incubator, Sal. They're not too sure at the moment how things will turn out. Anna is ... she wants you to come.' Of all my sisters, Anna and I are the closest. There is only a year between us, and we were mistaken for twins on more than one occasion growing up.

'I'll be there. Tell her I'm coming and I'll be there as soon as I can.' I hang up, and gasp as I realise you have been standing behind me, for at least the end part of my conversation. Judging by the look on your face, you heard me.

'What? Sal, where do you think you're going?' You're wrapped in a towel, water dripping from the ends of your hair.

'It's Anna. She's had the baby – it's too early and he's not very well.' I look you straight in the eye; I am not backing down this time, despite my heart beating double-time. Old, brave Sal is still there, just below the surface, spurred on by the feelings of success following my interview.

'So? That's your problem how, exactly?' You shift the towel slightly, not breaking eye contact with me. The air is charged with tension; there is no way I can get out of this now without a row.

'She's my sister, Charlie. He's my nephew. If I don't go now, I might not get to meet him at all.' I gaze at you, willing you to understand the enormity of it all, to not use this as an excuse to go off the deep end.

'It's our day out with Maggie, Sal. It's all arranged. Are you going to tell her she can't go? Because I'm not.'

'It doesn't mean she can't go. Why don't you two go, spend some time together?'

'It was supposed to be all of us, Sal. We are supposed to be spending the day together, as a *family*. It may have escaped your notice, but your family is Maggie and me – no one else. I work fucking hard to keep this family together, so the least you can do is be bothered to spend time with us. It's not like you do much else, is it?' you sneer at me, contempt radiating from every pore.

I have no idea where my bravery comes from – maybe the old Sal is closer to the surface than I realised – but I will not take this lying down any longer.

'No, Charlie. That's not the case. Anna is my family; she's my sister and she needs me. You two can still go and have a good time together, but this might be the only opportunity I have to meet my nephew. I don't think you understand, Charlie – he might not make it. Would you want to go through that on your own?' I stare defiantly at you, and feel some small sense of achievement when you are the first to break eye contact. Old Sal does a little cheer inside, while outwardly my palms are slick with sweat.

'Fine. You go, Sal. I'll take Maggie to Legoland. I won't let her down. I'm not guaranteeing that I'll bring her back, though – maybe it's time you learnt where your priorities should lie.'

You flounce your way back upstairs and, for the first time, I don't feel so afraid of you. I can't help but feel as though you are behaving in a slightly ridiculous manner. Calling Maggie downstairs, I explain to her that I won't be coming because Aunty Anna had her baby and he is very poorly, but that you will still take her. It's funny how a four-year-old seems to understand the situation better than an adult who is headed for forty.

I wave you off, standing at the end of the driveway blowing kisses to Maggie in the backseat, while you stare stonily ahead and pretend I'm not there. Grabbing my bag from the hallway, I set off for the bus stop – I had been hoping you would see sense and be reasonable about my going to the hospital, but you refused to discuss it any further, apart from to tell me, 'If it's so fucking urgent, go, but you can catch the fucking bus.' So, I find myself sitting at the back of a surprisingly empty double decker, the engine rumbling in the background, belching out exhaust fumes. As I get off at the stop right outside the hospital, I see Tony pacing outside the hospital doors, cigarette clamped firmly between his teeth. As I approach I see he's talking on his mobile – I am desperate to get inside and see Anna, but wait for him to finish his call. He smiles at me as he hangs up, dark smudges under his eyes. He looks exhausted.

'Hey, Sal. You made it. I didn't know if Charlie would let you.' I bristle slightly at that comment, but let it go. The man is worn out. Perhaps I haven't hidden your contempt for my family, or for me, as well as I thought.

'Of course I made it – she's my sister. Is she OK?' Tony throws his cigarette butt down, and motions towards the doors.

'Come and see for yourself. She's knackered and worried, but the doctors have been round this morning and it's all looking a bit more positive. I was just ringing your dad to let him know. Your mum's up there already.' He gives a tired smile, and I feel a beat of sympathy for him. He is another one who has no family of his own – his parents were killed in a car accident when he was a teenager and the elderly aunt who brought him up died three years ago. Tony, however, is the complete opposite to you and has embraced being part of a large family. We head up to Anna's room, and when I enter I see my mum leaning over the bed. My mum is worried, I know, but she'll be in her element having Anna and the baby to fuss over.

'Hey, you. Always the one to cause a drama.' I lean down and kiss Anna on the head, and she punches me on the arm.

'Sorry I stole your limelight.' She smiles up at me, glowing despite the exhaustion. 'Have you seen him yet?' A worried look flits across her face as she bites her lip.

'Not yet. I came straight to find you.'

'God, Sal, he's beautiful, but he's just so tiny.' Tears fill her eyes and I pass her a tissue. Mum bustles off, taking Tony with her, leaving Anna and I to have a moment alone.

'What has the doctor said?'

'They think he'll be OK. He's too small, so they want to keep him here until he puts a bit of weight on, and he needs help feeding, but the doctor says, all being well, he'll be able to go home in three to four weeks, which would have been around his due date anyway.' She gives a thin smile and blows her nose.

'Well, that's good news. You had us all worried, you know.' I squeeze her hand. 'Maggie will be so excited to meet her new cousin. What are you going to call him?'

'He's going to be James, after Tony's dad. Is Mags here? Where's Charlie?' She tries to peer past me, looking for her niece. Anna and Maggie have a special bond – they are both so alike; it's almost as though as soon as Maggie was born they were destined to be best friends.

'Not here. Charlie has taken Maggie to Legoland for the day. It was already arranged. We didn't want to let Maggie down.' I don't say anything more than that, incorporating myself into it so it doesn't look as though you are completely heartless.

'Oh, I'm sorry, Sal. I've ruined your day out.'

'Don't be silly – you're far more important than Legoland, and anyway, it'll do Charlie some good to look after Maggie alone.'

Mum and Tony come back, carrying coffees for everyone. Mum has also stashed a carrier bag of food in Anna's locker, on the understanding that now Anna is a mum she must keep her strength up, but hospital food won't do that for her. We all perch in various spots on Anna's bed, keeping her company until the doctor comes to check on her. Tony takes Mama and me down to meet Baby James. He is so fragile and tiny, lying there in his incubator, that it is almost frightening. It is such a relief to know he is going to be OK – Mama has finally stopped crying, her tears leaking soundlessly in a steady stream down her chin as she gazes at her new grandchild. My heart swells as I watch his tiny hands and feet waving in the air, his thin cheeks yet to take on the soft fullness of a full-term newborn. We all feel remarkably blessed.

I manage to spend most of the day with Anna, flitting between her bedside and going down to see Baby James whenever the nurses will let us. By the time I leave in the early evening, Anna looks completely worn out, and Tony has arrived back at the hospital after heading home for a quick shower and change of clothes.

'Listen, I'm going to leave Tony in charge now,' I say, leaning over to give Anna a kiss goodbye. 'He's beautiful, you guys. Anna, you did so well – I'll come back soon, when it's OK to bring Mags. She'll be dying to meet him.' We say our goodbyes and I jump back on the bus home. On the journey, I think back to when Maggie was born and feel relieved that she was born at the right time, safe and well, in the comfort of our own home. I resolve to speak to you when I get home, to remind you of how blessed we are.

It's not until I put my key in the door and enter the house to silence that I realise you aren't home yet. Lost in my own thoughts on the journey back from the hospital, I didn't even notice that the car wasn't on the drive. It's only six-thirty and realistically too early for you to be back yet, so I take the opportunity to shower off the smell of the hospital and fix myself something to eat.

By eight-thirty, I am starting to get a little anxious. I would have thought you would have been home by now, or at least called to say you were on your way. Maggie was up early and will be exhausted after a full day at Legoland, and she'll need a bath before she goes to bed. I feel mildly irritated that you have kept her out past her bedtime already, when it will be me that has to deal with her tired, fractious mood tomorrow. I try your mobile but it just goes straight to voicemail, and a shiver snakes down my spine. What was the last thing you said to me this morning, after I told you I was going to the hospital? *I'm not guaranteeing that I'll bring her back, though – maybe it's time you learnt where your priorities should lie.*

You wouldn't, would you? Beginning to panic, I try your mobile again, but to no avail. I debate whether to go next door and speak to Laura, but she already has ideas in her head about our relationship and I don't want to fuel the fire. She'll want to call the police and I'm not ready to do that yet. Maggie is with you and I know you won't let any harm come to her. I decide to call the hospitals before making any rash decisions. Maybe there's been an accident? I check the online traffic reports, but there are no reported major accidents. I call every hospital I can think of between here and Windsor, and not one of them has had anyone brought in under either your or Maggie's name. I even ring Tony, on the off-chance that you might have taken Maggie in to see

Anna on your way home, but he says he hasn't seen you, and from his hushed tones I can tell he is still at the hospital. Feeling sick, I pick up the phone to call the police when my mobile rings, Johnny Cash's 'Folsom Prison Blues' blaring out in the ringtone you hate so much.

'Hello?' I fumble with the phone as I bring it to my ear, fingers shaking.

'So you're home, then?' There is an undeniable sneer in your voice.

'Charlie! Where are you? Are you on your way home?' I am so relieved to hear from you, to know that you are OK, that I don't even care about the cold edge to your tone.

'No, we're not. I told you, Sal, that if you went to the hospital to see Anna, you would be taking the chance that I wouldn't be returning home.' You wait, triumphantly, it seems, for my response.

'Charlie, please. Don't be silly. Just come home. We can talk about it. Where is Maggie? Is she all right?' I just want Maggie home with me. It's nearly eleven o'clock and she should be asleep in her own bed.

'She's fine, but we're not coming back.' Your voice is flat, emotionless.

'Charlie!' I gasp, feeling my throat constrict with the weight of hot tears.

'TONIGHT. I won't be back tonight. Possibly, we will be back tomorrow – I'll see how the mood takes us when we wake up. But Sal, you should realise life could be like this for you all the time – not knowing where Maggie is, who she's with. I could take her and make sure you never, ever get her back. Do you understand?'

I hate you. That is the thought that floods my brain as I hear your spiteful, cruel words that hurt more than any punch, any kick, any burn you've inflicted on me. I bite back the words I long to say, reining it all in until I have Maggie back at home where she belongs.

'OK, Charlie. I understand. Please will you … please just consider coming home tomorrow? We can talk about things if you want to, but if you don't want to then that's fine, too. Just come home.' I wait, listening to your breath at the other end of the line.

'I'll think about it, but I'm not promising. You have to learn to get your priorities right, Sal. Your own daughter should come first, not some kid you've never even met.'

I am completely astounded. You have managed to make a newly born, premature baby – a part of our family – whose future was just about as uncertain as could be, sound like some sort of *teenage layabout*, one of those kids who hangs around outside the shops trying to get served with fags and beer. I decide to just go with it, in the hope that you will bring my daughter home to me tomorrow.

'Yes, of course. I will. Will you just please tell me where you're staying tonight? I just want to know where Maggie is, that's all, so I don't worry.'

'If you were here, you wouldn't have to worry, would you?'

You're deliberately being difficult and I feel like I can never win – if I hadn't asked, you would have said that I didn't even care enough to know where Maggie was staying. 'Please, Charlie. I've learnt my lesson, OK?'

'We're staying at the Legoland Hotel. Maggie was tired and I wanted to give her a proper treat. She was disappointed that you ruined the day by not coming, and this turned it into an adventure.' Ignoring your little dig, I apologise once again for letting Maggie down and hang up.

I am furious. Blood boiling, steaming, raging furious. How dare you keep my daughter from me and drag her into your games? I have put up with so much of your shit and for so long, all in the attempt to create a safe, family environment for Maggie to grow up in. I wanted Maggie to have the kind of childhood I had, with two parents who love each other. Combine that with your insistence that you can't live without me and I've always felt like I didn't have any other option but to stay and put up with it. It's always been me that takes the brunt of it all – your moods, your behaviour, your frankly disgusting treatment of me. But now you've decided to change the game and draw Maggie into it, even though she's too young to realise it. Now, I have to make my decision – something has to change. This, *tonight*, your attitude to tiny Baby James, who as far as you are aware, might not pull through – *this* is the final straw. The nail in our coffin. Old Sal is back, the Sal who would never have let anyone treat them like this until you came along with your control, and your power games, threatening to kill yourself if I ever left. I have made my mind up. I am getting out of this, once and for all.

CHAPTER THIRTY-TWO

CHARLIE

I drive away, ignoring Sal who is waving like an idiot from the doorway. A mild headache thumps away at the back of my head, caused by Sal's determination to spoil our day out, and another prickle of anger snakes its way through me. I am so angry – Sal's selfish, grasping family has ruined our entire weekend. Not content to pass judgement on my parenting skills, our relationship and anything else they think is their business, they have now ruined the only full weekend we have had together in months.

Maggie is singing under her breath in the back seat, seemingly not all that bothered that Sal has ditched us. A tiny spark of guilt wafts up – Anna didn't know she would go into labour this early, and Maggie doesn't seem too adversely affected – but I squash it down immediately, instead fuelling my anger by thinking about Sal's attitude this morning. Staring me down, telling me Anna is more important than Maggie and me.

I decide that today is the day I will teach Sal a proper lesson. Today, I'll show Sal what things *could* be like.

The weather is a direct reversal of my mood – warm and sunny, not a cloud in the sky – and, despite the long queues and miles of walking, Maggie has a whale of a time at Legoland. I try my hardest to get into the spirit of things, even though I am still feeling irate and resentful at Sal's absence. We ride all the rides that she's big enough to go on, twice when the queues allow, watch a pirate show which mostly consists of people wearing eye patches swinging from rigging over a tiny lake, and then head over to the Pizza Palace for all-you-can eat pizza and pasta. By this time, Maggie is looking worn out, and I decide to put my plan into action.

'Hey, Mags, you know there's a hotel here?' Maggie looks up from slurping her spaghetti and nods.

'Aunty Julia says next time she comes we're going to stay in it.' She takes another bite, and I feel a frown wrinkle my brow. *Bloody Julia.* This makes my mind up for me – there is no way bloody Julia is bringing my daughter to stay here, not unless I've brought her first. This is just another example of how Sal's family want to take over – giving Maggie all the exciting experiences and making all the best memories without a thought for how I feel about things. Presumably, Sal will know all about this idea of Julia's but will have kept it a secret from me. I store it up in the back of my mind, ready to throw out as more evidence of Sal's deceitfulness.

Maggie finishes eating, so we walk over to the hotel and book in. She is over the moon, babbling all the way up to our room and I feel a tiny bit smug that I beat Julia to it. Maggie wants to ring Sal and spill the beans about us staying at the hotel, but I remind her that Sal is probably still at the hospital.

'Aunty Anna's had her baby, hasn't she? So everyone has to go and see her, instead of coming here for a lovely day out with us. We can ring home later, once we've maybe … I don't know … gone in the pirate pool?' Maggie squawks with delight, and I help her struggle into her Little Mermaid swimming costume. Luckily, I remembered to pack one for her in the bag I stashed in the boot without Sal seeing. Although Sal is probably under the illusion that my saying, 'We might not come back,' is an idle threat, my mind is made up that this is the only way to teach Sal a lesson.

Maggie swims for a couple of hours, until she is so exhausted there is no other option but to go up to the room and get her to bed. It's ten-thirty, and we have been busy all day. Sal would never have allowed her to stay up this late, being a firm believer in routine – the fact that I have flouted the rules gives me a small sense of satisfaction. I carry her up, and by the time we get into our bedroom she is fast asleep on my shoulder. Tucking her straight into bed, I switch the kettle on and check my phone. There are seventeen missed calls from Sal, and I allow myself a tiny, self-satisfied smile. It looks like someone has been getting worried.

'Hello?' I can hear the note of panic in Sal's voice upon answering the phone.

'So you're home, then?' I can't help myself; the anger that has been simmering all day threatens to erupt again, just the sound of Sal's voice pushing me right to the edge. I tell Sal we are not on our way home, as expected, and wait to hear the panic rise up again. A tiny bubble of satisfaction bursts deep inside me as, sure enough, it does, and Sal starts babbling on about being worried.

I make my voice flat and completely devoid of emotion as Sal starts talking about how lessons have been learnt, blah, blah; the same old stuff that Sal comes out with every time I have to reinforce my rules, every time I have to remind Sal of who is the boss. Sal knows, and I know, that nothing will ever change. We go through the same old thing over and over again because Sal just doesn't remember the rules – rules I don't think are that difficult. It seems to me that Sal does things deliberately to break them, just in order to upset me. I tell Sal we may or may not be b ack tomorrow – the quiver of uncertainty in Sal's voice that follows is a balm to my ears – and once I am satisfied that Sal has been put back in place and is suitably cowed, I hang up the phone. I sleep like a baby.

***

Maggie is tired and crabby the next day, so instead of stringing out Sal's punishment for a little bit longer as I intended, I decide to just head for home. While I love spending time with Maggie, I am not good at dealing with her when she is in a tired, fractious mood, so it is easier all round if we just head back and then I can enjoy my Sunday while Sal takes over the childcare. We arrive home just before lunch and Maggie runs straight inside, shouting for Sal. I follow behind, carrying the holdall and the bags of Lego that Maggie has brought home. Sal sits at the kitchen table, and Maggie launches herself across the room into Sal's lap. I ignore Sal while Maggie sits and chatters about yesterday and *all the fun things* at Legoland, until, finally, she runs out of steam and goes into the living room to watch the Cartoon Network.

'You came back, then.' Sal's voice is tired and listless; worry lines and dark circles surrounding dark, chocolate eyes. It seems pretty obvious that Sal didn't get much sleep last night.

'Maggie wanted to. Otherwise we would have stayed longer.' I look into Sal's eyes, waiting for the apology that I believe is owed me.

'OK. I'd better get those clothes in the washing machine.' Sal stands and gestures towards the holdall at my feet. I don't move, staring at Sal until the penny drops that I am waiting for an apology. Sal reaches for the bag, not acknowledging me in any other way at all.

'Come on, then, pass me the bag. These things will need washing, especially if it's warm again tomorrow. I'll want Maggie's swimming costume so I can take her to the paddling pool at the park.'

I pass the holdall, feeling a little off-balance. Usually, after a row like this, Sal is falling all over me to apologise.

'Aren't you going to apologise to me? For causing all this upset?' Sal looks at me, blinking, as if the thought hadn't even occurred.

'Oh, of course. Sorry, Charlie, for causing all this upset.' Emotionless, Sal picks up the bag and walks away towards the utility room, evidently to put on this oh-so-urgent washing. I follow Sal through into the utility room.

'Is that all you have to say?' I go to grab Sal's shoulder, just as Sal spins away towards the cupboard where the washing powder is kept.

'I'm sorry, Charlie. I'm sorry you thought it was OK to take my daughter overnight and not tell me until the last minute. I'm sorry you thought it was OK to make me go out of my mind with worry. I'm sorry you thought I shouldn't go and see my critically ill nephew in hospital, despite there being a high chance he might not make it. And I'm sorry you thought it was OK to speak to me the way you did. What else did you want me to say?'

Sal's voice is still curiously devoid of emotion, not full of begging and pleading, as it would normally be. Something has changed between us, and although I'm not too sure what that is yet, I don't like it. Sal never reacts this way and hasn't talked back to me for a long time, not since Egypt and definitely not since Maggie was born. I don't know how to respond to this new Sal, shock making me flounder a little as I try to think of a response.

'I want a proper apology, and reassurance that you have learnt your lesson. I told you I could take her, Sal, and I did. Next time I will take her for good, and it doesn't matter who you call, you'll never find us. I'll tell the police you hit her and I took her for her own safety.' Finally, something that hits Sal right where it hurts. Looking up at me, dark eyes tired and sad, Sal's face creases with worry and I feel a spark of triumph. New Sal won't be sticking around for long, I'm sure.

'There's no need for that, Charlie. I've learnt my lesson. You don't need to teach me anything else. I understand completely.' Sal turns to the washing machine and starts stuffing clothes into it.

'Good. As long as we have an understanding. Make sure you don't forget it.' A wave of tiredness pours over me; looking after a child for twenty-four hours is far more taxing than I realised.

'I'm exhausted from yesterday. I'm going for a nap.' I march out of the utility room.

CHAPTER THIRTY-THREE

SAL

I have to bite my tongue hard when you return on Sunday morning, a tired Maggie in tow. You are cold and emotionless, and when you have the audacity to demand an apology from me, anger flames in my chest. I turn away from you and pick up the holdall of clothes you have brought back with you, under the pretence of washing them, so I can get five minutes away from you to try and douse my fury, but even that doesn't work when you follow me into the utility room. I apologise and tell you I've learnt my lesson – anything to make you leave me alone, to give me a few minutes to calm myself. I don't mean it. Not any more. I'll apologise to you to keep the peace for now, but I am most definitely not sorry.

Having the whole night alone last night to think things over, I have made my mind up. I am no longer prepared to put up with the abuse I have suffered at your hands for so long. I spent the night thinking about all the ways you have hurt me, physically and emotionally, and I have finally accepted that the problem isn't me – it's you. You have broken my fingers, burnt me and bruised my kidneys with the force of your kicks. You have perforated my eardrum. You have humiliated me countless times in front of other people, always telling them how I'm stupid, have terrible dress sense, am clumsy, always in such a way that you make it seem like a joke. You portray a façade of caring partner and parent to the outside world – how many times have I heard, 'Oh, you're married to *Charlie*. Well, you lucky thing, Charlie is just *lovely/ so clever/fantastic*.' People looking from the outside in would probably say we have the perfect life – nice house, beautiful daughter, wonderful relationship. If only they knew what went on behind closed doors. No one knows that the moments when we are the perfect family, when we are both happy and content, are few and far between – that now, the bad times outweigh the good and I can't honestly believe things will ever get any better. I don't think anyone would ever guess I am often frightened that one day you might actually kill me.

I am relieved when you say you are going upstairs to take a nap. It means I don't have to bite my tongue any longer and I can spend a bit of time with Maggie without feeling I have to watch what I say to her, as no doubt if I ask her in front of you if she enjoyed herself, you will take it as some sort of slight against you. You disappear upstairs and I wander into the living room to find Maggie. I missed her yesterday, and it seems she missed me, as she is reluctant to leave my side. We make squidgy, near-unrecognisable dinosaurs from Play-Doh, colour in some complicated swirly patterns in her colouring book and are just settling down to watch *Monsters, Inc.* when you reappear. You squeeze onto the couch, next to Maggie, and with me sitting on her other side the illusion of a perfect family unit is complete again.

It's Monday morning, and to my relief you once again head off to the office early. I have managed to act as normally as possible for the rest of the weekend, as though nothing occurred on Saturday, but now I have made my decision, I am keen to start planning. It's almost as though, if I don't plan and keep up the momentum, I will stall and never be brave enough to go through with it. I still feel terrified – at the thought of leaving, and at the thought of what you might do when I tell you I'm going, but I decide to confide in Laura. I'm going to need some help, and if Laura knows about it I won't be able to chicken out. Calling Maggie, I unlock the front door and we walk over to Laura's.

Maggie scoots up to Lucy's bedroom to play dolls as soon as we arrive, which I'm glad of, as I couldn't have the conversation I am about to have with Laura in front of her. Laura boils the kettle and looks at me expectantly, not appearing to notice my shaking hands.

'Well?' she demands. 'What's going on, Sal? It's not even eight-thirty and you're here already. Something must have happened.' I look down at the old kitchen table, pockmarked with the digs and scrapes of years and years of family use. Laura's kitchen smells like fresh, drying laundry, coffee and toast. It smells homely.

'I've made a decision, Laura, but I'm going to need your help. It's a big one, but it's been a long time coming and I'm ready.' Swallowing hard, I meet her eyes and see a frown flit across her brow. I feel slightly sick, nerves making my belly churn.

'Tell me more,' she says. 'Is it what I think you're going to say?' She reaches out, places her warm, milky-white hand on top of mine. Squeezing it hard I give a slow nod.

'I'm leaving, Laura. I can't put up with it any more; everything that you thought about Charlie is wrong.' Laura gives a little huff of a laugh.

'Oh, I don't think what I think about Charlie is so wrong, Sal. I think I've been incredibly polite in all the years I've lived next door to you, all the years I've been your friend. If you truly want to know, I think Charlie is a bully; one who does whatever it takes to get their own way. I've heard the things Charlie says to you, how Charlie puts you down. And I saw, *with my own eyes*, what Charlie did to you that day with the boiling water.' Her eyes flick to the bandage that still remains on my arm – the burn is healing, but slowly, and I am desperately worried it will get infected and I'll have to see a doctor. 'You say it was an accident, Sal, but I'm not stupid. I know it wasn't.'

Hot tears well in my eyes, and the relief that Laura believes me, no question, is indescribable.

'Oh, God, you have no idea how much that means. I didn't think anyone would believe me, no one did the last time I tried to talk about it. I mean, it's just not how things are done, is it? This isn't how normal people conduct a relationship. I've finally realised that it's not me, it's not my fault and I need to get away, but I need help. I can't do it on my own. I don't think I'm strong enough – will you help me?' As I look up at Laura, I see tears running down her cheeks, and realise that I am also crying.

'Sal, *anything*. I will do *anything* to help you. No one should have to put up with the stuff you have to deal with and I have been waiting for so long for you to realise that you're worth more than this. I never told you before, but I can hear Charlie shouting at you, most nights. And after you had water poured over you, well … I got some stuff together for you, for when you were ready. You're stronger than you think, you know – and no one is going to judge you for leaving.' Laura turns to the kitchen drawers behind her and pulls out a sheaf of pamphlets and leaflets, all relating to domestic violence and organisations that can help.

'What if they don't believe me, Laur? I don't reckon it's as common as you think, you know. And what do

I do if Charlie calls the police?' I swallow nervously. Now I've actually told Laura, I feel even sicker with nerves at the thought of going through with it.

'You'd be surprised, Sal, honestly. There are so many other people out there in your position and these guys have seen it all.' She waves the pamphlets at me. 'They are there to help you, to give you advice. Why would Charlie call the police, anyway?'

I explain that that is your reasoning now, the threat you hang over me every time I do something you don't approve of – you will call the police and tell them I hit Maggie, and then you will take her away from me for good.

'Bullshit!' Laura erupts, pacing around the kitchen. 'I'll back you up one hundred per cent, Sal, always. I've seen you with her; I know you would never hurt her.' Laura sits and grasps my hands again. 'We will not let Charlie win, Sal. We will get you out of this situation, you and Maggie, OK?' I nod and Laura shoves the pile of leaflets into my hands.

'Call one of them now, see what they say. Use my phone.' Laura hands me her phone and with trembling fingers I dial the first number. Beads of sweat pop up along my hairline, and as stupid as it may sound I feel as though I am somehow betraying you even after everything that's happened. But I have to think of Maggie. Every time I waver, I will just remember how you took her and threatened not to bring her back. I'll remember the fear I felt at not seeing her again, and that will strengthen my resolve.

An hour later, I am emotionally drained but clear-headed. The people at the refuge charity were amazing – they believed me, first off, and then gave me the advice that would take me on the first steps to getting free.

'What did they say?' Laura is hovering anxiously, waiting to hear what, if any, advice was given.

'They told me to keep a diary of stuff that happens, as proof, you know? And to take pictures of any injuries. To go to my GP or the police, so there is a log. I can't do that, Laur; Charlie would kill me if I went to the police. I just don't think I can do it.' Exhaustion washes over me as I heave a huge sigh, feeling overwhelmed with it all. There's no way I'm going to be able to go through with it; you will find out and kill me before I can get somewhere safe. It hits me just what a huge step I am about to take.

'You can, Sal. It will be hard, but you can do it. Look, we'll take pictures of the burn now, OK? And then you can just keep all the records here, so there will no chance of Charlie finding them. You can start the diary; we can make notes of rough dates when things happened. Go down to the surgery today and do the drop-in service to see the GP. He can document the burn in your records, give you some cream or whatever, and Charlie will never need to know because GP records are confidential. You can do this, Sal. I'm not going to let you carry on

like this. I'm not going to let you be bullied any more.'
Laura folds her arms across her chest and stares at me.
This is the reason why I needed to tell her, so she could
support me and stop me from being too frightened of
the consequences to carry on. I nod my assent, and
Laura carefully unwraps the bandages from the burn. I
hiss through my teeth as the gauze sticks slightly to the
wound, and Laura apologises. She grabs her phone and
takes pictures of the burn from all angles.

'There.' She sits back and shows me the phone. 'All
documented. Now I want you to get up to the doctor's
and get it looked at.' The burn looks red and sore where
the blisters have popped and the skin has come away. I
agree to visit the doctor, but only once we have made a
start on the diary. I get that feeling again – the one that
says, now I have started the ball rolling, I need to keep
up the momentum, as if I stop I don't know if I'll be
brave enough to start again.

'Sal …' Laura looks up from where she is scribbling
approximate dates in an old notebook she has dug out.
'How did I not know about all of this stuff? I've lived
next door to you, been your friend for so many years
and I *just didn't know.*'

'It's not the kind of thing you go round telling
people. I wasn't going to knock on the door and tell
you, *Sorry, I'm not able to go to the park today because
my other half has punched me in the kidneys and I'm*

pretty sure there's damage because I'm pissing blood, am I?' Embarrassment makes me snap waspishly and immediately I feel horrid. Laura is only trying to help me and it's natural she would be curious about it all. 'Look, I'm sorry. I'm just … I'm ashamed, I suppose. What sort of person lets their partner beat the crap out of them? Someone who's weak and pathetic, that's who. I don't want everyone to think that about me. I'm ashamed and embarrassed to be that person – the one who can't even stand up to their other half and say, "NO, enough is enough."' Laura nods, sadly, tears glistening in her eyes. I've made her cry more today than she probably has in months.

'No, Sal. You're not weak and pathetic. You're just someone who wanted to provide a stable, family home. Someone who put their child before themselves and then found themselves boxed into a corner. Someone who hoped, *wished*, that it would get better. And now, it's time to put you first, Sal. Maggie is going to be upset because she doesn't know the full story, but one day, when she's older, you can tell her and she will understand.' She pats my hand and I squeeze back.

'Now …' Laura is all business again. 'What about money? Do you have any? You're going to need something behind you to get you started.'

'Charlie controls all the money. I just get an allowance every week for food and things for Maggie. I've got a little bit set aside that Charlie doesn't know about.' Although you have started to ask to see the receipts after I have been shopping, making me think maybe you are getting suspicious. The plan to leave must have been formulating in the back of my mind unconsciously for some time now, as I have been managing to save a little of the housekeeping money every week and put it to one side, *just in case*. I was telling myself that it would be spending money for any holidays we went on, but realistically I know it was for this eventuality.

'That's good.' Laura is brisk, and it helps now that the tears are gone to look at things objectively. 'What about when you do leave? Where will you go?'

I have already decided that when I am ready to leave, and not before, I will call my mum and my sisters and tell them everything. I know my parents will be furious with you, but there will be a bed at their house until Maggie and I can get sorted.

'I'm just waiting to hear back from the job interview,' I tell Laura. 'I can go to Mum and Dad's, and if I get the job, I can start thinking about finding a place of our own. If I don't, then I'll just have to get a job doing anything else I can find. I just need to be able to support Maggie and stand on our own two feet.'

'It sounds like you've already been thinking about this for a long time.'

I nod – I suppose I have, without even realising it. Our relationship is over, and I think it has been for a long time. I've tried my hardest, and I even thought I did still love you. I suppose I still do in a way – you gave me Maggie and nothing that happens between us can ever change that.

Later that afternoon, I visit the doctor, who advises me how to look after the burn, and makes notes on my medical record. When he asks how it occurred, I still can't bring myself to tell him that it was you who did it, so I say it was an accident. It seems like, even when I have made the decision to leave, you can still control what I say to other people. I collect Maggie from Laura's and, when leaving, lean forward to kiss Laura on the cheek.

'Thank you. You don't know how much this means.' Laura blushes and twists her long, red hair around her fist.

'Don't be silly. It's what friends do. I told you before, I'm always here.'

You call at around eight o'clock to tell me you have a client dinner and will be home very late, possibly not even home at all. I go to bed early and fall into a deep, dreamless sleep for the first time in months.

CHAPTER THIRTY-FOUR

CHARLIE

I am up early on Monday morning and decide to head straight into the office. Things with the Otex deal are picking up apace, and it won't be long before Pavlenco seals the deal and gets what he wants, as usual. Since the delivery of the cheque to sad, sobbing Radu Popescu there has been no further word from him, which fills me with a huge sense of relief and I think it's fair to say that that little problem has been resolved. At least, I hope it is. I still wake up every night in the grip of that same nightmare – the one where Radu pops up unexpectedly to destroy everything I've worked so hard for, and I don't think it's going to stop until all the paperwork is signed, sealed and delivered.

When I get into the office, despite the early hour, I call Alex's direct line – I want to firm up our plans for dinner tonight. We have finally managed to pin down tonight as an evening we are both free after many rearrangements and after such a shit weekend dealing with Sal's appalling behaviour, I am looking forward to an evening out with someone who isn't out to undermine me every five minutes. An evening with someone who makes no demands of me and is happy to just enjoy my company without causing upset.

'Hello?' The phone is answered on the first ring and I hear Alex's husky tones, causing shivers to snake down my spine.

'Alex! It's me, Charlie. I just wanted to make sure we're still on for dinner tonight – no work talk, though, please. I need to leave it behind for one evening.' I give a little chuckle and relax back into my chair, Alex's voice soothing away the tension of the weekend.

'Of course – I'm looking forward to it. I know what you mean; the sooner this deal is done the better, and obviously even better if it's me who's the victor.' I can hear the smile in Alex's voice, and it takes me back to our uni days, when it feels like all we did was laugh, drink and enjoy ourselves. At the time we thought it was all so stressful. If only we had known what real, adult life was going to be like.

'I've booked Gaucho, a table for two at eight o'clock.'

'Sounds perfect; I'm looking forward to it. Don't be late.' Smiling, I hang up the phone; Alex knows that punctuality is my middle name. A huge argument would have been bound to erupt if I'd let Sal know who I was meeting tonight – Sal and Alex never got along, and it gives me a little shiver of delight to know that I have a secret to keep from Sal, even if it is only a dinner. After this weekend, Sal hasn't earned the right to know what I am doing and, as I said before, it's all about priorities; the sooner Sal realises that the better. It's OK for Sal to make demands on me, for me to work as hard as I do purely so that Sal can have the lifestyle Sal wants, but when I want the favour returned it gets thrown in my face. I can't help it; I am still angry about the way Sal abandoned us for Anna at the weekend. I haven't even been able to bring myself to ask about the baby and how he is, or how Anna is feeling. Although, to be perfectly honest, I'm not even really sure I care. If something docs happen to the baby it'll just be another excuse for Sal to put Anna first, ahead of me again.

The day passes quickly. Anita brings me lunch and I have a progress meeting with Mr Hunter, in which I hide my sweaty palms as I tell him I have everything under control and anticipate that the merger will be completed successfully within a couple of weeks. Unbidden, Radu Popescu's face pops into my head and I squash it down, back into the recesses of my mind, swallowing hard. I won't think about him now.

'Excellent, Charlie. You've done extremely well. I expect Mr Pavlenco will only want to deal with you in the future.' Mr Hunter stands to shake my hand.

'Thank you, Mr Hunter – I'll look forward to it.' We shake and I head back to my office. I am ecstatic that

Stan Hunter thinks I've done well, and his words can only mean one thing – that I will be made partner once this deal goes through. However, the thought of being the only one to deal with Lucian Pavlenco does make me feel nervous. I am the only one who knows the truth about him, and if anything did go wrong I would be at the top of his hit list – and I really do think he has an actual hit list. I pull myself together. *Come on, Charlie, you are the ONLY one who knows the truth so it's in his interests to treat you like royalty! Popescu is gone, no one else will ever know, and Pavlenco is a powerful man. This could be the start of something HUGE, bigger than you ever anticipated.* I smile to myself – nothing can go wrong.

I arrive at the restaurant at a minute to eight o'clock, but Alex has beaten me to it and is already waiting at our table for me to arrive – an unusual occurrence, as the Alex I remember is perpetually late.

'You made it.' Alex stands and we kiss both cheeks. I stuff my laptop bag under the table, even though the maître d' wanted to take it along with my jacket when I arrived; but as it contains everything I need relating to the Pavlenco deal, I don't want to let it out of my sight. Alex raises a glass in my direction.

'I took the liberty of ordering a bottle of champagne. I hope you don't mind.'

'Mind? Of course not. Who doesn't love a bottle of champagne on a Monday night?' I reach for the bottle and top Alex's glass up, filling my own with crisp, fragrant bubbles. We clink glasses and toast ourselves.

'Here's to making it as lawyers. Eventually.' Alex laughs, and we clink again.

'Work is not up for discussion, obviously, so how are things at home with Sal and … your daughter?' Alex takes a sip of cold champagne and eyes me closely.

'Maggie? Oh, fine. Maggie is just perfect – as perfect as a four-year-old can be, anyway. And Sal is … fine. Sal's fine.' I take a large gulp of my champagne, the bubbles making me cough a little, and am relieved when the waiter appears to take our order. I don't want to talk about Sal, not tonight. And definitely not with Alex. We both order the scallops and watermelon starter followed by the beef sampler, and sit back to wait for the food to arrive. The first bottle of champagne disappears quickly, and Alex orders another.

'So what about you?' I ask. 'What have you been doing since uni? Are you married, kids, what?'

'No, Charlie.' Alex gives a rueful smile, fiddling with the forks on the table. 'It took me a long time to get over you, you know, after Sal swooped in and pinched you from under my nose.' The subtle lighting casts a sheen on Alex's honey-gold hair, creating the illusion of a halo. I give a short, nervous laugh.

'Oh, Al, don't be silly. It never would have worked between us – two massive egos under one roof? I don't think so. And what about now? We wouldn't both be working on this deal if we were still together; one of us would have had to step down.' I pat Alex on the hand, the smooth, tanned skin warm under mine.

'Speaking of which …' Alex takes a bite of the scallop starter, which has finally arrived. The service is slow and we are already well into the second bottle of champagne. 'What's Pavlenco like? I've heard all sorts of stories about him; he just seemed to come from nowhere, with his millions and hordes of underlings ready to do his bidding.'

'Nothing to tell.' I eye Alex warily, not quite drunk enough to open up completely about anything regarding Pavlenco. 'He's a decent enough guy. If the communications company decide to go through with the merger with Otex I don't think they'll regret it.'

'Really?' Alex raises an eyebrow at me in that old familiar way, the way that used to make my stomach flip. It still makes my stomach flip and I fill my fork with scallop in an effort to disguise it. 'They might be better off with my guys – let's face it, Charlie, Pavlenco has a reputation as a bit of a shark. Do you honestly think he'll make them a fair offer?'

'It doesn't matter what I think.' I knock back the rest of the wine in my glass, and signal to the waiter to bring another bottle. 'Anyway, we are not supposed to be discussing it; we're supposed to be having a good time.'

'Is that so?' Alex raises that eyebrow again and I get the distinct impression that Alex isn't only here for the dinner, and that the evening is about to take a very different turn.

Ugh. Morning sunlight streams in through open curtains, blinding me and making me screw my eyes shut. A jackhammer is dancing on top of my head, making it completely impossible for me to lift it from the pillow. I twist my head round on the pillow, taking in the room. I am not at home. *Shit.* I squint at the clock on the bedside table, which tells me it's eight o'clock. *I am not at home, and I'm late for work.* I muster up the courage to sit up, and in doing so realise from the travel kettle and tiny sachets of coffee on the dressing table in front of the bed that I'm in a hotel.

Sinking back down into the pillows with a groan, I start to recall the previous evening. We had what I suppose must have been a very enjoyable dinner at Gaucho; although I can't really remember the food. After three bottles of champagne, some rather nice brandy and an Irish coffee, I don't think either of us really cared what the meal was like. Sparks were flying, and it was just like it was between Alex and I in the old days, pre-Sal and all the trouble that has come since. We reminisced about uni, old friends and some of the crazy times we had together. It wasn't long before the memories and the alcohol meant we were staggering up the road together to the nearest hotel. A wave of nausea makes my mouth flood with saliva. *Oh, God, is Alex still here?* I lift my heavy head from the pillow, but I can't hear any movement from the bathroom. Then I see it, a white envelope propped up against the television.

Struggling out from the tangled duvet and still fighting the urge to be sick, I rip open the envelope.

Charlie,
Thanks for a lovely evening. Just like old times eh?
Don't worry about Sal – my lips are sealed.
A xx

Sal. Last night was the ultimate revenge on Sal. I vaguely remember thinking as we made our way haphazardly up to the hotel room that, after the way Sal ditched me at the weekend, this was a fitting punishment. Proof that if Sal doesn't want to be there for me, there is someone else out there who does. I allow myself a tiny, private smile. If it were ever discovered that Alex and I had spent the night together, Sal would be devastated. And that would be no more, right now, than Sal deserves.

I drag myself out of bed, downing the glass of water and two paracetamol Alex has thoughtfully left next to the kettle. A twinge of regret pulls at my stomach – maybe I should have stayed with Alex. Sal certainly wouldn't have thought to leave me water and tablets to aid my hangover. After a hot shower followed by a hot coffee, I call Anita to let her know I'll be late.

'Anita, I'm running behind. Take messages until I arrive, OK?' I struggle into my jacket and reach for my laptop bag.

'OK, Charlie. Alex Hoskins called for you already this morning – just to say thank you for a pleasant evening?' The upward inflection in Anita's voice tells me she's dying to ask me what it's all about. Ignoring her questioning comment, I thank her and hang up. A pleasant evening, indeed. The thought crosses my mind that I must have been seriously out of it last night – I never even heard Alex leave, and it must have been some time ago for Alex to be at the office already. I pull my laptop bag out from under the table and pause as I heave it up onto the bed. The zipper is ever so slightly open, something I'm sure it wasn't last night. I always make sure I zip it up fully, especially if I have to travel on the tube; pickpockets are rife and it makes sense to keep it properly closed. Sighing, I pull the zip all the way open and tug everything out, fully expecting to see my laptop gone.

No. Everything is still in there, laptop, papers, charger all present and correct. I mustn't have zipped it up properly in my haste to get to the restaurant on time last night. Feeling relieved, I repack the laptop bag – I wouldn't have wanted to have to go into the office today and explain to Mr Hunter that I had lost the entire Pavlenco acquisition case files because I got robbed after spending the night with the opposing lawyer.

Leaving the hotel after a quick English breakfast – there is nothing like bacon and eggs, followed by hot strong coffee and a pulpy orange juice to sort out a rotten hangover – I decide to walk back to the office. The early-morning chill has disappeared to be replaced by another day of warm, late summer sunshine and I have a spring in my step, despite the hangover headache thumping away at the back of my head. Without even being aware of it, Sal has been suitably punished and I feel like I have scored the winning point, even though I am the only one in the relationship that knows about it. Judging from the few comments that Alex let slip over dinner last night, at least the ones I can remember, I am confident that Lucian and I have the upper hand over the deal and that everything is going to go our way without a hitch. I breathe in a huge lungful of hot, pollution-stained London air and smile. Raging hangover or not, life is good.

CHAPTER THIRTY-FIVE

SAL

By telling Laura what I am going to do, I seem to have cemented my plans in my mind, and the following week feels as though a weight has been lifted. Don't get me wrong – I am still terrified at the thought you might find out what I'm planning, but I start to think about what I can pack discreetly, things that can be squirrelled away into a holdall – the only bag I will take in the beginning – things of mine and Maggie's that you won't notice are missing. It's a difficult job; for someone who doesn't really spend a lot of time at home you don't miss a trick, so I decide to leave all of our favourite items of clothing, toys and books, and start to put away the lesser-worn, infrequently used items. Our favourite things will have to wait until we are safely away and then maybe I can send my dad over to pick things up. I don't tell my mum and dad my plans just yet – they always have bought into the illusion that we are a perfect family unit, and apart from my mum making the odd remark about how you don't seem to be able to attend many family parties, I am pretty sure she has no idea what has been going on in our relationship. Anna and Julia, on the other hand are a different story, and I think I am going to have to confide in them before I make the first step. Julia, as predicted, is pleased.

'Sal! To what do I owe this pleasure?' Sounding surprised, as usually she is the one to call me, her voice is warm honey pouring down the telephone line, evoking a lifetime of memories – Julia's voice has been in the background my entire life, comforting, bossing, and nagging; she's like another mother to me.

'Jules, I'm leaving Charlie.' I dispense with any niceties, blurting it straight out before I can change my mind, and hear Julia gasp, a quick intake of breath, and then:

'Thank God. Bloody hell, Sal, I was wondering when you were going to see sense. I've been biting my tongue for years, and so has Luca.' Julia's husband is a tall, dark, strong Roman she picked up on a gap year travelling around Europe. They met, fell in love and, needless to say, Julia never made it to university, choosing instead to move to Rome and marry Luca. If he hadn't been Italian, I don't think my dad would ever have allowed it. I explain to Julia everything that has happened, starting with the most recent incident of your taking Maggie overnight and going right back to the first holiday we had in Egypt and the cold-shouldering that followed. After hearing about the perforated eardrum, the broken fingers and all the other 'accidents' you have subjected me to, Julia is, in turns, shocked, horrified and disgusted. She had her suspicions but never, ever thought things were as bad as this. By the end of our conversation, she is in tears and furious, just about ready to head over to England and kill you. I am also in tears, relieved that she believed me and thankful she doesn't think I'm some weak, spineless idiot, as I was worried she would.

'Julia, please, calm down. I just have to wait and see if I have this job, and then I can leave. I've started packing, but I don't want to tell Mum and Dad just yet. I can't risk Charlie finding out and doing something stupid in an attempt to stop me, I have to think about Maggie.'

'OK.' Julia agrees to calm her typically Italian fiery temper. 'But I mean it, Sal – one word and I'll be there. Maybe you and Maggie should come over for a visit, get out of the heat for a while? I can't imagine Charlie will let you go quietly.'

I tell her I can't, especially if I manage to get the teaching job, but I hope she'll understand that I do appreciate it. I have to stand on my own two feet and show you that I don't need anyone else. Relieved to have her support, I thank Julia, tell her I love her and hang up. All that remains now is to find out if I have the job, or if I have to keep looking.

On Friday morning the postman delivers the plain, white envelope that will seal my fate. Sick with nerves and with trembling fingers I open the envelope and, once again, shake out the white paper bearing the St Martin's C of E Primary letterhead, almost too afraid to read it in case it's bad news.

'Dear Sal ... delighted to inform you ,,, please attend ... Friday, 21st August, ...' A wave of relief washes over me and tears spring to my eyes. I got the job. As of Monday, 7th September, I will be the Year Six teacher for St Martin's Primary. I rush next door to Laura, waving the letter in the air.

'Laura, I bloody got it!' I barge in through the back door, only to see Laura sitting at the kitchen table with a blond-haired man. 'Oh, sorry, you're busy, I'll come back.' I start to back away, back towards my own back garden.

'No, Sal, stop. Don't be silly! This is my cousin, Oliver. He's been travelling and just got home yesterday.' The man stands, towering over me, and shakes my hand. He must be 6' 4" at least – a direct contrast to tiny Laura who's lucky to hit 5' 3" in her stockinged feet.

'Nice to meet you, Sal. Laura's been telling me all about you.' I narrow my eyes at Laura and she gives a tiny imperceptible shake of her head.

'Well, nice to meet you, Oliver. Sorry for barging in on you two like that.' He sits back down and Laura gestures to the seat next to her.

'Tell me, then!' She smiles, holding out her hand for the letter. I give her a few minutes to scan over the details and wait for it to sink in.

'Bloody hell, Sal, I knew you could do it!' She jumps up and squeezes me tight in her arms. She leans close and whispers in my ear so only the two of us can hear, 'This means you're free.'

Oliver also reads the letter and we celebrate with a quick glass of wine – I have to go and pick Maggie up from a play date she's had this afternoon with a boy from her pre-school class and I don't want to be late, or stinking of booze. These things have a nasty habit of getting back to you, and now the end is so near I don't want any more drama before I leave. Laura says she will watch Maggie while I go and meet Mrs Prideaux next Friday, and I feel a sense of calm and contentment come over me. Everything is coming together and maybe, just maybe, I can start to look to the future.

The day of the meeting with my new boss falls on the Friday before your big final meeting regarding the Pavlenco acquisition, which is a relief as it means I don't have to worry about you coming home early and finding me out. You'll be finalising all your paperwork and making sure everything is in order to meet with the communications company on Monday and get everything signed, and no doubt will be preoccupied with it all weekend. I am nearly ready – everything essential I need to take is packed into the holdall, which is stuffed deep under the bed. While I think I am one hundred per cent ready to go, inside there is still a little voice that tells me I've failed; I didn't manage to keep a safe, family home for Maggie and she will end up just another child from a broken home

I take the train into town, after dispatching Maggie to Laura's, along with her wheelie suitcase of 'precious things'. This was the deal we made in exchange for her going to Laura's for the day – if her 'precious things' didn't go, then neither would she. I give in easily, not wanting the hassle, and Maggie is perfectly happy to wave me off from Laura's front doorstep.

Mrs Prideaux is waiting for me as I arrive at the school gates, and she ushers me straight through to her office, no Aurelie this time as it's the school holidays. The school is hushed and quiet, a completely different atmosphere to my last visit when the corridors rang out with the sound of children talking and laughing on their way to class.

'I'm very pleased you've decided to accept the job, Sal. We've been searching for teachers of a certain calibre and you definitely meet the standard we're looking for.' Mrs Prideaux smiles at me from across the desk, steepling her fingers under her chin.

'Thank you.' I blush slightly. It's been so long since anyone gave me a compliment I'm not entirely sure how to accept it graciously, or how to respond.

Mrs Prideaux runs through everything I need to know before term starts, including handing me the relevant forms for a DBS check, and before I know it, I'm laden down with paperwork and books. It's going to be a heavy workload but a frisson of excitement runs through me. I'll be back to being Sal again.

'It's going to be tough, Sal. The workload can be immense and some of the children are a handful, troubled even.' Mrs Prideaux looks sternly at me over her glasses. 'But we really believe you are the right person for the job.'

'I'm honoured to be part of the St Martin's team,' I say. 'I'm looking forward to the start of the new term. I've had a few things to get over lately and St Martin's is going to be a fresh start for me, and my daughter.' Mrs Prideaux smiles, and we shake hands as I leave. She hands me the plastic wallets full of paperwork in preparation for Term One and I make my way back towards the train station, nervous but full of anticipation for the weeks ahead.

My phone beeps as I struggle with my paperwork towards the train platform. Trying to dig it out of my pocket, while simultaneously juggling the slippery plastic wallets, I don't watch where I'm going and bump roughly into someone going the other way.

'Oh, God, sorry, I'm so sorry.' I reach out a hand to steady the person I've just collided with.

'Watch where you're … Sal? Sal Trevetti, is that you?' I look up, straight into the face of Alex Hoskins, your ex, the one you were with before you met me.

'Alex? Sorry, what a coincidence, bumping in to you!' I give a little laugh, before the plastic wallets slide right out of my hand, crashing to the pavement.

'Shit. Sorry.' Feeling awkward, I lean down and fumble with the folders, embarrassment staining my cheeks a hot red.

'Here, let me help you.' Alex leans down, completely unflustered, exuding the same ice-cold blondness that always radiated like a halo, making the rest of us feel bumbling and clumsy. Straightening up, Alex hands me the other plastic wallet, the problem one that really is full to bursting.

'Fancy meeting you,' Alex says, raising a single, blond eyebrow in the familiar manner I remember from our university days. 'I only just bumped into Charlie the other day. We had dinner at Gaucho one Monday evening; it was just like old times.' A ghost of a smile passes over Alex's lips. *Monday evening?* I pause for a moment, as realisation dawns. Monday evening, a week or so ago, when you said you had an important dinner with a client and would be late home. It was the day after that awful weekend when you took Maggie overnight, the day I confided in Laura and felt relieved you wouldn't be home until late. In fact, that evening, you didn't come home at all, if I remember correctly.

'Really? Charlie didn't mention it.' Heart hammering in my chest, I pull myself up straighter and meet Alex's eyes. Not a whisper of guilt, but then that doesn't mean anything. Alex has always been ruthless. I've heard Alex referred to as 'calculating' on more than one occasion in the past. You must have been a formidable team together.

'Oh, yes.' Alex smiles knowingly. 'Just like it used to be, back in the day. In fact, it was like we saw each other just yesterday. You know how it is, Sal, when you have that kind of connection with someone, right? You don't see them for years, but then you pick straight back up where you left off, like you've never been away. I hope Charlie wasn't *too* hungover – we did have rather a lot to drink. Anyway, it was nice to see you, Sal. Good luck with your … with everything.' With that, Alex sweeps past me towards the train platform, leaving me open-mouthed with no chance to formulate any of the questions that are bursting on my tongue.

There is absolutely no doubt in my mind that you were with Alex last Monday night, the night you didn't come home. Alex made it perfectly clear that that was the case. I feel sick, humiliated. No matter what has gone on between us, I have never, ever contemplated cheating on you and I always thought you had more integrity than that. Swallowing hard, the taste of vomit at the back of my throat, I look towards the platform, but Alex is nowhere in sight, presumably having bagged a seat on the train that is leaving the station now, the train I should have been on. I walk slowly towards the platform to wait for the next one. I feel hot and shaky, my hands trembling. Any last traces of doubt have been washed from my mind. I couldn't stay with you, even if all the other stuff hadn't happened, not now you've cheated on me. And the fact that you've cheated on me, humiliated me, with *Alex* of all people just seals our fate. I am leaving and there is no way I will ever come back. The hold you have had over for me for so many years is broken.

CHAPTER THIRTY-SIX

CHARLIE

I spend Friday in a panic at my office, trying desperately to make sure everything is prepared for Monday, and Geoff is no help whatsoever. I need to get all the paperwork finalised, all my ducks in a row so to speak, and he hovers anxiously in the background for most of the day. Although the acquisition is my deal, Geoff is the head of my department and if it all goes tits up Geoff will also be in the firing line. I am so tired through lack of sleep I feel as though I'm wading through mud, and I long for the whole thing to be over, if only so that I can get a decent night's sleep. I just have to get through to Monday evening, and then it'll all be done – Mr Hunter will have me lined up for partner and some of the pressure will be off me at last. By six o'clock, I am losing patience, but everything is ready.

'Geoff, please, just relax. It's all under control. I've got everything ready to go – all we need are the signatures on it and it's done.' I lean over to shut down my computer. It's early for me to leave, but I know if I stay any longer I'll either go back to the files and start obsessively checking all the clauses again, or I'll want to punch Geoff.

'Are you leaving?' Geoff is sweaty, his forehead beaded with tiny dots of perspiration. He always sweats when he gets anxious and today he has been off the scale, even for him, making me cringe by mopping at his forehead with a grubby white hanky all day.

'Yes, Geoff, I'm leaving. And you should, too. Monday is a big day for both of us. If this all goes to plan, *which it will*, the communications company will hand themselves over to Lucian, everyone will sign, the communications guy will be rich, Lucian will be even richer, and I will be a partner. Oh, and your department will have the knowledge that you orchestrated the entire thing, OK? You'll probably get an even bigger, even fatter bonus this year than last year. Just go home and have a weekend, for God's sake.' My patience is wearing thin, and I can't wait for Monday when this deal goes through and I get my office on the sixth floor. Then I will never, or rather *will rarely*, have to deal with Geoff and his anxious sweating. I eventually get his twittering voice out of my office and pack the rest of my things into my laptop bag. Reaching the door, I turn and survey the office one last time. This could be one of the last times I work in here. Monday could mean the start of a whole new journey – starting with a brand-new office. I smile, switch off the lights, and shut the door.

'Are you sure you're OK, Sal?' Sal has been quiet all weekend and for a moment it flits across my mind that maybe my night with Alex has been discovered. I shake the idea away, dismissively. *It couldn't have been. When would Sal ever see Alex? It's not like Sal ever heads into town, or even leaves the village for that matter, choosing instead to just lounge around at home while I trek into town every day to bring home the bacon.* It must be something else bothering Sal, something little and inconsequential, no doubt.

'I'm fine, honestly, Charlie.' Sal looks up from the newspaper. We are actually managing to enjoy some quiet time this Sunday morning. Maggie is parked in front of Cartoon Network, which is her favourite place to be, but Sal is normally so strict about how much TV Mags can watch it's unusual for her to get a whole Sunday morning. Another sign that maybe something isn't quite right with Sal, but I'm not going to let it bother me.

'So, how is … ummm … Anna's baby?' Sal is still staring at the newspaper and I feel a flicker of annoyance. It's not often we get a morning to spend together like this and I'm really trying to make an effort here, by feigning interest in Anna's baby.

'What? Oh, fine.' Sal doesn't even look up. This is not acceptable. I am working so hard, and under so much stress, and now Sal can't even be bothered to spend Sunday morning with me, preferring instead to read about slutty celebrities and political scandal. I feel my blood start to boil.

'Sal ... WILL YOU FUCKING LOOK AT ME!' I roar, no longer able to keep my temper under control. Sal startles and pushes the newspaper away.

'OK, Charlie, calm down. What do you want?' Sal glances anxiously towards the closed living-room door, checking to see if Maggie has heard me shout.

'What do I want? I want you to fucking speak to me, that's what I want. I don't work all the fucking hours God sends for you to spend the weekend reading your shitty newspaper and ignoring me!' A tiny figure appears in the doorway.

'Daddy? What's going on? Why is there shouting?' Maggie's frightened face is peering round the door frame, eyes big and wide, looking anxiously between us. Something crosses Sal's face as we make eye contact, something that looks suspiciously like disgust, before I blink and it is gone. Sal gets up and goes to pull Maggie into a hug.

'It's nothing, baby, don't worry. Just grown-ups being silly, that's all. Go back to your show.' Maggie eyes us both warily, before tiptoeing back into the living room and snuggling back into position on the couch.

'That's not acceptable,' Sal hisses at me, pulling the living room door closed again. 'I don't want her to see that. I don't want her to hear you screaming at me.'

'Then maybe,' I hiss back, 'you should stop being such a fucking useless moron. You deserve everything you get, Sal, and if it's not good for Maggie then maybe I *should* take her away.' I slowly, deliberately grab the skin at the top of Sal's arm and twist, hard. Yelping, Sal pulls away, rubbing at the angry red mark that has appeared just below the sleeve of Sal's T-shirt. I just laugh.

Later that evening, Maggie is asleep and I sit next to Sal on the sofa. Taking Sal's hand in mine, it lies there warm but unresponsive.

'Sal, I'm sorry, OK?' I squeeze gently, but Sal's hand still just lies there. 'I just … I work so hard and I miss you so much because I'm not here, so I just want a bit of attention when we are together, that's all. I work hard for *you*, Sal, so that you can stay home with Maggie. When you ignore me it just makes me angry and you make me lose my temper. It's only because I love you so much, Sal. You know that, right? It's me and you, together for ever, remember?' I squeeze slightly harder until I get a response.

'Yes, Charlie, of course. I'll remember that in future.' Sal gives my hand a brief squeeze and turns back to the television. I can't help feeling that same sneaking sensation that something in our relationship has changed. Something is not quite as it usually is and I'm not too sure what.

I don't sleep well that night, Sal's response to me on Sunday evening and the meeting scheduled for Monday morning playing on my mind. I rise early, and after a shower, I kiss Sal's sleeping head and sneak out the front door.

By ten o'clock, when Anita buzzes through to me that Lucian Pavlenco has arrived, all the paperwork is ready and complete and I am nervously waiting for the meeting to begin. The director of the communications company Lucian is planning on buying has arrived ten minutes earlier, so I gather up all the paperwork and walk slowly along the corridor towards the boardroom. I pause outside, taking a moment to catch my breath and gather my thoughts. Once I have these papers signed, I've done it. I've made Hunter, Crisp and Wilson a ton of money and launched myself to the top of my tree. I will be a partner in the firm, a success story, and with Sal and Maggie by my side, I really will have it all. The perfect life. Taking a deep breath, I push the door open and enter the boardroom, smiling an acknowledgement at Lucian and Mr Hunter, who is sitting at the top of the table.

'Good morning, gentlemen.' I put my papers down and shake hands with everyone. 'Stefan' – I turn to the director of the communications company – 'thank you so much for your patience regarding this process.

We are incredibly pleased you decided to sell to Mr Pavlenco. You've made the right decision.'

'Thank you, Charlie.' Stefan winks at me. He looks groomed and polished today, whereas on the previous occasions I have met with him he just looked kind of scruffy and grungy, not at all how I imagined the kind of guy who owns a very successful company and is about to make his fortune.

'These are the papers that need to be signed in order for everything to be formally completed.' I lay out several sheets of A4 paper, all closely typed, with various spaces for signatures. 'Once these are all signed, that's it. The agreed amounts will be transferred to Stefan's account and Mr Pavlenco will have full control over the company, enabling him to merge completely with his existing communications company, if he so wishes. Everybody understand?' The table is a sea of nodding heads. 'Well, seeing as there are no further questions, in that case I think we should get on and sign, don't you? No point in delaying completion.' Mr Hunter smiles at me, a warm, approving smile that tells me I've impressed him. I pass the paperwork to Stefan first, and as he is reaching for a pen the door bursts open. Alex is standing in the doorway, blond hair standing out in a bright halo, eyes blazing fire. Anita puffs into the doorway, slightly behind Alex.

'I'm sorry, Charlie,' she huffs, clearly out of breath. 'I tried to stop them, I really did.'

'Don't worry, Anita. Go back to your desk.' I narrow my eyes. *What the hell is Alex doing here?* 'Alex, you don't need to be here. You are aware Stefan has decided to sell his company to Mr Pavlenco – not your clients – so there is absolutely no reason for you to be in this office right now. Please leave.' I stand and move towards Alex, who stares at me, unable or unwilling to break eye contact.

'Mr Pavlenco, you say, Charlie?' Alex stands tall, and refuses to move from the doorway. From the corner of my eye, I see Stan reach for the telephone. 'See, the way I hear it, there is no Mr Pavlenco in this room.' A hush descends, and Mr Hunter replaces the phone he has picked up to call security. A hot wave of fear prickles its way down my body. *Oh, God, please, no. This cannot be happening. After everything I've done to try and prevent it, the worst cannot happen now.*

Lucian stays seated, still as calm as ever, and appraises Alex coolly. 'Please,' he says. 'You might care to explain yourself?' *Oh, God, no.* I fumble for the pen on the table, my fingers shaking. I need to get these contracts signed if it's the last thing I do.

'Alex, please,' I interject quickly, 'let's talk about this outside. There's no need for this.' I take Alex's arm and move towards the doorway, avoiding Mr Hunter's quizzical gaze. Alex shrugs me off, roughly.

'No, Charlie. It does need to be said. You see, I have proof that Lucian Pavlenco is not who he says he is.'

Alex waves a sheaf of papers. Mr Hunter gets to his feet, spluttering with rage.

'Out of here now!' He points to the stairwell, his face turning an interesting shade of purple in his fury. 'Get out of here – I don't know who you think you are, but your bosses will be hearing about this.' Mr Hunter is quivering with anger, and I watch helplessly as he moves towards the doorway. Alex just smiles, quite unruffled, still clutching the wad of papers in one hand.

'Yes, Mr Hunter, I am rather hoping they do hear about this. You see, Lucian Pavlenco is *not* Lucian Pavlenco and I have the evidence right here to prove it. His real name is Radu Popescu and he entered our country illegally sixteen years ago, when he was twenty-four. He was born in Bucharest in 1975, and came to England after the death of his father meant his family were struggling to survive. His best friend, the *real* Lucian Pavlenco, had already come to England a year previously, but legally. Upon his arrival, Radu convinced Lucian that, if he would just lend Radu his identity, he could do well and support both of them. It's all there.' Alex throws the bunch of paperwork down on the desk with a thud, and I recognise printouts of the emails and documents that Radu, *Lucian*, had emailed me as proof of his identity. *Oh, Jesus, no.* 'The only thing is, Radu didn't stick to his side of the bargain, did you *Radu*?' Alex sneers in Lucian's direction. I feel my face flaming as the taste of vomit hits the back of my throat. Alex has betrayed me – my laptop bag was slightly open that morning in the hotel and now I know why. I knew I closed it properly when I left the office. *Oh, God, how could I have been so stupid?* Lucian is pale, a single bead of sweat growing at his temple.

'This is preposterous.' Lucian stands, and makes to grab the paperwork, but Mr Hunter lays his hand on top of it.

'If you please, Mr Pavlenco.' Mr Hunter picks up the paperwork and begins to scan through it, flicking through page after page. His gaze rests on a printout of my email correspondence with Radu and he makes a small noise at the back of his throat before meeting my eyes. 'Charlie, you knew about this? And you kept it quiet?' There is no mistaking the shock and disappointment in his voice. Shame floods through me, and I open my mouth before hesitating, unsure of whether to brazen it out or not.

'Stan – I did what was best for the company. I only wanted to do what was best for us all.' I can't meet his eyes. Stefan gets to his feet, looking from one to the other of us.

'Hang on a minute,' he says. 'So, *he*' – he points a finger at Lucian, who is sitting pale and quiet, not making eye contact with anyone – 'is not Lucian Pavlenco? He's actually an illegal immigrant who stole someone else's identity and made a ton of money doing it? And then he ripped his mate off?'

'That's about the size of it,' Alex says. Stefan looks at me incredulously.

'And you, the lawyer, you knew about it? Jesus, I knew lawyers were unscrupulous, but this is ridiculous.' He shakes his head in disgust, while Alex smirks in the doorway.

'I did what I thought was best!' I shout, slapping my hand down on the boardroom table. 'I tried to do what was best for everyone concerned, that's all! I'm not the one who's done anything wrong here; I only tried to do the best thing for everyone, for me, for Sal, everyone. Stan, please ...' My breathing is ragged and I can feel the tight arms of panic squeezing me, as I rake my fingers through my hair. Everything is ruined. Everything that I've worked for has gone up in smoke, just like it did night after night in my nightmares. Anita appears in the doorway again, hands fluttering nervously.

'Umm ... Charlie,' she begins, as three immigration officers enter the room. *Oh, God, it really is all over. There's no coming back from this.* Alex's eyes meet mine triumphantly as the immigration officers explain to Lucian, Radu, whatever his bloody name is, that he will now be arrested and taken to a detention centre until his case is processed. Lucian nods, defeated. As he rises, his wrists held out in front of him to allow the officers to handcuff him, he nods in my direction.

'It was fun while it lasted. Don't worry, Charlie, I'm sure we will meet again,' he says, his eyes a cold, grey lake, and I shiver. I hope to God this is the last time I see ruthless, calculating Lucian Pavlenco. As Lucian is escorted from the building, Mr Hunter stands in front of me.

'Charlie, it's over. You need to clear your desk and go home. There is no position available for you here any more. You have disgraced the name of Huntor, Crisp and Wilson, and I'm sure the police will be wanting to discuss this matter with you in the near future, so I suggest you don't stray too far from home. Jesus, Charlie, what were you thinking?' His manner is cold and emotionless, nothing like the Stan Hunter I have come to know.

On shaky legs I leave the boardroom, staggering past Anita's desk. She tries to stop me, reaching out with one hand as I pass, but I ignore her, unable to speak. I leave my things – there is nothing I want so badly from my desk that it is worth facing the other people in the office, particularly Geoff. Despair swamps me as I walk through the glass front doors for the last time, not even looking back. It's over.

CHAPTER THIRTY-SEVEN

SAL

The weekend is weird and awkward. Knowing what I now know makes it difficult to pretend that everything is going to be OK, but I put on a brave face and make my best effort, trying my hardest to be responsive to you when inside I feel nothing. Even so, it's still not good enough and you scream at me on Sunday morning for reading the paper instead of giving you the attention you feel you deserve. I bite my tongue, resisting the urge to tell you to go and get some attention from Alex if you need it so badly. Maggie hears you shouting and I have to squash down my anger, your behaviour just reinforcing to me that I have made the right decision. Not long to go and we will be free. Your reign of terror will be over.

On Monday morning, I wake and you have already left for the office. I am thankful I don't have to pretend any more this morning, pretend any more *at all*. By this evening, I will be gone and you won't be able to control me any more. I get up, checking and rechecking that the holdall is packed, my heart beating double-time all the while. I am so nervous that something will go wrong, that you'll find out before I can get away. My plan is to drop Maggie off at my parents', and then come back to get our things and lock the house up. Maggie is excited to be going over to see her grandparents and I decide to take your car keys and drive over there. Fuck it; what's the worst that can happen now? My mother is shocked to see us – I haven't told her anything because she is a typical, fiery, Italian woman and I couldn't risk her contacting you to give her a piece of her mind.

'Mama.' I lean in and kiss her cheek, her plump hands holding my face.

'Sally! What are you doing here?' She smells of baking and hand soap; she smells like my childhood. Tears threaten and I take a deep breath.

'Mama, I'm coming home.'

An hour later, I have explained to my mum briefly what has been happening in our relationship, while my dad keeps Maggie occupied out in the workshop. There are tears, anger, more tears, and by the time Mama has calmed down we are both quite exhausted.

'Sal, why did you never tell me before?' Her eyes fill with tears and I hate myself for hurting her.

'I was ashamed, Mama. Worried that people would think I was just some weak, useless idiot with no backbone. What kind of person lets their partner treat them like that? I just wanted Maggie to have a family, a childhood like we did when we were growing up. I got it so wrong.'

'Don't be silly, Sal. You did everything you could. Now we have to get you away. Leave Maggie here and go get your things. If you're not back here in an hour and a half then I'm coming to get you.' I smile; my lovely, brave, feisty mum, not afraid of anything. Everything is going to be OK.

The house is silent when I let myself back in, and I take a moment just to drink in the peace and quiet. I had such high hopes for us, you and me and then later on the three of us, when we bought this house. It's hard to think that all this is over, that I won't be coming back. I wanted this place to be a haven for us, to bring up our child in a calm, safe environment. Instead, this house has seen anger, pain, blood and suffering and now my decision is made I can see the bad times far outweigh the good. The brief perfect moments when we were a happy family never made up for the bad times, I can see that now, and I should never have stayed as long as I did. I climb the stairs, and stand in the doorway of Maggie's room one last time before pulling the holdall out from the back of her toy cupboard. I've moved it from place to place so many times, terrified you would come across it before I was ready to leave. There is only one last thing left to pack, a small stuffed tiger that Julia and Luca bought for Maggie when she was born. She's slept with it every night since and to pack it beforehand would have been a dead giveaway. I stuff it into the bag and make my way downstairs. Sitting at the kitchen table, I pull out a pen and try to draft some sort of note to you. I can't just leave, can't just take Maggie without letting you know she is safe, even though it shrieks against all my best instincts. I begin to write:

> *Dear Charlie,*
> *I can't do this any more. I have tried for so long but it is not fair on Maggie, or us ...*

My head jerks up as I hear the front door slam. Surely it can't be you, home already? The signing of the contracts is today, and I was sure you would all be out celebrating until late this evening. It's only three o'clock – maybe it's my mum arrived early? I rise from the table, heart hammering in my chest and sweat prickling across my palms, just as you crash through the kitchen door. The fug of whisky rises from you and your eyes are bloodshot, blonde hair standing out at all angles.

'Charlie? What the ...? What's happened?' I discreetly try to kick the holdall under the kitchen table, out of your sight, and tuck the pen into my back pocket.

'It's *FUCKED*, Sal, is what it is. Fucking fucked. Everything I've worked for, all the fucking effort I've put in *for you*, has gone down the drain. I am out of a job. The End.' You drag your hands through your short blond hair, and judging by the state of it it's not the first time you've done that today. Sitting down at the kitchen table, you slump forward onto your forearms. I don't know what to do, or what has happened. You've obviously been drinking, but Maggie isn't here and, drunk or not, you're sure to notice.

'Do you want to talk about it?' I ask, moving to fill the kettle to make you a strong coffee.

'No, I don't want to fucking talk about it, Sal, you fucking idiot. Jesus Christ, you have no fucking idea. This whole fucking thing is your fault, for Christ's sake.' *My fault?* You raise your eyes to mine, face contorted with anger, noticing the notepaper on the table just as I realise it's still there. I move to grab it but, even though you're half-cut, you reach it first.

'What the hell is this? *Dear Charlie …*' You start to read through it, and I pray you're so drunk that you can't take it in. My heart is pounding and I feel sick. This is it. I reach down to grab the strap of the holdall and as I do so you drop the letter and punch down with your fists, full strength onto the top of my head. The force of the blow knocks me off my feet and I fall to my knees, smashing them hard into the tiled floor.

'What the FUCK IS THIS?' you roar, punching me over and over. 'Do you really think I'll let you go? You think you're going to leave me after everything I've done for you? After I've put myself on the line for you? I'll NEVER let you go!' You're screaming at me as you hit me over and over, blood pouring into my eyes as the skin above my eyebrow splits. I struggle backwards, digging my heels into the floor to push myself away from you and get to my feet.

'No, Charlie. STOP. This is why; this is why I can't do this any more. Stop and I'll stay, I promise.' Gasping for breath, I back away, blood dripping steadily into one eye, my eyebrow throbbing where the skin has split. Both knees throb in sympathy and I keep begging you to stop, but you are so angry you don't hear me. You just keep coming for me. Your breathing is ragged, anger making you breathless as you come ever nearer. As you reach out and grab a chunk of my hair I feel a wash of anger pour over me. NO. I am not going to let you do this. I won't let you hurt me, or worse. This time might be the time that you do actually kill me. Thinking only of Maggie, I reach up and shove your chest with all my might, pushing you hard away from me. You hit the kitchen sink, bouncing off it slightly, a stunned look crossing your face at my retaliation. Taking my chance, I grab the bag and back towards the kitchen door, my vision blurry from the blood pouring from my cut eyebrow. I reach for the door handle, my eyes stinging from the sweat and blood that drip down my face, but you are on me before I can get a strong enough grip to turn it. Rage makes you stronger than ever and a blow to the kidneys winds me, doubling me over, making me gasp and retch. I drop the bag as I turn and try to push you away, the phrase 'that old chestnut' flickering through my mind as I feel the wash of sickness and familiar dull ache that a punch to the kidneys brings. I don't notice the carving knife in your hand and it's as though I don't even feel the knife at first, as it slides between my ribs.

CHAPTER THIRTY-EIGHT

CHARLIE

It happened so quickly, and now there is so much blood. More blood than I ever thought possible. I back away, pushing myself up against the kitchen counter. I feel light-headed, sick. He reaches up to me, a shaky hand, slick with his own blood. A coppery, iron tang fills the air and I want to retch. Turning, I lean over the kitchen sink, where I heave and heave but nothing comes up. I wipe my mouth and try to think calmly, rationally. I need to phone for an ambulance, and I need to get my story straight. I'll tell them that he slipped and fell onto the knife, a brutal carving knife usually used for carving the Christmas turkey, not carving into other people. I can't tell them that I snapped. That a red mist descended and for just a few seconds I felt like I just couldn't take it any more, the shouting, the aggression and the lies. That after everything I had done for him, all the hours I had worked, all the lies he had told me, he was going to leave me, and I just couldn't have that. In just a split second, all rationality left me and I grabbed the knife and thrust it firmly into my husband's stomach. They'll believe me – they'll have to. Who would ever think that an eight-stone woman could stab her much bigger, stronger husband?

I wipe my mouth with a shaky hand. Sal is lying on the kitchen floor, half slumped against the kitchen counter, a cut on his eyebrow leaking blood down his face. His still, white face. The hand he reached out to me lies still and unmoving in his lap. The knife handle sticks out from between his ribs, blood soaking into the white shirt he wears, a shirt I bought him for our last anniversary. I'll sort this out. I'll tell them it was an accident. Sal won't leave me, not now. I flex my hand, knuckles protesting in pain where I slammed them into the top of Sal's head in anger, knocking him to his knees.

The sound of the back door being thrown open startles me and I look round in panic, as suddenly Laura bursts into the kitchen, closely followed by Sal's mum. Laura gives a little shriek and goes straight to Sal, crouching over him and whispering in his ear. I always knew there was something more between them.

'Did you call an ambulance?' she asks, as Sal's mum flutters over him, stroking his curls back away from his bloody forehead, the cut still oozing down the side of his face. 'Charlie, did you call an ambulance?!' Laura shouts at me and I shake my head.

'It was an accident, Laura. I don't know what happened – we were just talking and then … he slipped and fell onto the knife.' I wring my hands together, blood making my skin tacky. Wiping them on my skirt, I try to stop the sticky tackiness that makes them feel dirty; I am overcome with the desperate need to wash them. I give a soft laugh at the thought of needing to wash my hands while my husband is lying bleeding to death on my kitchen floor. Laura shoots me a look full of hatred as she hands Maria a clean tea towel from the kitchen worktop, instructing her to press down on the wound on Sal's stomach to stop the bleeding. She pulls her mobile from her back pocket, pacing backwards and forwards across the kitchen floor, as I watch in numbed silence.

'Ambulance,' she barks into the phone, not taking her eyes off me. 'And police. My friend has been stabbed.' I slide down the kitchen cabinets and close my eyes. It was your own fault, Sal. I only did it because I love you. You were going to leave me, after all the promises we made of you and me together for ever; after all the lies you told me, Sal. After everything we've been through together you were just going to go. I had to stop you leaving somehow.

CHAPTER THIRTY-NINE

FOUR MONTHS LATER …

SAL

Laura laughs as I hand her another bag to stuff somewhere in the boot of her ridiculously small car. We are packing to take Maggie, Lucy and Fred to Cornwall for the Christmas break and, despite the fact that it's bloody freezing, we are all looking forward to spending some time on the beach, getting away from the horror of the past few months.

I try not to think too hard about that day, the day that Charlie completely snapped. I was unconscious before Laura and my mum broke into the house, my mum panicking because it was long past the hour and a half I had said I would be. She had driven over to find Laura on my doorstep about to force her way in after hearing Charlie screaming at me. Together they broke in, called an ambulance and managed to stem the bleeding, all while Charlie stood and watched. I lost a lot of blood, but the doctors said I was extremely lucky that Charlie didn't manage to hit any vital organs.

It turns out that Charlie lost her job at Hunter, Crisp and Wilson that day after a scandal surrounding Lucian Pavlenco and his immigrant status, or lack of it. I knew nothing of what had been going on, and so for Charlie to come home drunk and find me packing my bags to leave was the last straw for her. She tried to tell Laura, my mum and the police that I fell onto the knife myself, that it was an accident, but the fact that only her fingerprints were found on it soon blew her story out of the water. That, and the fact that I had other injuries consistent with being beaten. Following on from that, she tried to tell the police it was self-defence, that I had attacked her after beating her for years, despite the only mark on her being a small bruise on her breastbone, where I had shoved her away from me into the kitchen sink. Laura soon put them straight and handed them the diary and photos we had put together, just a short while before all this happened. Charlie was arrested and is now on remand.

Laura has been a tower of strength – she looked after Maggie with my mum while I was in the hospital and I couldn't have got through it all without her. We're not in a relationship – I'm not ready for another relationship and I don't know if I ever will be – but our friendship has deepened into something stronger, and we spend a lot of time together, something that seems to help Maggie. While Maggie didn't witness anything, she knows that her mummy did something mean to her daddy, so Mummy has had to go away for a while. We'll just leave it at that for now, until she's older.

Mrs Prideaux has kept my job open for me. Obviously, I couldn't start in September, following the events of the last week in August, and I thought my chance was blown, but Mrs Prideaux, *Lana*, came to visit me in the hospital after she heard what had happened and said she would be prepared to hold my position until the January term.

'You are an excellent teacher, Sal. We understand that these events are out of your control and don't want to lose you. Are you still happy to take the job in January?' She eyes me over the top of her glasses in that teacherly manner she has.

'Of course! I was worried that this would have blown my chances.' I struggle into a sitting position, wincing as the stitches in my wound pull. Lana pats my hand, and tells me, 'Sal, you have no idea just how special you are.'

I smile at the memory. Lana is right. After years of being told I was useless, a moron, someone pathetic whose opinion was worth nothing, it's taken these events to make me realise I am special – not the total loser my wife was so fond of telling me I am.

In the past, I was told so many times by so many people how lucky I was – my life, to others on the outside looking in, was pretty much perfect. I had a beautiful home, a clever, beautiful and successful wife, an adorable little girl and I didn't even need to work – according to those on the outside, I had it all. On the inside, however, a very different story was being played out and it just goes to show that not everything is always as it seems.

'Come on, Sal, hurry up!' Laura is waiting in the car, blowing on her freezing hands while she waits for the heater to warm up. With one last look at the house, I lock the front door – I have finally been able to return after spending three months at my parents' – the police said I could go back before then, but it all felt unsettling and slightly terrifying – and turn back towards the car. To Laura, and Maggie. To the future.

CHAPTER FORTY

CHARLIE

On remand. How did I go from being at the top of my game, about to become a partner in one of the most successful law firms in the South-East of Britain, with a beautiful family, a big house and a brand-new car, to being *on remand*?

Sal was just lying on the kitchen floor, slipping into unconsciousness when that stupid bitch Laura forced her way in, screaming and calling the police. I tried my hardest to defuse the situation – to tell them that Sal slipped and fell onto the knife himself – but my lawyer told me that was a stupid thing to do; that only my fingerprints were found on the knife. So I told them Sal had been beating me for years, that it was self-defence, but the lawyer told me it wouldn't stand up in court; that there was evidence to the contrary. And now I'm stuck in here, awaiting trial for attempted murder. It wasn't attempted murder – it was just a knee-jerk reaction to an unbelievable situation and I'm sure the jury will see it that way. There was no way I was going to let Sal leave me – I love him so much, and everything I ever did was *for him*. I lied for him, covered up illegal activity for him; everything I ever did was for him. I had to do the things I did to Sal; he drove me to it and, even when I really tried, he would always push me just that little bit too far. It's all Sal's fault that I am in this hideous place.

I tried to get someone from the criminal law department from Hunter, Crisp and Wilson to represent me – they are the best in the South-East, after all – but Mr Hunter, my old friend Stan, said they wouldn't. A conflict of interest, apparently, as they would be involved in the charges regarding the illegal status of Lucian Pavlenco. I am still waiting to hear what charges, if any, will be brought against me for that. Pavlenco is apparently being detained in a detention centre, awaiting deportation back to Romania. His funds have been frozen and his wife, who believed herself to be Mrs Pavlenco, not Mrs Popescu, has left him and taken their children back to her wealthy family in Romania. As much as I hate being held here, it probably is the safest place I can be right now, at least until Pavlenco is gone. I don't think he will take my mistake of leaving Radu's emails on my laptop lying down, and I'm pretty certain that he has a taste for revenge.

Sal hasn't been to visit me, nor has he responded to any of my letters. I have demanded to see Maggie, but I have had no response. No doubt his family have stepped in and are probably burning my letters before Sal even knows they have arrived. Sal would never ignore me deliberately, so he mustn't even know that I've written to him. It's OK, though. Sal and I are destined to be together for ever, that's what we always said, and once this whole mess has been sorted out, we will be together again, somewhere far, far away from all of them, where they can't interfere in our lives any more.

I have received one letter since I was brought here. Not from Sal, but from Alex. Just to let me know that Stefan decided to merge his company with Alex's client – it all went swimmingly, apparently, and now Alex has been made a partner at his law firm. He thanked me for giving him the opportunity to succeed. I screamed with rage and tore the letter into a million tiny pieces when I read it – Alex is living my life, the life I should have had, until he destroyed it. There is a bitter taste in my mouth that I can't get rid of; no matter what godawful prison food I eat, no matter how many times I brush my teeth.

This isn't the end for Charlotte Trevetti – I will get out of here, at some point, and then I'll have my chance to make sure everything is put right, that everything reverts to how it should be. That they all get what they deserve.

ACKNOWLEDGEMENTS

Firstly, a huge thank you must go to my fantastic editor, Victoria Oundjian, whose creative brilliance helped pull this manuscript into shape, all whilst simultaneously holding my hand every step of the way.

More enormous thanks to my early readers – your input was invaluable and you have no idea how grateful I am.

Special thanks must go to Amy and Dave Jacobs, Victoria Goldman, Rebecca Raisin and Sarah Cole – without you guys, it's highly unlikely that this novel would ever have landed on the desk at Carina - your encouragement and support kept me going when it seemed like the writing would beat me.

And finally, thank you to my crazy, amazing family – Nick, George, Isabel and Oscar – thank you for supporting me, thank you for the wine and the bacon sandwiches, and thank you for putting up with my needy writer ways – I love you all more than you'll ever know.

From the New York Times Bestselling author of *The Good Girl*

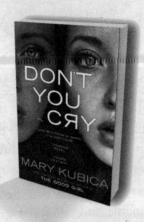

In downtown Chicago, a young woman named Esther Vaughan disappears from her apartment without a trace. A haunting letter addressed to My Dearest is found among her possessions, leaving her friend and roommate Quinn Collins to wonder where Esther is and whether or not she's the person Quinn thought she knew.

As Quinn searches for answers about Esther, so unfolds a twisted thrill ride that builds to a stunning conclusion and shows that no matter how fast and far we run, the past always catches up with us in the end.

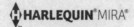

Everyone has secrets…

Sarah Quinlan's husband, Jack, has been haunted for decades by the mysterious death of his mother. But when Jack's beloved aunt Julia is involved in a serious accident, Sarah begins to realise that nothing about the Quinlans is quite as it seems.

Caught in a flurry of unanswered questions, Sarah dives deep into the rabbit hole of Jack's past, but the farther she climbs, the harder it is to get out. And soon she is faced with a shattering reality she could never have prepared for…

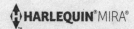

Bringing you the best voices in fiction
🐦 **@Mira_booksUK**

DI Richard Poole returns in this brand new
murder mystery from the BBC1 series
Death in Paradise

When famous supermodel Polly Carter is found
dead at the bottom of a cliff, all signs point to
suicide. But as the evidence continues to mount,
DI Richard Poole declares it to be a murder. At
the same time that his mother is arriving from
England, throwing his whole perfectly ordered life
into turmoil, Richard is now faced with a
houseful of suspects, and must discover who the
murderer is before it's too late.

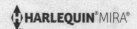

Bringing you the best voices in fiction
🐦 **@Mira_booksUK**

M435_TKOPC

Everyone knows a couple
like Jack and Grace

He has looks and wealth, she has charm and elegance.
You might not want to like them, but you do.
You'd like to get to know Grace better.
But it's difficult, because you realise
Jack and Grace are never apart.
Some might call this true love. Others might ask why
Grace never answers the phone. Or how she can never
meet for coffee, even though she doesn't work. And
why there are bars on one of the bedroom windows.

Sometimes, the perfect marriage is the perfect lie.
#StaySingle

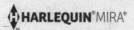

Bringing you the best voices in fiction
🐦 **@Mira_booksUK**

M437_BCD

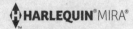